PRAISE FOR
and her cap

"Tiffany Clare writes a ███████████████████
with rich details and vivid characters. Any readers wishing for a bold and sweeping historical romance need look no
further—Tiffany Clare is a treasure of an author!"

—Lisa Kleypas, *New York Times* bestselling author

The Secret Desires of a Governess

"With its irrepressible heroine, deliciously dark and dangerous hero, and suitably atmospheric setting, Clare's
latest impeccably written novel cleverly references the
classic gothic romances of Victoria Holt and Madeleine
Brent, while at the same time incorporating plenty of
the steamy passion and lush sensuality found in today's
brand of sexy historical romances."   —*Booklist*

"With its brooding hero and dark backdrop Clare brings an
updated gothic twist to her latest novel. By incorporating
the themes and red herrings of a classic Victoria Holt or
Daphne du Maurier, she entices readers to keep turning
the pages to uncover the mystery and savor the highly
sensual romance."   —*RT Book Reviews*

"This is an entertaining throwback to the Victoria Holt
legendary Gothic tales as Tiffany Clare employs all the
elements from the innocent female, to the foreboding
castle to the brooding hero inside a romantic suspense
thriller. Abby and Elliot are terrific lead characters while
the support cast, especially his son, the villagers, and her
family, make for a wonderful Victorian Gothic romance."

—*Midwest Book Review*

Also by Tiffany Clare

The Secret Desires of a Governess

The Surrender of a Lady

The Seduction of His Wife

Wicked Nights with a Proper Lady

TIFFANY CLARE

St. Martin's Paperbacks

This is a work of fiction. All of the characters, organizations, and events portrayed in this novel are either products of the author's imagination or are used fictitiously.

WICKED NIGHTS WITH A PROPER LADY

Copyright © 2012 by Tiffany Clare.

All rights reserved.

For information address St. Martin's Press, 175 Fifth Avenue, New York, NY 10010.

ISBN: 978-1-250-00802-2

Printed in the United States of America

St. Martin's Paperbacks edition / November 2012

St. Martin's Paperbacks are published by St. Martin's Press, 175 Fifth Avenue, New York, NY 10010.

10 9 8 7 6 5 4 3 2 1

Scott, darling, you invent activities just to keep the kids out of my hair when I need time to write and that makes you my biggest hero.

Acknowledgments

Elyssa Papa, Maggie Robinson, and J.K. Coi, where would I be without our go-to place? Sara Lindsey, you are always there for the small things that seem to count the most, and I can't thank you enough for your help.

Thank you, Dad, for proudly displaying my books on your shelves at work even though you're not allowed to read them.

Thank you, Mom. Who knew you had a stash of my books on hand and ready to sell to your friends at any occasion, even at your own birthday party?

Helen & Monique, you ladies truly are amazing. Thank you for believing in this series.

Wicked Nights
with a
Proper Lady

Chapter 1

Death causes the oddest affectations in the upper echelons of society. The Countess of F—— certainly took the death of her husband to loftier heights of aberration in her latest display, and in Kensal Green *of all places. Her exhibition was wholly . . . distasteful, and left much to be desired by all who were present.*

Why the infamous Countess of F—— should be immune to censure from society has always baffled this writer. Though judging from the glances received by others in true mourning, *she'll not likely be allowed to carry on her usual dramas in widowhood.*

The Mayfair Chronicles, May 26, 1846

London

As the oak coffin lowered into the muddy hole before them, Leonidas Harrow, the Earl of Barrington, muttered none too quietly, "He always was a jackass."

An elderly matron dressed in heavy bombazine better suited to two decades past tittered. Her companion hissed in a horrified breath, narrowed her gaze briefly on him, and then returned her focus on the solemn grave as the vicar droned out his sermon.

Not that he gave a damn what anyone thought, but perhaps in this instance, it would have been better for him to keep his opinion to himself. It couldn't be helped that it was nothing more than the truth.

And it wasn't as though the onlookers wouldn't expect him or his friends to utter such shocking words. They were known as the four degenerates of society—pleasure seekers with no other purpose than to make a mockery of their position and standing in the *ton*. Or so they were categorized.

Too rich to snub and too risky for the youth to befriend; they stood together on the outskirts of polite society. Though they were all invited into the inner folds of the elite class much like one might warily invite the devil in to better watch their back.

Leo stood next to the Countess of Fallon—now the dowager. She'd always been Jezebel, or Jez, to his small group of friends.

At least Jez was a widow now. Her husband really had been a boar's ass right up till his passing.

Mr. Warren, the man who would inherit the earldom, stood across from them, a severe look of disdain set in his dark brows as he stared at Jez with barely concealed contempt. One of his hands was wrapped around the stylized dragonhead atop his black lacquered cane. His jacket was crisply pressed, his starched cravat done in so elaborate a knot that it must have taken his valet a good hour to accomplish the ostentatious display. The gleam in his eyes was smug and sure.

Leo suspected Mr. Warren, the great-nephew of the previous earl, might prove no kinder than Jez's late husband. This whole situation didn't bode well for Jez.

Jez fixed the edge of the black lace veil and dabbed

away her tears—more likely derived from anger than from grief.

She then tucked the handkerchief under the edge of her sleeve and yanked her bodice down to reveal another inch of bosom. The crimson of the gown was like the color of a harlot's painted lips, and wholly improper for the occasion of her husband's funeral.

She placed her satin-gloved hand on Hayden, the Duke of Alsborough's coat sleeve. Both he and Hayden each held an umbrella over her.

Leo turned to better see the duke, who stared down at the bleak grave filling rapidly with rainwater. Hayden's jaw was squared, his stance stiff. Of their party, he was the only one wearing a somber expression befitting the occasion.

Tristan, the Marquess of Castleigh, stood to Leo's right, stifling a laugh with his gloved hand by pretending to cough.

"Yes." Jez gave another sniffle, or was that a laugh? The lacy veil obscured not only her expression but also a faded bruise inflicted by Fallon shortly before his heart gave out. "Though *jackass* isn't quite the word I'd use."

She released her hold on Hayden's sleeve and kneeled to the ground to pluck the head of a white rose from one of the funeral bouquets.

The vicar continued to read a passage that Leo would bet his finest racing stud Jez had chosen with great care.

" 'Those who have done good will rise to live, and those who have done evil will rise to be condemned . . .' "

Her husband was definitely roasting in hell for his sins. But all that mattered was that Fallon would never again be able to lay a hand on her.

Even though the earlier downpour of rain had trickled to a spit, Jez's hairpiece flattened against her head and face as she pressed beyond the reach of the umbrella.

Leo watched her curiously. She'd been acting most peculiar since her husband's death, as though she were simply going through the motions of living every day when she should be celebrating her newfound independence. Instead, he knew she was fighting to keep the Fallon estate and its entailments in her possession. But the will had been clear: all the monies and properties went to the successor in title.

There was nothing allocated to her.

Absolutely nothing.

Whispers started among the procession, drawing Leo's attention back to the present. The clergyman prattled on, but everyone else was focused on Jez as she plucked the petals from the head of a white rose, placing each feathery white piece at the center of her palm, and blowing them into the grave pit to land on the lowered coffin.

He was sure he was the only one close enough to hear her hushed words when she spoke.

"A thousand years of soul-burning agony will not be enough to right your wrongs. May your evil spirit blister in hell for all eternity. Not only have you wronged me in life, you have managed to cheat me in death."

In her voluminous skirts, she struggled to find her footing in the mud as she stood. Hayden grasped her elbow and hauled her to her feet.

She peeped her head over her shoulder to look at the dark pit one last time, then turned back to them. "Let us be rid of all this . . . death."

Leo could care less if they left the funeral early. He nodded his intention to leave to Tristan and Hayden. The crowd parted like the Red Sea, and the train on Jez's dress flowed outward like froths of watery crimson silk as they departed Kensal Green.

Hoisting the lady on his arm into the waiting carriage, he climbed in after her. Leo called out their direction to the driver as he mounted the final step. Tristan and Hayden followed them in and took the leather bench opposite. With neighs and snorts from the horses, the carriage jolted forward.

Jez lifted the veil from her face and stared first at him with her somber, resigned expression and then at Tristan and Hayden.

None of them said a word.

Jez pulled the shade of the window aside and stared out at the rain-filled streets with a sigh.

Leo closed his eyes and rested his head back against the seat. Perhaps time with friends would cheer Jez up. They could work up an old trick or two to distract her from the melancholy that had fallen on her this past week.

Leo had never liked Jez's husband, but if the bastard weren't already dead, he'd kill the old blighter with his bare hands for the undue suffering he continued to cause from beyond the grave.

Jez was vulnerable right now, and he hated to see her helpless when she was normally on top of the world.

"Whatever you need right now, just name it," Leo said.

Tristan leaned forward in his seat and placed his elbows on his knees. "Yes, what can we do to cheer you up, dearest?"

"Must we do anything at all?" Hayden removed his hat and settled it over his knee.

Tristan gave him a look of bemusement. "If it were up to you, we'd mope about for a week."

"Enough." Jez twisted her finger absently around the tassels tying back the small curtain. "Knowing what I now know about the will . . . and my husband's abominable final feat on his death bed, I wouldn't hesitate to push him down a flight of stairs to be rid of him sooner had I been given the opportunity."

"Jez . . ." Leo reached for her hand and gave it a comforting squeeze.

When she turned back to them, a trail of tears carved a damp path down her right cheek. "I wish I could carry on with life as though none of this mattered."

"Of course it matters," Tristan said. "That bastard knew exactly what he was doing to you."

"There never was any love lost between us. Perhaps this is my punishment for marrying for convenience instead of for love?"

Leo couldn't recall a single day where Jez had been content with her marriage.

"Fallon was an ass," Tristan pointed out again. "There was nothing you or any other person could do to change that fact. And besides, many a woman would have wanted to be in your position, so there was no fault in your choice."

After the hell her husband had put her through, and Leo had seen some of the damage left by the earl's heavy hand—though Jez had denied any wrongdoing by her husband—you'd think he'd leave her *something*. Mr. Warren didn't seem disposed to spare her any humiliation by offering her a small settlement from her long-suffering marriage, either.

Leo wondered if the only steadfast thing Jez had in life now was her friendship with them. She'd been labeled as one of their set shortly after her introduction into society as the Countess of Fallon because she eschewed society's rules of conduct for a young lady.

"We should head back to my townhouse. Let's call it a day, Jez." Hayden was always the voice of reason.

"There wouldn't be nearly as much fun in that, old man," Tristan said.

Leo also wasn't inclined to let his friend out of his sight just yet. "Jez, name your preference for the evening."

"Hmm . . ." She swiped away a few remaining tears and pasted on a smile for them. "I'm sure there are a number of activities that might brighten my mood."

Hayden's gaze narrowed on him; Leo smiled in return.

Jez drummed her fingers along her beaded reticule, the sound reminiscent of a snare drum readying soldiers in line for war. "The Randalls are hosting a ball tonight. And I certainly wouldn't want anyone to assume I'm in mourning."

Tristan clapped his hands together. "Excellent."

"We'll have to stop at my townhouse. I don't want to be seen wearing my funeral rags to the duchess's ball."

"Nor I, for that matter," Tristan concurred, fixing his skewed black cravat.

"And no more feeling sorry for myself. I'm never maudlin." Jez raised her chin high. "It's better to be angry. If ever there was a woman scorned, that woman is I. And I will not be kicked down a moment longer."

The carriage turned toward Mayfair, quickly approaching Jez's townhouse.

"My solicitors will look over the will first thing in the morning," Hayden insisted for the umpteenth time.

The man was determined to find a loophole and no one would begrudge him that. Hell, Leo still couldn't believe that Fallon had so thoroughly tied up his funds in his successor. All Jez had was the paltry sum she'd gone into her marriage with.

"I'll worry about the will tomorrow, Hayden." Jez gave them all a droll look. "I deserve a short reprieve from the reality of my situation for at least one night."

The carriage rolled to a stop.

"Are we sure this is wise?" Hayden interjected as the door opened and Jez took the footman's hand to be let down.

Tristan ducked his head and exited. "Should we hide behind our mothers' apron strings?"

Leo laughed and slapped Hayden on the shoulder as he stepped down from the carriage. "Come on, Hayden. It's

meant to be a night of celebration now that the old scala-
wag has kicked the bucket."

"I'm willing to do just about anything to cheer you up,
Jez." Tristan offered his arm. "I'll see you to your townhouse."

With a pointed glare aimed at Hayden, Jez batted her
lashes at Tristan. "I couldn't ask for a better or more willing companion."

"What have you planned for the evening, Jez?" Leo
asked, trailing behind Jez and Tristan up the steps to her
townhouse.

"This particular ball is full of debutantes . . . ripe for
plucking. I do believe Mr. Warren has his eye on one of
the ladies in attendance. There was something he said at
the reading of the will to indicate such."

Not sure how he should interpret this tidbit of information, Leo only quirked one brow. No one knew how to ex-
act revenge quite like Jez. That was what had set her apart
from most women of his acquaintance: she thought and
acted as ruthless and as cunning as a man.

It brought a smile to his face when he remembered the
first time he'd met her. It had been gentlemen's night at
Hastley's and she'd been smoking a cigar and playing cards
at a table with ten other men.

"What do you have in mind?" Leo asked, intrigued.

"I'm only thinking of the girl," she said with a sweet
pout tilting her mouth down. "I wouldn't wish the life I had
on anyone. She mustn't marry Mr. Warren."

Chapter 2

Though a host may turn away any guest without an invite, it would be bad judgment to refuse the Duke of A—— entry anywhere, even with friends considered to have the lowest of morals in tow.
The Mayfair Chronicles, May 26, 1846

"You're to stay by my side this evening, as your grandmother instructed. I will not be impressed if I have to search for you in the gardens with your newest beau," Genevieve Camden scolded her cousin.

Her younger cousin, Charlotte, had debuted in society this past spring and all had gone swimmingly well between them for months. Everything had changed with Charlotte's father's insistence that his daughter be courted and married to a man of his choice come fall—one Mr. Warren.

So far, Charlotte had only disappeared twice into a garden and dark alcove with gentlemen this past week. Still, the suddenness of her impending marriage—to a man neither knew well—did not mean that Charlotte could eschew proper conduct.

And, really, it could be far worse for her cousin.

Genny guessed Mr. Warren to be in his early to mid-thirties. He was handsome enough with his lithe, strong-looking frame. More importantly, he had a full head of hair and was in possession of all his teeth. There were far too many bald-headed, gum-grinding gentlemen for Genny's liking. All in all, she thought her uncle had chosen well.

"Pooh." Charlotte pouted. "You really aren't any fun at all."

"That is why your father asked me to accompany you around Town," Genny retorted before she could rein in her frustration. "I'm sorry, I didn't mean to be so harsh."

"Yes you did." Hurt was etched in her cousin's face. "You should never have sided with my father."

"What else could I do?" Genny couldn't stand up to her uncle, else he'd have her removed from the house and cut off his support.

"You could have made excuses on my behalf. Instead you just stood beside me and nodded in agreement with everything my father said."

"It won't matter how often I apologize, you'll never forgive me, will you?"

"This isn't the place for this." Charlotte looked around the room before turning back to Genny with a forced smile. "We are at a ball, and I should be dancing the night away."

Genny did sympathize with her younger cousin's plight. But that didn't mean Charlotte should risk damaging either of their reputations, especially since Genny relied upon the generosity of her extended family to keep her clothed, fed, and comfortable now that she was firmly considered an unmarriageable spinster without an income to sustain a life of independence. It wasn't so terrible having to rely upon family. Genny did have more freedom now than she had when she was a debutante.

"I am headed for the punch table," Charlotte said,

smoothly changing the topic when Genny made no response. "Can I bring you a refreshment?"

"I will pass, thank you. I have already partaken of the punch and it's quite bland." She took a deep breath and tried to summon a reasonable tone. "Please don't leave this room without me, not under any circumstance, or your father will hear about it."

Charlotte's brows puckered closer together and she let out an annoyed huff. "You really are a spoilsport. I promise to do no more than converse with my friends and wait for gentlemen to fill in their names on our dance cards. You'll see me directly across the room. Does that meet with your approval?"

"I wouldn't have to scold you if you acted like a proper young lady."

Charlotte looked affronted. "The best years of my life are going to be wasted in marriage. Why shouldn't I experience what life has to offer before then?"

Before Genny could come up with a reasonable response, Charlotte was halfway across the ballroom, weaving through guests and dancers with sure footing. The heavy pleats in Charlotte's green silk gown seamlessly flowed through the crowd instead of dragging behind her. Heads turned, but her cousin gave no notice to anyone until she reached her friend Ariel's side. Ariel had on a blush silk gown with pearls sewn right into the fitted bodice, making her look almost like a fairy princess with all that opalescent shimmer and pale blonde hair to give her an ethereal quality men seemed to adore.

Genny looked down at the drab affair she wore with a slight shake of her head; it was better suited for a funeral than a ball. She felt too young to be a spinster and sometimes wished that life could be as easy for her as it was for her cousin.

Genny had been born to a modest family with an equally humble income. But she knew that wealth came with a few disadvantages of its own. She supposed she was lucky to have been sponsored at all and had at least experienced a debut at eighteen. She had not made good use of her great-aunt's generosity and married well, though.

She blew out a frustrated breath and looked away from the small gathering of debutantes and young, marriageable gentlemen that surrounded Charlotte and Ariel.

Genny was *not* envious. Well, maybe slightly since she had wanted to marry, just not to any of the men who had offered.

Taking a step back, Genny pressed her shoulder against the wall. Would it really hurt anyone's sensibilities if a few chairs were placed in the ballroom? She didn't wish to stand all evening.

Though it hadn't been that long since she had debuted into society, she was no longer cut out for the late nights and early mornings. Not after playing the role of companion these last three years to her aunt Hilda, the very woman who had sponsored her. Her aunt was in her sixth decade and in bed before the evening clock struck eight once she'd retired from society.

Now, from luncheon to the latest hours of the night, Genny was at her cousin's side. She swore by the time she closed her eyes to finally sleep that the girl's grandmother, too aged to escort her granddaughter around Town herself, was ringing that dratted servants' bell and demanding Genny's attendance. Sometimes Genny was summoned before the sun even had a chance to rise—like today.

A commotion at the ballroom entrance had Genny standing taller and firmer where she'd perched herself against the wall. Unladylike, she knew, but she couldn't find it in her to care at the moment. All she needed was one decent night of sleep and she'd be in top form for the remainder of the month.

The clamor came from a great many voices talking all at once. Newcomers to the ball, Genny concluded.

She scanned the candlelit room for Charlotte and spotted her still standing near the punch table. Charlotte leaned into Ariel, her fan flicking rapidly at her reddened cheeks as she whispered something next to her friend's ear. Both girls laughed then turned their attention back to the gentlemen who surrounded them; two men actually blushed at whatever her cousin said.

Just as Genny turned back to the entrance of the ballroom, the Earl of Barrington appeared, arresting her attention.

Her breath hitched, her heart beat frantically in her chest, and a sound that was a mixture of hurt, anger, and longing welled in her throat. Stepping away from the wall, she clutched her hands in front of her, unsure what to do. Hiding seemed ideal, but not when she needed to keep a sharp eye on Charlotte.

She'd known it was possible that she might chance seeing him about Town now that she was back in society with her cousin.

Four years hadn't changed him one whit. He was still as handsome and dapper as ever. It was probably better she hadn't pursued a match with him; she'd look rather plain next to such a striking specimen of man.

He was tall and imposing, at least a couple of inches above six feet. His deep brown hair curled like that of some Adonis of old. She recalled the soft silky texture of it as she'd run her fingers through the curly tresses and held him tightly in the midst of the most earth-shattering pleasure she'd ever experienced in her life.

His eyes were as dark a brown as the most decadent

chocolate and his brows were perfectly trimmed, giving him that devil-may-care look. His nose was crooked; he had boasted that it had been broken not once but twice in his younger days. Why she had found it attractive at all was testament to how blinded she'd once been by his dashing looks and charming wit. However, such meaningless things could no longer sway her.

Hair grew down the side of his face along his jaw, which he kept clipped close to his skin. She well remembered the feel of his face rubbing over her bare thighs, her naked breasts . . .

She had to stop visualizing those memories.

He was a solidly built man. His frame wide, his arms had been well muscled and strong and still looked to be so. She had once traced the blue veins that stood out on his arms as they lay in bed together. She had grasped his wide shoulders tightly as he pushed her up against the headboard and did very wicked things to her.

Closing her eyes to gather her fast scattering imaginings, she mentally chastised herself and focused on the here and now. Though it was hard to forget the pleasure and the mind-numbing delight they had shared so long ago. Goodness, it was nearly impossible to forget *him* at all. And if she were honest with herself, which she did not want to be, her focus had strayed to memories of him far too many times to count over the years since she'd last seen him. Had things been different, maybe they would have married. She'd been foolish not to demand it of him after everything they had shared.

Three others of *his* set stepped down from the landing above the grand ballroom. The duchess, and hostess of the ball, emerged from the throng of matrons occupying her attention; a tight, somewhat forced smile formed on her face the moment she caught a glimpse of the Dowager Countess Fallon in a sapphire-blue dress, her red hair knotted back into an intricately braided bun with iridescent green feathers sticking elegantly out the top.

Did the dowager plan on making a scene? Hadn't the funeral for her husband been held today? Genny wasn't one to judge but it seemed odd that the dowager would attend a ball so soon after her husband's passing.

Genny spun back in the direction of her charge. Charlotte was chattering with her friends, unaware of the tension that suddenly thickened the air and lulled the conversations around them.

Focusing again on the entryway, Genny wondered why *they* had come to a ball with mainly debutantes in attendance. She doubted any of them had marriage in mind—or, for that matter, good intentions.

The host of the ball crossed a short span of the ballroom and took the Duke of Alsborough's hand in a familiar gesture. The duke had deceivingly angelic features with his blond hair and sharp blue eyes. He was tall and lean, but she could see the strength all but radiating from him.

The Marquess of Castleigh kissed the back of the duchess's hand. The man wore black from head to toe, except for the stark white cravat about his neck that further sharpened his handsome features and dark slicked-back hair. He was a perfect contrast to the duke . . . sweet heaven and tempting hell.

And then there was the devil in the Earl of Barrington. Leo—as she had familiarly addressed him so long ago—also kissed the back of the duchess's hand, offering some pleasantry that had the woman smiling coyly back.

Genny pressed back into the wall, wishing she could simply disappear from view. Not a possibility with her cousin half a room away and in need of an eagle eye to keep her from a danger she couldn't possibly understand.

Even though a quadrille played in the background, the new guests seemed to capture the attention of most of the attendees milling about the room. Dancers abandoned the dance floor to discuss the turn of events.

With added bravery, Genny forced herself away from the wall and took a step in Charlotte's direction. She doubted she had anything to worry about where her cousin and these men were concerned, but she remembered the temptation Barrington represented all too well. And since her father's declaration, Charlotte seemed to smell a bad decision a mile away.

Hopefully, Barrington didn't notice Genny as she made her way around the room.

She snorted.

He wouldn't.

Besides, it wasn't as if Barrington would ever take stock of the colorless women that had found a comfortable spot along the edge of the room with only the odd wallflower to offer some color among them.

It hadn't been hard for him to forget her after he had ruined her for any other man. It was a small blessing she'd been spared the humiliation from society for what she'd done. She'd grown into a spinster of sorts, a steady companion for elderly family members, and now a chaperone to her young cousin. No one knew about Genny's past—with *him*.

She'd had other suitors: two to be precise. But she could not bring herself to settle with either of them when her heart had belonged to Barrington. He could not possibly have returned the sentiment; if he had he wouldn't have left her.

While keeping a close eye on Charlotte, Genny conversed about the weather with Ariel's mother, Lady Hargrove.

The other woman frowned as she watched the Dowager Countess Fallon's every move. "It's unfathomable that the duchess would allow *that* woman in here. The nerve she has to present herself in society with her husband's funeral held only this morning proves what incredibly poor taste she has."

"It is quite scandalous." Genny nodded her head in agreement, though she could care less what her current companion nattered on about. Genny didn't miss the tongue wagging or speculation that ran rampant behind everyone's backs.

"Simply impossible to believe Her Grace would invite the dowager. I heard the earl simply stopped breathing at the end. I'm sure he wanted nothing more than to be rid of that woman."

Genny didn't want to know how Lady Hargrove had come by that information.

From that point forward she only paid half a mind to what the woman said. Genny was completely absorbed by Barrington's presence. She couldn't help that her eyes strayed toward him like a compass pulled by the magnetic poles.

Had she known all those years ago that he'd leave her after she'd so fully given herself to him, she couldn't say for sure if she would have refused his attentions, even those of a carnal nature. He was a very hard man to resist and utterly charming when he wanted to be.

Had she never met him, she would never have known the touch of a man. Then again, she wouldn't have been ruined for all others when she constantly craved the touch from only that particular man. It had always been *him* in her thoughts. Perhaps that was her own foolishness. She couldn't fully blame him for her current marriageless state; she'd been an active participant in their affair. He had never needed to persuade her of anything, she'd leaped into the pond with both feet forward, hoping not to hit the bottom too hard. She had fallen in love with him in the two weeks they'd spent together, but she had never been able to utter that truth to him in fear of being rejected. And then he had left and it was too late.

Oh, dear Lord.

All Leo had to do was step into a room for her to become a slavering mess of emotion. Tamping down any flicker of desire for him that lingered, she studied him with a critical eye, as the mothers in the room might, and were very likely doing at this moment.

As a potential husband he had many an attribute. He was as handsome as the devil, as rich as Croesus since the majority of his money came from import. The Caribbean, she was sure. He owned a decent estate in Hertfordshire and a large townhouse in the city. And he was in possession of a title built on the bluest of blood.

If a mother was willing to overlook his greatest flaws—his reputation as a player and his dabbling in trade—he might be considered a great candidate for marriage.

Leo's gaze went around the room, skimming over the guests with a disinterested mien. He didn't so much as slow his perusal as his gaze passed over the spot she stood in. Had she expected any other reaction from him?

If she ever thought she could settle down a man like Barrington again, she'd take a step back, pinch herself to the point of bruising, and force herself to walk away without so much as a glance back.

A rake of the first order was what he was. He'd taken her innocence without any qualms. Technically, she'd thrown it at him, but that was beside the point.

With more difficulty than it should have taken, she tore her gaze away from the temptation that man offered and returned her attention to reality.

Charlotte had two new gentlemen at her side. One filled in his name on her dance card while the other made her laugh in her flirtatious, raucous way. Genny knew the young men vying for her cousin's undivided attention.

Both were from decent families and both were of an age with Charlotte. The poor things had no way of knowing she was already spoken for.

Genny shouldn't begrudge the girl any fun over the next couple of months. So long as Charlotte remained a young woman of purity then Genny's task would be all but accomplished.

Next year, Genny would either become a companion to her cousin after her nuptials—possibly help Charlotte rear her children should she bear them for Mr. Warren—or she would remain a companion to the girl's grandmother.

She hated this uncertainty in her life, never knowing what her future held, or where it would take her. However, she always landed on top, so it wasn't worth fretting over right now.

Leo thought Jez was nervous to be at the ball with her husband not yet cold in his grave. She'd laughed too gaily when the hostess had met them at the entry. It was also apparent in the way she clasped his arm tighter when they entered the room. Everyone's attention had swung like a restless pendulum in their direction. Did Jez harbor regrets for going out in society so soon?

He held her close, knowing she'd imbibed a little too freely of his rum earlier this afternoon in a poor attempt to drown her sorrows.

After kissing the ring on the duchess's hand, he surveyed the room full of debutantes, wondering who the poor chit set to marry the next Fallon was. Before he could choose for himself whom to weed from the herd of unsuspecting young ladies, Jez released his arm, drawing his gaze away from the nervous flock.

"I'm of a mind to try my odds at cards. I'm feeling a spot of luck because of how the day has unfolded in my favor."

"Tell me about the young lady we are looking for before you leave," Leo said.

"Lady Charlotte Lindsey." With a slight tilt of her chin in the general direction of the punch table, Jez fingered the gold pendant that dangled above her décolletage. "The brunette with the green dress, cut low off her shoulders, and the emerald pendant."

A trickle of unease slid down his spine. "Warren plans to marry the Ponsley girl?"

"There was that card game a few weeks back," Jez reminded him.

She'd been sitting across from him, and he'd lamented on his dealings in the House of Lords. "The very card game where I expressed a certain amount of interest in crushing the opposition on the new sugar imports act?"

Ponsley's parliamentary act would destroy Leo's plantations in the West Indies, increasing his taxes and making it impossible for him to continue profiting on his imports. It was well known that Ponsley had plantations in South America and used slaves to harvest his sugar products, yet the conservative bastard thought to levy a tax in the West Indies where slavery had finally been abolished.

"That's the one. I knew you'd remember," she responded.

"Do you honestly think we'll be able to charm and win the chit over when her father despises me?"

Leo also doubted that courting Ponsley's daughter would sway votes to his favor.

"I say." Tristan put his arm around his shoulder and joined their conversation. "I'll bet you that fine filly you brought back from the Americas last month that I break her in first."

Before Leo could respond, Tristan headed in the direction of the lady in question. Leo held back, taking Jez's elbow before she could retreat to the card room.

He still wasn't sure what to think of this new piece to the puzzle.

"Just think what she'd have to look forward to if she married a man like Warren." Jez subtly smoothed the back of her hand down her faintly bruised cheek. "This would make everything immensely better for us both."

"Understood."

"And also think of it as killing two birds with one stone, dearest."

"Can Ponsley be brought to heel with his familial connections?"

"In all likelihood, yes. He indulges her every whim."

That *could* well work in Leo's favor. But more importantly, this would ensure the girl's safety from Warren. "It's difficult to deny you anything, Jez."

"I know." She batted her lashes. "It's part of my charm."

Releasing Jez's elbow, he made his way through the crush of guests and toward the chit. Tristan was already at Lady Charlotte's side, whisking her away from the admiring beaux who surrounded her. The young lady laughed gaily as Tristan spun her onto the dance floor. His friend was already halfway to seducing her, and she would be deflowered before summer came. Not that Tristan intended to ruin the girl; but that was what happened when a lady found herself charmed by him.

Some moral warning bells went off within Leo. Decisions on the best course of action hampered his forward momentum, until he recalled his stepmother and the life she'd endured before marrying his father. Warren would not treat this young lady like the previous Fallon had treated Jez. Leo simply wouldn't allow that.

Tristan twirled Lady Charlotte into the next dance—a country gigue. The girl was more than pretty, and it surprised Leo that she didn't resemble the staunch Ponsley with his bulbous nose, beady eyes, and balding head. He was thankful that she apparently took after her mother in looks.

Tight ringlets fell on either side of her temples, framing her heart-shaped face and narrow nose becomingly. Her eyes were round and bright, twinkling like stars among the dancers. Her dress was of the latest fashion and swept off her shoulders front and back. A large bow tied at the base of her spine enticed a man to let his hands wander lower than was polite.

As Tristan brought the beauty toward him, Leo stepped forward, not wanting anyone else to steal Lady Charlotte's next dance. Judging by the wary looks he received from her admiring beaux, they wouldn't dare interfere.

A petite woman, more than a head shorter than him, stepped right in front of him. He saw nothing but the top of her brown head, a low bun knotted at the base of her neck, the high collar of a drab navy blue dress with a small lace frill that wrapped around to the front. She smelled of lavender, an odd thing to observe but familiar.

That was when she turned only a hairbreadth away from him, and her gaze caught his.

Genny.

Chapter 3

*With Lord C—— one never knows if the young la-
dies of decent reputation should run in fear of their
virtue and good name . . . or not. He doesn't distin-
guish between the diamonds and the ugly ducklings
who occupy the outskirts of any occasion when offering his gallantry. Shouldn't the latter be entitled
to enjoy compliments given freely from a lord of
marriageable age?*
The Mayfair Chronicles, May 26, 1846

This was a terrible plan.

She'd wanted to avoid Leo and forget she'd ever seen
him again, but she'd been forced to do otherwise the moment that rapscallion Marquess of Castleigh had swept
Charlotte onto the dance floor before she could intervene.

Confronting Barrington was a very, very terrible idea.

Whispers all around her had started the moment the
marquess had spun her cousin into the last set. Thank
goodness it was a simple gigue and not a more intimate
dance. Every nerve in her body had been put on edge, as
she waited—no, counted—the seconds till the dance
concluded.

She saw perfectly well what the man was doing. Especially since he hadn't bothered to write his name on Charlotte's dance card. Then Barrington had stepped toward Charlotte as the marquess walked off the dance floor.

All Genny wanted to know was why they had aimed their sights on Charlotte. How unfair to be not only dealing with a young woman who had the sudden whims of a girl bent on ruin but also to have Charlotte singled out in a room full of other beautiful women—plenty of whom probably wanted to be courted by one of these pleasure seekers.

At least the marquess had only kept her cousin on the dance floor for one dance—and had done nothing that would have the gossips' tongues wagging . . . yet.

Genny looked up at the *other* man she had every intention of stopping from swooping in on her unsuspecting charge. She saw what they were doing—weeding Charlotte out from the flock so they could do their damage.

She was glad to put a damper on his evening. Her cousin would *not* become one of his playthings.

He tugged at the tight knot of his cravat as he attempted to step around her. She followed as if they were in the midst of their own dance. Genny didn't dare take a glance around the room. Not on her life would she give her enemy her back or an opportunity to slip from her grasp to pursue Charlotte. She would not fail in her duty as chaperone. Charlotte would marry the man her father chose, and that was the end of it.

"A bloody bulldog in my path," he muttered.

"You'll stay away from that particular young lady, Barrington." Genny kept her voice just above a whisper.

His eyes narrowed as he focused on her. Only her.

Ha! She had his full attention now.

One down, another degenerate to go.

She really did have her work cut out for her this evening. She would bet a week's worth of pin money that Charlotte had probably encouraged the marquess's flirtation.

When Genny was done deterring Leo from his current conquest, she'd make sure the marquess also understood that his behavior was intolerable and unacceptable. She'd not stand idly by while her cousin fell to ruin.

Barrington remained silent as he studied her. Did he recognize her? Or had their time together all those years ago been so forgettable? No use lamenting a past long forgotten. Well, not completely forgotten to her. At least he wasn't trying to dodge around her anymore. She had quite effectively stopped the charging bull from following his determined path.

"Isn't this a surprise?" he finally said.

Before she could respond, he clasped her hand and twirled her into the middle of a throng of dancers and the quick steps of a mazurka. If she danced, she'd not be able to find Charlotte, but she couldn't leave the dance floor now that he'd dragged her there.

"It's been a long time."

"For dancing?" She knew perfectly well that wasn't what he meant.

He gave her an assessing look. "Among other things."

He pulled her along with the fast pace of the music. She'd be hard-pressed to talk if they kept up with the vigorous tempo.

"Who is the young lady to you?"

"A vested interest." At his raised brow, she added, "She is my cousin."

He laughed and spun her around faster, taking their steps at the correct speed instead of slowing down enough to let her catch her breath. And how unfair that he wasn't out of breath.

His fingers rubbed over the backs of hers as though searching for a ring beneath the fitted gloves. "You never married."

Was this an absent observation or was he truly curious? What right did the man think he had to comment on her status as a spinster?

"Not for want of trying."

She'd just chosen the wrong man to set her sights on.

If anyone had bothered to tell her that Barrington was not the marrying sort, she wondered if she would have listened. It was too late to wonder about the what-ifs. What was done was done. She'd made the most of the lot she'd been given in life. As much as she'd like to turn the clock back and try it all over again, life didn't work that way.

"What do you want, Barrington?"

"How do you know I didn't just want to talk to you?"

He smirked. Actually smirked as though she'd just told the funniest joke of the evening.

"You shouldn't look so amused. It's unbecoming for a man of your ilk."

"Why hasn't anyone ever told me?"

"Because you are a blackguard."

"How wonderful to be showered with compliments by you." There was a teasing quality to his comment. "How long has it been, Genny?"

She sighed. She supposed it wasn't so terrible to be in his company since he *did* remember her. But she couldn't help saying, "It shouldn't surprise me you don't know the answer to that."

The heat of his breath fanned over the shell of her ear. "Perhaps I wish to hear it from your lips, talking about your memories of our wickedly delightful nights together. I have missed you more than you can imagine all these years."

What was that supposed to mean?

He pulled her in a little closer as they rounded the outskirts of the dance floor. To an observer, it would look as if he merely had a good hold on her through the turns instead of holding her inappropriately closer so he could whisper sweet nothings in her ear. Well, inveigling words would not sway her in whatever game he played.

Afraid it would look too obvious if she fought his tight hold, she relaxed into the steps, letting him lead the brisk pace and the direction for their rapid turns and jumps and twirls.

Goodness, she hadn't danced a mazurka since . . . since forever. They spun so fast, moved so quickly to the two-four beat, that she couldn't utter another word. That was probably his intention, while his friend made off with her cousin.

She tried to focus on the room around them to ensure her cousin was still present but couldn't concentrate her gaze long enough on any one spot while they danced.

Leo's hand was firm and steady around hers. The muscles of his biceps moved and flexed beneath her hold on his other arm.

The citruslike smell of his cologne enveloped her. The underlying smell of male musk brought to mind the unwanted memories of hot sweaty nights, when they had embraced and been so thoroughly entwined with each other that nothing else had existed in all the world. She closed her eyes and swallowed back a lump that had formed in her throat, trusting him to guide them around the other dancers.

With those unbidden thoughts, her body swayed closer to his. Close enough to feel the shush of her skirts brushing against his legs. Close enough that his every breath moved the loose tendrils of hair around her temples. She looked away from his knowing gaze, realizing he understood exactly which direction her mind had wandered in.

When the song ended, she dropped her hand from his arm and attempted to slip away. She searched the crowds around the outskirts of the room for her cousin.

To her relief, Charlotte was still in view. Had the earlier warning that Genny would be displeased if her cousin so much as dared to wander off rooted firmly in the girl's mind? Unfortunately she was still in the company of the marquess.

While Genny slackened her hand in Barrington's grip, he did not release her. She turned to face him, eyebrow raised. What was he about?

"Our dance has concluded, my lord." She tried to tug her hand from his, but he held tight. "You are making a scene."

His smile was slow and so very wicked that it felt like hot flicks of his tongue dancing erotically against her heated flesh. She didn't like or trust that expression one bit. It was one she'd grown used to during their summer liaison and it was full of mischievous and assuredly lascivious intentions.

"We are far from garnering anyone's attention."

A waltz—Chopin, if she wasn't mistaken—started for the next set. Couples stood ready, then bowed and curtsied. Barrington twirled her on the spot, hand above her head briefly, and then he pulled her intimately into the circle of his arms, as though they were the only ones in the room and no reproach would come from their actions.

Two dances in a row.

She wanted to kick him in the shin for his bold behavior. Maybe she would if she ever came upon him without an audience.

She attempted to push away from him. "What are you doing?"

His grip tightened.

"Dancing." That charming, nonchalant tone only added to her ire. "You?"

"My duties lie elsewhere. I'm not at liberty to play whatever game it is you have devised."

"I assure you that you are much more than a passing amusement. Besides, everyone should be *at liberty* to enjoy a dance or two, princess."

His use of that old endearment prickled unsettlingly at her pride. That was the nickname he'd used for her so long ago. For all she knew, he called every woman princess.

Purposefully, she stepped on his toes, giving him a wide smile as she ground the ball of her foot onto his instep.

"I know exactly the kind of man you are. And I know firsthand what you are capable of. You'll have to find another woman to seduce."

"Are you offering?" The teasing quality of his voice only irritated her further.

"You had your chance with me, Barrington. Never again."

"Phrasing it that way, you don't sound so sure."

"That's where you are sadly mistaken." She wished she could walk away, and she would—just as soon as this dance ended. Never had a man infuriated her more than Barrington.

Forget bulldog. She was a hellcat, nails unsheathed and ready for a bloody battle.

To say he was reluctant to release her hand might very well be an understatement. He remembered Genny all too well, though he enjoyed goading her to believe otherwise when he could see clearly in her expression that she didn't think he did. How could he ever forget a woman who had wormed her way under his skin and had made him restless whenever she was near?

It had been summertime when he'd last seen her. Though "seen" wasn't exactly an apt way to recall their sultry nights and sensually charged evenings.

There had been nothing tame about her four summers ago.

What he did recall with perfect clarity was that she'd been dressed in the height of the season's latest fashion back then. The garb she wore now was hardly fashionable. Hardly becoming. The only thing she needed to make it complete was a mobcap.

Even though her clothes might say she was here in a different capacity than that of finding a husband, he couldn't relinquish the images of their entwined naked forms. He remembered what the heat of her skin had felt like against his. Recalled, too, the taste of her passion and the sound of her cries as their bodies came together.

The very idea of having her again fired his blood, and that thought alone was enough to have him raring and ready to go like a stud in season.

He couldn't be expected to keep his liberties to a minimum with his thoughts diving so quickly southward. Bloody hell, he knew the woman more intimately than anyone.

More importantly, she'd meant more to him than she could ever fathom. He had thought himself in love with her, and had intended to ask for her hand before his father had convinced him that was the wrong move to make. He had cared enough to leave her behind at the house party when the first scandal broke over another couple engaging in an illicit affair—his only concern had been to protect Genny's reputation.

His hand flexed around her hip. Her curves felt as lush as ever where his hand rested just above the curve of her bottom—he slid his hand to the left, placing it on the small of her waist between her hip and breast. Her bosom was unfortunately covered completely from view. A man could bury and happily smother himself in all that plumpness . . .

Genny was quick to pull away this time when the dance ended. His intention had been to keep her away from the girl, or so he led himself to believe, but really, he'd just wanted to feel her in his arms again.

Much like lead tossed in a bucket of water, the thought of charming and winning Genny's cousin sat heavy in his gut.

Tristan had had the girl to himself for fifteen minutes. That was enough time to endear Lady Charlotte in his favor for eternity. Tristan had a certain *je ne sais quoi* that ladies of all ages found irresistible. So what was Leo to do? Tristan never left anything unfinished. And once Jez had made up her mind about something it was not easy to divert her attention elsewhere. It wasn't as though they'd ruin the girl, simply steer her planned path in another direction—one far from Mr. Warren.

Leo was one step behind Genny as she weaved her way through the dancers. A few threads of her straight hair had escaped her low chignon; it must have come undone during their dance. Thank the heavens she didn't wear a mobcap. He liked seeing her slightly disheveled, especially when he was the one to cause the disheveling.

Mamas watched their daughters from the edge of the dance floor while he followed hot on Genny's tail like a buck in rut. There those rutting thoughts came again. He wanted to throw his hands up in exasperation. Why did this little woman turn his thoughts primitive?

Lady Charlotte's back was to them; her hair had been coiffed with an array of perfect, corkscrew spirals. The satin bow that tied off her necklace at her nape was an enticement to all men in the vicinity. It was an invitation to touch and explore the soft feminine curves of her shoulder blades. Yet . . . yet, he had no desire to reach for her, not when he was closing the distance on a certain temperamental Fury.

Leo nodded to Tristan and gave his friend a meaningful glace in the direction of the woman three paces ahead of him—who just so happened to have every intention of spoiling any plans Tristan had laid the groundwork for.

Leo was torn as to whether or not he should let Genny put a stop to their devised amusement. Certainly the Ponsley chit's feelings would be involved and she'd be crushed when she realized neither of them had any intention of marrying her once Mr. Warren found another woman to chase after.

Leo saw clearly that this was an irrational wager decided on the spur of a moment.

No, this was the right thing to do.

Mr. Warren was a product of his great-uncle, who had been an abuser of woman. They'd be saving the chit from going down the same path Jez had taken with her husband. Save her from experiencing what his stepmother had experienced before she'd met Leo's father.

There was no reason to stop what they had planned. The girl would gain a life experience, and she could find a man more deserving of her.

Genny slid her arm under Charlotte's, intent on taking the girl as far away as possible from both men currently in their company.

"We are needed elsewhere."

"Cousin, you are being discourteous." Charlotte's blue eyes sparked in annoyance. "Let me introduce you to the Marquess of Castleigh."

Genny pinched her lips together in an effort not to say she knew very well who he was as did every other person in attendance tonight. Everyone would want to know what the pleasure seekers had said to them and why they had singled them out.

Smooth and cunning, Castleigh bowed neatly and took Genny's hand in his. "It's a pleasure to make the acquaintance of the two most beautiful women at the ball. And to have you both to myself."

His voice was like warm mead that melted down your throat and loosened any inhibitions you might have despite knowing better than to spend time with such a man. He'd weaken a woman's sensibilities with a few pretty words and an admiring glance. A skill only the greatest rakes had, she was sure, but her experience with rakes did not extend beyond Leo.

Genny glanced at her cousin, whose gaze was raptly focused on the marquess. She herself had once been that innocent and admiring of the handsome gents who had courted her. But this man did not engage in decent courtship. She needed to guide her cousin away from the marquess. Perhaps a heartfelt conversation would enlighten Charlotte as to the man's true nature?

"I know precisely who the Marquis of Castleigh is. You'll do well to know, cousin, that his type is better suited to a den of iniquity than to a respectable ball." She pulled Charlotte away from the scoundrel. "Lady Carleton wanted to discuss the seating arrangements for her upcoming dinner party."

"Firmly rebuffed, I daresay." Tristan laughed as though this were the greatest fun he'd had in ages.

Charlotte pulled away from her with a pointed glare. "Why should I have any say about her seating plans? You're being incredibly rude, Genny."

"I am positive that Lord Castleigh and Lord Barrington are not in the least offended. After all, I only speak the truth, don't I, gentlemen?"

"How could I ever forget that you had such a sharp bite, Miss Camden," Leo said drolly.

Before Genny could riposte, Charlotte interjected, "I really must apologize for my cousin." Charlotte flicked her fan open. "The heat in here has obviously gone straight to her head."

It took everything in Genny not to make an unladylike noise. Her cousin was only trying to dissolve the fast-building tension, so Genny pinched her lips shut and narrowed her gaze on Castleigh and then Leo, hopefully making her disdain known without the necessity of words.

While the marquess watched their exchange with barely concealed amusement, Leo was so raptly attuned to Genny that she thought him angry on her behalf.

Leo stepped toward her. "Take another turn around the room with me, Miss Camden."

"The attendees might think you intend something of a permanent nature where I'm concerned, Barrington."

"No dancing, I promise. Just a few words shared between *friends of old*."

"And leave Charlotte in the clutches of your friend?" She put her shoulders back and canted her chin up. "I have a great deal more sense than you seem to give me credit for."

Leo turned back to the marquess. "Keep company with Lady Charlotte while I take Miss Camden around the room. We'll be but a moment."

Then Leo had the gall to take her arm and lead her away. The hold he had on her arm was so tight that the only way to escape him would be to yank harshly away, which would cause a scene. Being on his arm was enough gossip fodder for the next week, so she wisely chose to follow him.

"What is it you think you are going to accomplish with me watching and anticipating your every move?" she asked.

He had the decency to keep her in view of all party attendees, leading her to the edge of the room but far enough from any burning ears.

"Giving us some much needed space, my dear."

"I'm not *your* anything, Leonidas Harrow."

"You once were many things to me, Genny."

"I suggest you hold your tongue, unless you plan to ruin me in society's eyes after all these years of doing the right thing by staying away."

"I don't wish to cause you any lasting damage. I merely wanted you to myself for a moment." He grew quiet as he studied her with a critical eye. Finally, he said, "Four years is a long time."

"What is it you are so eager to say that you had to drag me away from my cousin?"

"I want only to know how you fare. Why is it you play the role of chaperone instead of filling some house with babes of your own?"

"A bold question from the man who practically destroyed any chance I had at marriage."

This time he was the one to narrow his eyes. He opened his mouth to say something only to close it again as they weaved their way farther away from her cousin.

"We never agreed to anything beyond that house party."

How right he was. There had been no promises of tomorrow, only a few weeks of mutual pleasure, and a yearning on her part for more. True, they hadn't had *that* conversation until after their first night together. She'd wanted more, of course, but had been reluctant to broach the subject with him for fear that their time would end prematurely. How stupid she'd been.

"There was more than one way to preserve my reputation." Why was she even having this conversation with him?

His hand tightened briefly around her arm.

"At the time, you were being courted by two other men at that house party."

What was left unsaid was that he thought she'd choose one of her other suitors to pick up the pieces of her tender broken heart. Not that he knew he'd broken her heart.

The day Leo had left the house party, without a promise to return for her, she knew that she would never marry without love. The funny thing was, she hadn't realized she'd really loved him until it was too late.

"They didn't suit." She dropped his arm and gave him a defiant glare. "Now, if you'll excuse me, I have much to discuss with my cousin."

He tried to keep her on his arm, but Leo eventually had to let her go or risk drawing eyes in their direction. With a polite nod at those standing near them, he followed after her, his fist clenching, itching to grab her back into the fold of his arms. Finding her here tonight felt as though he'd been given a second chance to prove himself worthy of her.

Tristan headed his way when Genny all but pulled Lady Charlotte off in another direction.

His friend grinned. "I do believe that horse will be mine before the week is out."

"Is that so?" he asked absently, watching the women converse with Lady Carleton at the other end of the room.

The cousins were a great contrast.

While Ponsley's daughter was all done up in the latest fashion without a care for the expense considering all her fine jewels and the diamond-studded picks in her hair, Genny wore a plain gown of navy blue. There was not one embellishment to be seen on her dress, or any piece of finery added to make it more stylish and becoming for the grand duchess's ball. And though Genny had never been wealthy—she was a vicar's daughter as he recalled—she'd never lacked for anything. Then again, she was far more stunning in her simple clothes than all the finery that filled the room.

Had he been the cause of her current circumstance? Guilt like nothing he'd ever felt before filled his chest uneasily.

Was this what Genny had been reduced to after their time together? Why hadn't she married? She had been a pleasant, biddable woman.

When they'd met, he'd been young and incredibly stupid. He'd lost himself in her all those years ago, and he had felt something a lot like love for her. Yet, he'd walked away at his father's bidding. His father had insisted that chasing after Genny would be the greatest mistake of Leo's life, a mistake that could not be fixed. And he'd trusted his father blindly.

Their liaison had been unplanned but it had still happened. They'd been diligent about keeping their evenings together a secret. No one, not even Tristan, who was his oldest friend, knew about it. Why should he share that information? It had been a very private matter between just the two of them. He had liked her not only because she was a woman of great beauty but because she made him want more for himself. And he simply liked to spend time in her company. Had he been the right man for her, would he have left her to her own devices after taking her innocence? He thought not.

Feeling a niggling of doubt, he reminded himself again that they'd made no promises to each other. Not once had she asked that they marry, nor had she admitted to having strong feelings for him . . .

The prickle of doubt grew stronger.

Tristan chuckled beside him. "You can't be serious, my friend."

Had Tristan noticed where his focus lay?

"We agreed to help Jez," Leo said thoughtfully. "And

I have a feeling you can't charm Ponsley's daughter with Miss Camden standing over you, watching and noting your every move."

Besides, Tristan was voting in Leo's favor against the import duty. His friend could just as easily charm Ponsley's daughter. Really, it didn't have anything to do with him having another woman in mind altogether. Second chances weren't meant to be squandered.

Tristan slapped him on the back. "That's the spirit. We'll take them both down."

Leo glared at his friend. Swaying the Ponsley girl toward another course was officially the worst idea he'd ever had in his life, especially if it meant indirectly involving Genny. Genny had never been part of this equation.

In the end, however, they were protecting Lady Charlotte from Mr. Warren. Leo reminded himself again that Jez had endured hell for the past six years, and he would not allow another Fallon to harm a defenseless woman again. He wasn't leading Lady Charlotte astray, he was simply helping her find a better path in life.

This was why he'd avoided Miss Camden all these years. She made him question himself: his morals, his wants, and his true desires in life. And now that Miss Camden had matured nicely and was no longer young and docile, she could defend herself against a man of his nature. She could put him in his place and keep him begging for more, no doubt.

But would she let him close again?

One thing was certain: if he was going to go along with his plan of stopping Lady Charlotte's impending marriage, he had every intention of courting Miss Camden down a delectable path of sin once again. This time, there was nothing to make him walk away.

Chapter 4

Rumors abound about the Earl of B——. I've not had good gossip to share about him since his torrid breakup with that actress Mrs. W—— of Drury Lane some nine months past. Not one attendee at the most talked about ball last night failed to see the bond between Lord B—— and someone not well known in the ton. The interest has everyone abuzz and twittering in speculation.

Could she be a relative? An old friend or acquaintance? This writer thinks not. Oh, how my hands tingle with excitement with this latest on dit. Perhaps there is a much more sordid past between these two yet to be revealed? Let it be known that this writer intends to find out the whole truth and report back to my readers' burning ears.

The Mayfair Chronicles, May 27, 1846

Genny's head fell back on the chaise as Charlotte's grandmother read Scripture from the Bible. It truly was the most ungodly hour to be awake for this kind of challenge. Shouldn't there be rules on when the Bible was read? Saved for Sundays and religious holidays? Most of all, it should never be attempted until well after the sun rose for the day.

Genny's head bobbed forward as she focused on the gray-shrouded windows on the southeast wall in the morning parlor. Though it had to be a quarter past five, and the birds chirped and whistled out of doors, there was no sign of sunshine. Perhaps it would be a dreary, rainy day.

The amber, emerald, and aquamarine stained glass in the upper portion of the windows remained dull without the sun's golden rays illuminating it. Only splotches of the rose-patterned paper on the wall could be made out in the dim glow of gaslights set around the room.

"Genevieve." Her companion rapped her knuckle on the side table to get her attention. "Do keep up."

"Yes, Aunt." The woman insisted on being addressed as Aunt or Aunt Millicent by anyone who was not a direct blood relation. "I must apologize for my absentmindedness. The duchess's ball was a tiring affair last night."

"Yes, dear. I imagine so. But it's not you who dances all evening long."

Not normally, she supposed, but she did have to be on her feet the whole evening. "Of course, Aunt. I didn't mean to imply otherwise."

Genny covered a yawn that nearly overtook her face and focused on keeping her dry, tired eyes open. Half-mast would have to do; she truly did not have the energy to keep them fully open. Thank goodness Aunt Millicent couldn't see clearly without an eyeglass firmly tucked inside the unflattering wrinkles around her eye. Said blue eye was focused on the tiny print of the Bible held open in her hands.

Genny didn't even know which chapter they were reading from; her thoughts were occupied by very unholy images of Leo.

She'd woken twice in the short sleep she'd had, and

both times Leo had been in her thoughts. The first time she'd awoken, she'd been covered in sweat, her pulse racing in excitement. The second time—she was almost embarrassed to recall what had her nearly jumping out of bed—but the juncture between her thighs had ached and pulsed in time with her frantic heartbeat. She hadn't been able to fall asleep again and before she knew it the ringing of Aunt's bedside bell had called her to the old woman's side for the morning.

"I had word of your escapades at the ball."

That had Genny snapping to attention. Her head whipped up and focused on Aunt Millicent. "I'm not sure what you mean by escapades. I can assure you that the majority of our night was passed in Lady Carleton's company."

"And what of the Earl of Barrington?"

First, who had told her any such thing? Second, how could she have found out details of the ball when they hadn't arrived home till after midnight and had gone straightaway to bed? Aunt Millicent should have been asleep by the time they'd arrived home.

Would Charlotte have gone to see her grandmother before retiring for the evening? If so, it didn't escape Genny's notice that there was no mention of Castleigh in the veiled accusation.

Maybe Charlotte wished to have Genny sent away? Anger bloomed in her chest and made her hands shake where a moment ago they had rested calmly in her lap. Did Charlotte not understand how badly Genny needed to keep this appointment? Who would she stay on with if she were turned out of the Ponsley residence?

"I'm sure you know the type of character Barrington is, Aunt. He made poor judgment dancing with me and we wouldn't have partnered had he not caught me unawares. I promise you, he was firmly rebuffed shortly afterward."

"A dance, was it?" She put down the Bible and focused her enlarged eye on Genny. "You are here in the capacity of chaperone for my granddaughter. You are to make the correct judgment call in all situations."

Genny fisted her hand in her lap. "I can't express how thankful I am for the generosity of this family. I will endeavor never to be caught unawares again."

"I objected to my son hiring you, since you are still too young to play the role of a proper and respectable chaperone, but he took pity on your situation and your need for another appointment after Hilda passed away."

She had expected this type of lecture from Lord Ponsley but not from Aunt Millicent. Did Lord Ponsley have a bigger heart in his chest than she imagined after all?

"Dancing is not allowable under any circumstance for a chaperone, especially with someone of Barrington's reputation. How can you possibly keep an eye on Charlotte if you are indulging in wickedness of your own?"

Damn it. Why had she even mentioned dancing? Regardless of whether or not Aunt Millicent heard of her *escapades* from one of her many acquaintances later on, Genny wished she hadn't plainly spelled out what she'd done wrong.

What made all this worse was that Genny had a feeling she'd see Barrington and Castleigh in the coming days. And she was not looking forward to the battle that was sure to arise when she informed Charlotte she would have to strive to ignore the two degenerates vying for her undivided attention.

"I can assure you there will be no misjudgment on my part again. It was uncouth of him to approach me when I didn't even have a dancing card. I put him firmly in his place." Genny reached her hand out to pat her aunt's arm reassuringly. "Don't you worry, Aunt Millicent. He won't dare approach me again."

When her aunt didn't pick up the Bible again, but stared at her probingly, Genny thought she'd have to come up with a better explanation. Thankfully, they were interrupted by Lord Ponsley's entrance into the parlor.

"Here you are, Mother. I looked for you in the break-fast room first, but I suppose the day is still too early for consuming anything aside from tea." He came forward, ignored Genny, and pressed a kiss against his mother's softly wrinkled cheek. "I wanted to wish you a good day. I'm off to my club and then Parliament meetings. I shan't be home till nigh on the dinner hour."

"You work too hard, my boy." Aunt Millicent patted the side of Lord Ponsley's face. "You should spend the day with your daughter. She expressed interest in purchasing a new bonnet and a few dresses for some upcoming dinner engagements."

"I would if I could. But I haven't the time for fripperies just now. You know how it is, Mother."

"Yes, my darling boy."

Genny folded her hands in her lap and waited for his lordship to address her, if he even thought to do so. She was usually invisible to the man, which, come to think on it, might be a good thing today. Did he know anything of what happened last evening? Certainly not, or he would have berated her for the indiscretion.

He kissed his mother on the cheek again and turned to leave. Before exiting, however, he turned and said, "Miss Camden, do take Charlotte out and appease her senseless need to shop. Tell her I'll see her tonight before you leave for the Carletons' dinner party."

She dipped her head in acquiescence. "Of course, my lord."

When the door shut behind his tall, somewhat paunchy form, she slouched back into the comfort of the chaise.

"Do sit up straight, Genevieve. It is no wonder that you failed to marry when your posture is so wretched."

Yes, surely marriage depended solely upon one's ability to stand and sit ramrod straight. Genny corrected her posture to appease her aunt.

Once her aunt picked up the Bible again, Genny leaned against the arm of the chaise and fought very hard to keep her eyes open. Maybe she'd be able to sneak in a short nap between breakfast and shopping. She'd have to have her wits about her if she was right about not having seen the last of Barrington and Castleigh.

Leo sat heavily in the chair across from Hayden. A fizzing glass of water—the best hangover cure to be had anywhere in London—was set before him.

Hayden motioned to the glass. "I ordered it when I heard you talking to Brett at the front. You'll feel immensely more human after half a glass."

Leo eyed the cloudy water distastefully. He knew he needed something to settle his foggy head and jumbled stomach. After the ball, they'd spent a greater portion of the night at his townhouse. Between the four of them they had split two bottles of rum before the night had concluded. And the only reason he knew they had consumed so much was by the empty glass jugs lying about in bald evidence come morning.

Leaning forward in the chair, he slid the glass closer so the fizzing bubbles tickled at his nose. His stomach protested at the very thought of drinking liquids of any type at present.

"What was it Jez said we were doing tonight? Can't recall this early in the day, my head has not had time to wake up with the rest of my slow-moving body." Leo closed his eyes to block out the light. Good God, what had he thought to accomplish by drinking so much last night? He didn't normally imbibe this freely, and hadn't since his college days.

"Tristan managed to get an invite to the Carletons' dinner party. He spent half his night charming the lady and her husband to secure two seats at her coveted dinner party—you being an automatic choice."

The Carletons were old family friends of his father's.

"Those who attend are more oft than not invited to her annual house party in the country in June." Hayden leaned back in his chair, amusement coloring his expression. "I sit this one out, old chap."

Right, Leo thought dourly as he recalled bits and pieces of his night now. Apparently they were to steal the Ponsley chit out from under Mr. Warren's nose.

A plate of toast, eggs, and bacon were set in front of Hayden. Leo's stomach roiled. He had to focus on the pattern in the Turkish rug off to the right of Hayden's shoulder, though that didn't help the spinning of his head any better than the sight or smell of food.

"Drink up, so you'll be able to eat something."

"I met an old acquaintance last night." Leo wasn't sure why he mentioned it, perhaps because it was worth mentioning?

"And . . . ?"

"The chaperone—did I mention she was the girl's chaperone?—well, she'll be a problem." An enjoyable one, but a problem nonetheless.

Hayden put up his hands. "Jez is right stubborn whenever the mood strikes and she told me quite frankly that she'll not have me interfering with her plans. I think you should humor her for the time being. It keeps her from doing anything . . . rash." Hayden took a healthy bite of his eggs before continuing. "What she really needs is a break from society, but when I suggested we spend a week at my country estate, she outright refused. She said the moment she leaves, Mr. Warren will have all her belongings tossed out of her house and into the middle of Mayfair for all to witness."

"Has Mr. Warren threatened her?" Leo felt his ire rising with every shared detail of Jezebel's predicament.

"I believe the only reason he's not thrown her out is that it would damage his reputation considerably by doing it so soon after her husband's death. Society has always been divided on their opinion of Jez."

"Too true. Those who hated that blighter husband of hers feel something very close to pity for Jez." Leo rubbed his temples in an attempt to ease the pounding migraine he felt coming on. He was never going to drink again.

"And those who find her actions and candor distasteful side with her husband," Hayden finished.

Leo downed half the contents in the glass and cringed as he set the revolting concoction back on the wooden table with a thunk.

"Jesus, man. What is this crap that I'm pouring down my gullet?"

"Something that'll help you eat." Hayden waved over the steward. "My friend here is ready for your breakfast specialty. Something to cure his cotton mouth and uneasy stomach." Hayden looked to Leo and said, "You can thank me later for the cure-all you're throwing down your *gullet*."

"Much gratitude, Hayden." He scrubbed his hands roughly over his eyes, wishing the spinning would settle long enough for him to drink up the remainder of the fizzing mixture in front of him. "Back to Jez for a minute here. Have you seen your solicitor yet?"

"Not for another two hours. But I should warn you, changing the outcome of the will is about the only way she'll listen to reason. I'll try and have it held up in court.

Perhaps Mr. Warren will draw up a settlement to appease Jez if he's made to wait a lengthy period."

Jez's choices were few: she could marry again, and hope the man was decent, or she could figure out a way to live on a small fraction of the money she was used to.

Leo pulled out his fob, and flipped the gold case open. Nearly eleven and he wanted nothing more than to sleep off his headache. Though it seemed to be receding with every minute that passed.

"Right, then," Leo said. "I'll take myself about the shops and buy something nice to cheer her up. What do you reckon she desires most?"

Between bites of his poached eggs, Hayden said, "Aside from dashing Mr. Warren's chances of ever marrying, I suggest something frivolous and completely useless. She does love her baubles and she was admiring a fan inlaid with jade on Bond Street last week. Or perhaps some new hair combs?" With a shrug of his shoulders, Hayden wiped his mouth on his napkin and tossed it down on his finished plate. "I have some errands to attend. Will I see you at Tristan's before you make your way to the Carletons?"

Leo nodded and pressed his fingers to his aching temples again. Saying no to Jez was not something he or Tristan had ever been able to do. "I believe 'after eight' were his words, though I can't be sure."

Hayden laughed at him as he stood, doffed his hat, and slapped him on the back of his shoulder. "Till this evening," were his parting words.

Once Leo finished his meal, he felt marginally better and called for his jacket and hat. It was time to head over to Bond Street to buy something for Jez. And he would shamelessly use said gift as a bribe to persuade Jez that she should plan a trip to the countryside. She did need to get away from the hubbub of the city at least for a short time.

As he turned off Piccadilly, whom should he see but

Miss Camden and her cousin? He paused at the corner of
Old Bond and watched them for a moment. The driver of
the coach helped Genny's cousin down the last step of the
carriage. Done with his task, the driver held out his hand
for his coin, which Genny placed in his ungloved palm.

Well, didn't this just make his day a little brighter? He
did enjoy the fact that he could fluster Miss Camden so
early in the day—maybe he enjoyed doing that a little too
much.

Genny's dress was a white-sprigged muslin, with little
yellow flowers dotting her bodice and skirts, simple yet
elegant. Though her companion wore a pink and green
checked silk day dress with a slight dip in front and back,
and of a much finer material, his gaze swung immediately back to Genny. She clasped a white parasol in her
delicately lace-gloved hands. Unfortunately, a silk moiré
bonnet shaded her face from his vantage point.

She would not see him coming, then. He'd have the opportunity to take her unawares. What would her reaction
be on seeing him today?

A smile tugged at the corners of his mouth, and he
picked up his pace, heading in their direction. They disappeared behind the dark-stained wooden door of a jeweler's.

Leo pushed his way through the same door they had
entered a few minutes later. A brass bell jingled above his
head, heralding his arrival. It was busy—there were about
a dozen patrons looking over the wares—so no one turned
or took notice of him, aside from the shopkeeper who
smiled brightly and approached to offer assistance.

"Good afternoon, my lord."

"Afternoon."

"Might I be of assistance?"

"I intend to catch up with the ladies." He nodded in the
direction of Lady Charlotte and Miss Camden.

The proprietor stepped back with a bow. "I will not keep you, my lord. Let me know if you require any assistance."

"I will. Thank you." He stepped farther into the store and closer to his quarry.

A store clerk was showing Ponsley's daughter a hatpin. He placed the emerald-studded piece through the young woman's hat and showed her the image she made with a handheld mirror. Miss Camden looked like the most patient woman in the world, standing off to the side, hands folded demurely over her front, head nodding as she said something too quiet for him to hear from this distance.

Should he approach the cousin or Miss Camden first? Maybe he should approach the salesclerk helping them, since he did plan on buying some sort of bauble for Jez and this was just as good a store as any. That settled it then, two birds with one stone as the saying went.

He stepped out from the melee of people crowded around the glass cases situated at the front of the store.

Lady Charlotte turned to him with an inviting smile, fingers clasped to the soft yellow brim of her hat as the clerk pulled out the hairpin lodging it in place.

"Lady Charlotte," he said, tipping his hat forward. "Your very presence has made my morning all the brighter."

For the briefest moment, there was a glint of wickedness in her smile before she schooled her expression into something more becoming for a lady fresh out into society. It was practiced coyness and far too knowing for a woman who was under the age of twenty and unmarried.

And it was in that moment—after not having spent any time alone with her the previous evening—he understood she was not a woman easily taken by surprise. He would have guffawed at the realization if they were the only two people in the room. Maybe he need not worry about her virtue. He had a suspicion the young lady knew precisely how to handle Tristan. It might be wiser to worry for his friend.

"Lord Barrington. Fancy we should find you here. I don't believe we've had the pleasure of running into each other before now."

"Evidently, it is my good fortune that finds me here while you are out shopping."

Charlotte's gaze slipped past his shoulder. It was brief, but he noticed her attention was momentarily distracted. A shame he hadn't thought to invite Tristan along for his outing. The wastrel was probably still abed.

"Alas, my lady, I am alone in my travels today."

Her perfectly plucked brows arched just as Miss Camden's arm slipped through hers.

Genny inclined her head politely, but he didn't miss the flash of annoyance in her light brown gaze. "Lord Barrington," she said tersely. At least she acknowledged him. To her cousin she said, "I saw the most beautiful hairpiece. I must show it to you at once."

She tried to tug her cousin away from him, but Charlotte budged not an inch.

Did he have an accomplice in monopolizing Miss Camden's time?

"What brings you to Bond Street, my lord?" Charlotte asked.

"I am on a mission to find the most nonsensical frippery possible."

"For whom do you purchase this gift? Maybe—"

"Charlotte," Miss Camden scolded. "You cannot ask such things."

Charlotte's cheeks pinkened and he doubted it had anything to do with her boldness, but was instead a result of Miss Camden's firm, public reprimand. "I only meant that we could be of service and help you pick something out."

"I cannot refuse such a generous offer." He looked to Miss Camden, his smile slow and easy. She chewed on her lower lip as she stared at him questioningly. "The frippery is for Jez . . . I mean the Dowager Countess of Fallon."

Charlotte covered her mouth too late to hide her amusement over the nickname. Miss Camden's lips pinched together in disapproval.

"I'd be honored if you could help me pick out something suitable for a lady."

"I daresay our tastes differ greatly and I doubt we would be of any help in this quest of yours for the dowager countess." Miss Camden turned away from him after she spoke.

"Come now, Miss Camden. Surely all women appreciate the same types of fripperies?" He spread his hand out to indicate the array of jeweled picks and tortoiseshell hair combs in the glass display cabinets that lined the walls. "What would you choose for . . . yourself?"

Her eyes dropped to the pieces in question. Charlotte remained silent on the topic as Genny stepped forward with a barely audible sigh of defeat.

The first of many concessions he would garner from the lady. Leo had to cover his amused grin with his gloved hand so as not to prick her mood again. She gave him a distrustful glare, then looked at the glass case, her finger running along the seamed edge. Her gloves were lace and frilled out in layers just above the delicate bone at the side of her wrist; her fingers were long and slender beneath, bringing back memories of them searching across his broad, naked chest.

He swallowed and focused on the hair picks and tried not to imagine those hands sliding along his skin as teasingly as they did along the glass.

It wasn't long before she pointed to something for the proprietor to retrieve.

He leaned closer when the item was placed on a small piece of black velvet. Charlotte also stepped closer to view what was displayed before them.

"Oh, cousin," she said, mirth sprinkled in her voice.

Genny had picked a hair comb with a mishmash of red octagonal beads roughly the size of the tip of his pinky, glued above long lacquered black tines. Six-inch feathers dyed orange shot straight through the middle of the pasted jewels.

"I daresay," Leo responded, "that has to be the ugliest hair comb I've ever laid eyes upon."

Genny put her chin up defiantly. "As you might have surmised, our tastes differ greatly."

Leo full out laughed at her quip. Miss Camden really disliked his attentions. Disliked that he'd put her in an odd situation by asking for her and her cousin's assistance.

He would sway her opinion of him to something more favorable. There had been a time when she had adored him and it would be his goal to charm her a second time. And he wasn't doing this for the sake of Jez; he *liked* Miss Camden more than he ought. She was a wicked temptation he didn't want to resist.

"Genny, do pick something else. Show his lordship that you have a modicum of good taste. You *did* help me pick out most of my millinery needs for the season."

"I'm glad to know what displeases you most, but I'd be interested to see what does catch your eye from the display." Leo motioned to the cases lined up before them.

Miss Camden let out a frustrated air as she stared back at him. "Very well. But why ask me? Do you not buy baubles for your lovers or mistresses?"

They'd been relatively quiet up to this point and had

only attracted the attention of a few of the other women in the shop. But that comment had a few heads turned in their direction.

His smile slipped for the briefest of moments. Ah, so she only thought the worst of him. Yes, he'd taken her innocence, and he was somewhat of a playboy in society, but the idea of a mistress was repugnant even to the likes of him. And he did not pay his lovers with fripperies, nor would he ever treat them as one might a shameful mistress.

"I've never needed nor wanted to acquire such an item, madam."

She must have heard the displeasure lacing his voice for she turned away and stared down at the glass case before them once again.

Nothing seemed to catch her eye as she moved on to the next case and then the next. He followed slowly behind. Twice she stopped suddenly to closer inspect the pieces beneath the glass and it caused her skirts to brush against his calves. He wanted to press forward and feel a little more of her, but he daren't act so bold as to harm her reputation. He forced himself to step away and settled for watching her move from case to case. He'd have to be content with the fleeting touches he'd received thus far.

Finding something she liked, she nodded for the proprietor to join them and tapped her finger against the case, indicating another piece she wished to inspect. "This one, as well."

The proprietor laid out his small strip of black velvet again and placed the two hair combs Genny had chosen atop it. One had two twisted sterling silver prongs; the top portion was done in an intricate floral pattern and it was no larger than the casing of his timepiece. The second was made of tortoiseshell with a French ivory cameo molded into the center and six tines spiked down from the center.

The pieces were equally stunning. She'd chosen jewelry fit for a princess. Not surprising since she'd always been *his* princess, hence the moniker he had given her.

With his forefinger and thumb rubbing thoughtfully at his chin, he gazed down at her choices. Now that she'd picked them out—and done an exceptional job of it—he had to find another way to keep her in his company. Perhaps it would be best to remain undecided?

Sliding her selections to the side, he pointed out a few more pieces that caught his eye from the case. As the proprietor pulled each item out, Leo turned and faced Miss Camden.

"Would you be so kind as to try them in your hair?" Leo asked. "I daren't make my purchase without seeing how they fare in conjunction with your beauty."

She raised one dainty brow. "Flattery will do you no good, Lord Barrington. Besides, it would be a travesty to don any of these pieces with my hair not properly dressed."

"Genny, you're being dreadfully unhelpful." Charlotte drummed her gloved fingers over the edge of the case beside her. "Lord Barrington has implored our help, and therefore we could do no less than he asks. It's simple enough, really."

Lady Charlotte stepped in front of him, nearly blocking his view of Miss Camden as she loosened the wide ivory silk bow tied beneath Genny's chin. Genny said something under her breath that he could not make out. Probably berating his character. Why it brought a smile to his lips was anyone's guess.

Genny looked discomfited and out of sorts once her bonnet was removed. With her gloved hand, she brushed loose strands of her chestnut-colored hair from her forehead and reached behind her to adjust hairpins in the simple bun she wore.

Wisps of hair had escaped the small braids that wrapped

around and held the rest of her hair in a knot at the back of her head. Had she cut her hair over the years? Or did it still fall to the middle of her back? A memory so vivid of her riding him came to mind, the ends of her hair brushing his thighs as she arched her back and pressed her breasts into his face. He clearly recalled kissing, licking, and delivering love bites to her tender flesh as she leaned back in his arms in the throes of passion.

He swallowed tightly, hoping his gaze wasn't as sexually charged as his thoughts.

Genny's sharp eyes stared at him briefly, as though she'd seek retribution for his request. He didn't mind a little tit for tat with her when her growl was far worse than her bite could ever be.

She leaned over the selection of hair picks and picked up the tortoiseshell one first—perhaps that one was her preference?—and brushed the long tines gently through her hair before sticking it into the base of the bun.

Her hands moved methodically and easily as though she'd done this a thousand times without the aid of a mirror or maid. The sight of her hands made him itch to peel off her gloves and press her bare hands against his chest. He wanted to feel the heat of her naked flesh seeping into his skin.

He craved her touch as much now as he had all those years ago. It had been pure foolishness leaving her behind at the Carleton house party. He really couldn't recall now why he had left.

It was in that moment that he decided he would not keep his interest hidden. Not that he had tried very hard since dancing with her at the ball. His thoughts were suddenly consumed with her.

How did she manage it?

He'd had lovers over the years but none had compared to her. It would be impossible to let Genny slip through his fingers a second time. And he'd not let her escape him until he had her figured out.

Plucking up the green jade comb he had selected, he took a step in her direction. If he acted quickly, she'd be helpless to stop him from obtaining this liberty. One he coveted most right now.

Whispers behind them started up the moment he raised his arms to his task. The green was offset nicely against the silkiness of her chestnut hair. The slightest hint of red and the odd strand of blonde that indicated she spent some time in the sun without the protection of her bonnet could be clearly made out standing this close to her.

She raised her hands as though to push him away but seemed to realize she'd only draw more attention their way. She clasped her hands in front of her instead.

The pick slid easily through her soft hair, the tips of the tines massaging along her scalp before he settled the jewelry firmly in place, burying it as deep as he could in the bound tresses.

Lowering his arms, he brushed the back of his hand against the nape of her neck and over the small bone. Her skin was warm and soft. He wanted to dip his head and trail his tongue over the fine line of her spine. Her breath hitched; his froze in his lungs.

With more effort than it should have required, he took a step back. He doubted anyone would have seen what he'd done, as his larger frame blocked her smaller one from everyone behind them.

Miss Charlotte broke through the hushed din that was no subtler than a field of crickets suddenly disturbed from their reverie.

"It looks lovely, cousin."

The proprietor came around the case. "Miss," he said, showing her with his hand that she should turn to see her reflection in a tall looking glass. The mirror rested on the floor and stretched nearly ten feet high in a large ornate gilt frame.

Leo nestled the tortoiseshell comb back on the velvet and stood close behind Genny as she fixed imaginary loose strands of hair. As she gazed into the looking glass, her amber-colored eyes caught and held his gaze.

Her lips parted marginally and a hint of color rose in her cheeks. He was sure he only noticed the slight blush because they were staring at each other and in such close proximity.

Did she crave his touch as he did hers? Was she remembering their past and the passion they had shared night after night?

She had to be thinking of their past. Words weren't needed to convey *that* message between them. If they were alone their passion could be rekindled. All it would take was one simple look to indicate she wanted more, or one simple nod that said yes. Even one word that invited his touch and he'd do as she bid.

He wanted to undo every button that held her bodice snuggly in place. Then peel away the chemise that covered her shoulders beneath, and kiss a path along her nape. He'd not stop there; next he would draw a soft line down her spine till he reached the top swell of her buttocks to caress tiny circles over the dimples above each cheek, and follow those touches with a kiss and lick of his tongue . . .

The wicked things he fantasized doing to her . . .

Thank goodness his valet had chosen a long jacket today.

Lady Charlotte softly and pointedly cleared her throat next to him. He forced his gaze away from the wicked temptation of Genny. Had he and Genny been anywhere else, alone, nothing would have stopped him from acting on all his imaginings.

Locking gazes with the proprietor, he said, "Wrap them both."

Genny turned to him, a frown wrinkling her brow.

"The countess will be thrilled with the pieces." His voice croaked a little and he had to clear his throat. "I can't thank you and your cousin enough for the assistance."

"I'm glad we could help." Genny turned her attention to Charlotte, who aided her in putting her bonnet back on.

"We must go to the milliner's before they close for the day, cousin. Let us leave Lord Barrington to wrap up his business here."

Surprisingly enough, Lady Charlotte did not argue with her cousin's dictate this time.

"Good day, Lord Barrington," Genny said, her cold demeanor back in place.

With a curtsy from each of them, he watched them head toward the exit of the jeweler's shop.

It seemed as though everyone had watched his and Genny's exchange since they all stood silently by, waiting for someone to snap them all back to attention.

Those who knew him or of him would remark that he'd never paid mind to another woman so openly as he had done with Genny just now. At least he'd never been so attentive to a lady in the public eye. The wickedness associated with his name was derived from dabbling in trade and of the reputation-tarnishing information he had on at least half the peerage that made up the *ton*.

He didn't give a damn what anyone might speculate; he'd always been circumspect where his relationships were concerned. And he'd done nothing to blemish Miss Camden's good name today.

He would take great care to protect Genny's reputation just as he had in the past. Even though he had every intention of renewing their *friendship,* Leo would never allow her to be fodder for the more vicious gossips.

The store's patrons stared outright at Genny and Lady Charlotte until the bell above the door jingled its final toll behind their retreating figures.

Leo turned back to the shopkeeper and fingered another hair comb. "Wrap the first two together, but this one separately."

The man nodded. "Shall I have them delivered, my lord?"

"No, I will take both packages with me and make all the necessary arrangements."

Now the only question that remained was, should he deliver one of the combs directly to Genny or have his valet discreetly deliver her present? He had a sneaking suspicion she'd return it, but that didn't mean he couldn't try again and again to give it to her until he succeeded in winning her favor.

Chapter 5

This writer fails to see how the classes can become indistinguishable. The revered Lady C——'s intimate dinner party invites have gone out. It should be no surprise to anyone that the list of names includes members of the haute ton *who have for one reason or another caught this writer's attention over the course of the season.*

Not to mention, there are some unknowns who have been invited, too. The only thing this writer knows with certainty is that this first exclusive invite will match that of the most sought-after country stay in less than a month's time.

The Mayfair Chronicles, May 28, 1846

The Carletons' dinner party was going to be a delightfully quiet affair. Wide comfortable chairs, divans, and settees were strewn about the room, inviting the guests to rest their tired feet, as Genny was currently doing. There was even a beautifully appointed retiring room for the ladies, offering a tranquil place to kick off tight slippers and put your feet up without censure.

The evening would be intimate with less than twenty-five at table. Genny covered a yawn almost a second too late. No one paid her any mind, however, so no harm done with her faux pas.

Everyone's focus lay solely on the center of the room where Charlotte, her friend Ariel, and the young girl's mother chattered.

Ariel and Charlotte were the diamonds of the season, and attention was lavished upon them as if they were prized mares to be bid on at auction. Had it been like that for her when she'd debuted? She couldn't recall since she hadn't had the dowry both these young women had—though Ariel's was not as grand as Charlotte's.

"Miss Camden," Lady Carleton called over to her, her opal and lace fan wafting cool air against her slightly reddened cheeks. "Do join us. We need a level head to help settle our disagreement."

Genny stood from the reposed position she'd assumed for far too long and strode toward the hostess of the party. Lady Carleton's dress was of fine ivory satin. Simple strands of diamonds wrapped around her neck and wrist, her silvery-blonde hair was pulled up into a twisted chignon and adorned with tall snowy-colored marabou feathers. Her face was aged but still beautiful. Her easy smile had always been a welcome sight, and for some reason Genny was reminded of her mother whenever she looked at Lady Carleton.

"We need clarification on the events earlier today," her cousin said, a wicked smile lingering on her lips.

How much had her cousin said? Better yet, how much had she speculated aloud?

"I heard," Ariel piped in, "that Lord Barrington was so bold as to buy you a trinket at the jeweler's." The young lady's fan twitched a little faster with the declaration, as though she couldn't contain her excitement over a possible scandal.

If Genny chanced seeing Leo again, she had every intention of thoroughly castigating him for his actions. How dare he act so forward in front of no less than five society misses and their mamas, not to mention Charlotte? And Genny wasn't sure that Charlotte wouldn't keep this from her grandmother, which in turn might find its way to Lord Ponsley's ears. What a muddle she was in.

Pasting a smile on her face, she made her way into the throng of tittering women all wanting to be the first to know the latest on dit.

"Oh, no, no," Genny started to say with a slight shake of her head, eyes wide as though shocked at being the center of gossip. "The trinket was certainly not for me. Can you believe that Lord Barrington thought to consult with *me* on what he should purchase?"

Who should she say it was for? Even if the trinket was for his friend, it was still inappropriate for him to have been so forward. To have insisted she remove her hat and try them on herself. Not to mention the slight touches he'd stolen. With a great deal of agitation, she flicked her fan open to cool her cheeks. She refused to blush. Refused to think of his touch and the way it made her skin tingle in awareness.

His liberties had been so glancing she almost thought them a figment of her imagination and wanted nothing more than to convince herself that she was mistaken.

"It was for a female relation of his. He thought I might be able to aid him in picking out something simple." She wasn't sure why she had lied, but it had seemed important to do so.

"He didn't dare insult you so!" This voiced concern came from Ariel's mother, Lady Hargrove.

Whatever gossip these ladies thought to speculate on where Genny and Barrington were concerned . . . it stopped now.

Genny would not allow herself to be distracted by a man ever again. Genny would much rather this group of ladies pity her than offer scorn for something she had no control over.

"I can hardly believe it myself," she said.

"And did you pick out something *plain* for him?" Lady Carleton asked.

"He looked so out of sorts over what he should choose that I couldn't refuse his entreaty. Yes, I assisted him and then we left him with the proprietor to conclude his business. I don't even know which bauble he purchased."

"For whom do you think he purchased the piece?" Charlotte said, rubbing the closed edge of her fan thoughtfully beneath her chin.

"I couldn't say. Though I do hope he made out well."

Lady Carleton looked at her oddly before declaring, "I feel inclined to tell you that my husband invited Barrington and Castleigh for dinner tonight. Perhaps I'll seat him next to you since he seems to have found a friend in you."

He was coming here?

Of course he was coming here. How had she not realized that possibility sooner?

She closed her fan with an audible snap and folded her hands in front of her. No one would guess that she actually pinched her fingers together in frustration. It took every ounce of her good manners to school her features so she didn't give away her true thoughts on spending an evening with Leo—though she was annoyed with the prospect, she was also intrigued that he'd gone to the trouble of securing an invite to dinner tonight.

God, she hated society niceties. It was as if everyone waited for her to make one slipup so they could declare her a pariah. How much had Charlotte's father and grandmother already heard about this afternoon? Should she worry about her reputation?

She'd have to stay close to her cousin's side tonight. Castleigh wouldn't swoop in without Genny readily available to interfere. Nor would that roué Barrington make another pass at her.

To Lady Carleton, she gave a neat curtsy. "I defer to your superior hosting skills to determine if I am the best dinner partner for either gentleman. In fact I'd be delighted to sit with Lord Barrington so we might renew our acquaintance. It's been so many years since we've mingled at the same functions."

That warm, comforting smile was back in place on the hostess's face.

"Perfect. Walk with me a while," Lady Carleton suggested.

Genny didn't hesitate to take her arm. They headed toward the verandah, probably so they could have privacy for whatever the countess wished to say.

A cool breeze settled around them. Millions of twinkling stars above their heads greeted them into the fold of the clear night like a lover's embrace. The smell of lilacs and late-blooming peonies wafted up from the gardens.

"I'm not surprised to hear the rumor," Lady Carleton started. "Lord Barrington has taken a liking to you, my dear Miss Camden. Perhaps something will come of his attentions this time."

"I'm afraid your rumor source has exaggerated the facts. I think most members of society forget that Lord Barrington and I have a prior acquaintance."

"I, however, do not. To this day I question why he didn't offer marriage when he seemed smitten with you all those years ago."

Genny couldn't hold back the sound of humor that escaped her in the form of a snort. "We were both so young. And, I admit, we developed a friendship. But a *tendre*? Hardly."

"Yet that friendship did not hold up over the years. One would wonder what type of bond you shared."

The countess could not be suspicious after all these years. She and Leo had been incredibly discreet.

"We come from much different circles. It is no wonder our friendship could not hold up when I went to live with my great-aunt as a companion," Genny said.

"But now you are back in society, making the necessary rounds with your cousin." Lady Carleton leaned against the balustrade and stared out on her darkened garden. "It might do you well to reacquaint yourself with his lordship."

"We will always remain friends, my lady."

Very distant friends if she could help it. Lord Barrington was a complication she did not want or need at present.

Leo looked around the parlor as the butler took his and Tristan's hats. His gaze skimmed over the company present, searching for one person in particular.

He looked forward to spending more time with Miss Camden. This afternoon, he'd come close to asking her and her cousin if he could purchase them an ice and take a stroll through Hyde Park. Not only would the suggestion have been presumptuous, it reeked of actual courtship, which he doubted Miss Camden would appreciate. Honorable was not what he would call his intentions where both ladies were concerned.

Regardless, he had plans tonight that involved segregating the current lady of his desires from everyone present. He didn't precisely have a reason for wanting to do so other than a desire to be alone with her.

Who was he fooling besides himself? What wasn't honorable about courting a lady he enjoyed spending time with? Well, there was the small fact that he was aiding his friend in a false courtship of Lady Charlotte. He'd have to figure out the right and wrong of it another time.

Finally, he laid eyes upon her among a throng of ladies and a couple of gentlemen—all of his acquaintance.

Carleton approached Leo and Tristan as they entered the parlor. They'd agreed to come to this party on the grounds of discussing their mutual interest in the sugar imports act. All three owned land in Barbados. All three of them would be forced to either sell their plantations or risk losing any money generated from their sugar business in the Caribbean.

"So glad you could make it. My wife is pleased that you agreed to even out our numbers for dinner." Carleton took Tristan's hand with fondness and then Leo's. Lord Carleton had been a close friend to Tristan and Leo's fathers.

"We're glad for the wonderful company," Tristan said to the older man. "Besides, when will a better time arise to strategize our next move? The party tonight makes everything more convenient."

Leo did not miss the stressed enunciation on "everything."

"Shall we mingle to even out those numbers you spoke of?" Leo gestured to the room all the while eyeing the gaggle of women at the center.

Miss Camden wore a less unappealing navy-colored dress this evening. Still drab, but prettier than the one she'd worn to the duchess's ball. He had to wonder if she owned anything that complemented her shapely figure.

She avoided his gaze, so he stared at her cousin, suspecting she'd be quick to include him in whatever conversation they were currently immersed.

She did not disappoint.

"How do you fare this evening, my lords?" Lady Charlotte gave Tristan a smile that revealed dimpled cheeks.

"Well, my lady," Tristan answered. "I daresay, with the luck I've had in spending time with you two nights in a row, I should test my hand at the craps table before the night is through."

Lady Charlotte blushed for all in the company to see.

Well played, Leo thought.

Miss Camden chose that inappropriate and outrageously flirtatious comment to intervene. "Perhaps," she said, a coy smile tilting her lips, "we should all try our hands at cards since we seem to bring about such luck."

"You must know, Lady Hargrove," Lady Carleton said when everyone around them seemed wide-eyed and agog at Genny's open rejoinder. "That Lord Barrington and Miss Camden go back a number of years. I do believe they met at my house party four summers past."

"You are correct," Leo responded, giving her a flash of mischief in his slow smile.

"It was an interesting time." Lady Carlton laughed. "So much happened at that house party. There was that matter with a young woman and another of the unattached guests." Everyone's focus was naturally on Lady Carleton as she gave them this old bit of gossip. Audience captive, she continued, "Of course it was so long ago that none of it is worth hashing over now."

There was an undercurrent of significance to her tone that Leo didn't fail to notice. Was it directed at both him and Miss Camden? He couldn't be sure. He suspected Genny thought the same thing because she did not raise her eyes to his.

"Yes," Genny said, "it was an age ago. And let it be a lesson to the young ladies that you can never put your eggs in too many baskets. I had two suitors at that house party."

He didn't fail to notice she neglected to include him in that number. He was slightly hurt by that fact. It wasn't as though he could gainsay her. He'd never made his intentions clear where she was concerned. It surprised him how much he regretted that now.

"Then why ever did you not marry?" Charlotte asked.

"Not every man is worth marrying, darling. Besides, we learned over the course of the party how ill suited we were. I am happy to report that both gentlemen are now happily settled."

"A shame you didn't meet someone else," Ariel said.

"I don't regret my decision to remain unattached. I hate to think what would have happened to my great-aunt had I not been there to offer my companionship to her before coming to Charlotte. I have no regrets."

"None?" Lady Carleton asked, her tone disbelieving.

"None," Genny assured everyone present.

Interesting. Leo wondered if the "no regrets" extended to the time they'd spent together.

The countess's husband came around, took his lady wife's arm, and announced dinner. They all filed out of the drawing room and into the dining room. Leo wasn't far behind Genny; not that she paid him any mind; she was busy chattering with Lady Hargrove.

"Just like old times, I see." Genny gestured to the nameplates at the table that lacked proper order. No one sat by rank at a Carleton party; everyone was treated as an equal. "You'll have to suffer my company for the evening, Lord Barrington."

She looked at him from beneath her lashes, quite satisfied with everything turning in her favor. On the other side of her was Castleigh's nameplate.

It seemed that Charlotte was allocated to the opposite side of the table, next to Lord Chester, a distant relation to the host. Lord Chester was a man of indeterminate age with a jovial laugh and he sported a shock of white frizzy hair that matched his long gray beard. To Charlotte's left was Mr. Torrance, who was a scholar and poet.

Genny looked back to Leo and clasped her hands together. "Lady Luck is on my side this evening. Lord Castleigh to my left, as he should be," she added under her breath. "Though it would be equally satisfying to put you in that position, Lord Barrington."

The way Leo tilted his head and looked at her full of raw intention had her breath freezing in her lungs.

"I'd enjoy playing your devil, Miss Camden," he responded, equally as private as her comment had been. "I have always thought it better the devil you know than to invite a new one into your midst." He leaned in close to her ear. "And though you cast the marquess so, I am a far greater threat to your virtue, my dear."

"Don't flatter yourself." How she managed to keep her voice cool and calm when she felt rather parched by his insinuation was quite a miracle. How could anyone be aroused by mere banter?

"Let me share a secret with you, Miss Camden. Once you have had your first taste of ambrosia"—Leo waved the footman away when he came to pull her chair out and instead did it himself—"you cannot so easily resist its allure again."

He flicked out her napkin, placed it over his bent arm, and gave her a deep bow. "I am ever your servant, madam."

As Genny sat, she hissed, "Ever the ass." A shame she didn't have a better retort, but the man knew how to fluster her.

With a chuckle, Leo placed the napkin in her lap. Lest she feel the urge to further insult him, Genny turned from him and focused on Castleigh, in the hope that she could better understand his character before dinner concluded. She would like to understand where his desire stemmed from in his obvious attempt to court Charlotte.

"I don't believe we've had the pleasure of dining together at previous social events, Lord Castleigh."

"We have not." His smile was all charm. "I don't make it a habit to indulge in decent affairs."

"Only the wicked will do for you, then?" she teased.

Castleigh's gaze slipped past hers and to Leo's. "This one will put you in your place." To her, he said, "Wicked is as wicked does."

"Don't you grow bored of all the wickedness after a while?"

"You're quick, Miss Camden," Tristan said. "It's no wonder you were paired with Lady Charlotte this season. You are quite the match."

"We are cousins," she reminded him.

"I will not forget it."

It was hard to tell if Tristan was goading her into compliance or if he was heeding her advice to remember that they were both strong-willed women and not easily taken advantage of.

"Are you always so agreeable?" she asked.

He gave her a wide smile and winked at her. "I try to be as accommodating as possible when the situation warrants it."

"And what kind of situation would this be?"

"Well, Miss Camden, I find I like you. If you wish to warn me away from your cousin, then I will do my best to comply with those wishes." He bent closer to her and whispered, "But you should know, she seems to have a mind of her own when it comes down to doing what she wants. I cannot curb her desire to befriend me any more than you can fend off the friend sitting on the other side of you."

"Lord Barrington and I have a long history." She heard the defensive quality in her own voice and cursed it.

"So it seems," Tristan mused.

Her mouth flapped open once, then she snapped it shut realizing she was at a loss for what to say. Leo slid his chair farther under the table; his hand brushed the side of her thigh quite intentionally and it startled her.

"You're mighty jumpy tonight, as though there were a mouse at your feet."

"It's not a mouse, my lord. It appears to be a very large rat."

Both gentlemen on either side of her laughed just as the first course was set down in front of them. Dinner couldn't end fast enough.

Chapter 6

Ah, won't you be pleased with what has been un-covered about the chaperone. Yes, you read that correctly—the chaperone *of one Miss C——, daughter of Lord P—— was caught in company with Lord B——. My ears are humming at what is slowly being uncovered about her past, which I will share with my dear readers after the full history is revealed to this writer.*

The Mayfair Chronicles, May 29, 1846

Where had Charlotte disappeared to now?

With a quick look over the heads of every guest in the room, Genny could not find her cousin. Or for that matter Lord Castleigh.

How had she let her attention be occupied for even a moment of nonsensical chatter? Genny could not find Lady Ariel, either, so it was possible the girls were off giggling and gossiping together as they were wont to do whenever the occasion presented itself.

Genny excused herself from Lady Carleton's company, hinting she might have to loosen her stays in the powder room after all the food she'd consumed since it had been so delicious and since eating had given her a reason not to converse with the imps on either side of her.

Donning a serene look of calm as she headed toward the powder room, she picked up her pace to a near skip once she was out of view of the rest of the dinner guests.

There was a small chance her cousin and Ariel had sequestered themselves in the powder room and not somewhere else. How had her cousin escaped her eagle eye while she'd been on the balcony with Lady Carleton for no more than a few minutes?

That apparently was all the time Charlotte needed to disappear.

Genny checked the resting room, where not a soul was to be found. The house was a simple enough layout: a narrow hallway stretched about forty feet in front of her, two doors on both sides, one a pocket door at the end that she assumed was the library.

Her slippered feet made no sound as she traversed the beige marble floor. Marble eventually made way for dark-planked wood flooring in the first room. Moss-green papered walls with inlaid gold molding and a simple furniture arrangement were all she saw. Shutting the heavy door behind her, she made for the next one, and came to a sudden halt on hearing whispered voices.

The voices were too low to determine who was inside, and she couldn't be sure everyone had been present in the main parlor before she'd gone in search of Charlotte. Not wishing to catch anyone in a compromising situation, she pushed up the latch. The hinges were well greased for the bolt clicked over and the door slid smoothly open.

Genny peered through the crack but it was no help. Whoever was in the room was on the other side of the door and she would have to enter fully to see who resided within.

"How convenient that I should find you all alone." The whispered words came from behind her.

Genny turned her head and peered at Leo over her shoulder. "Why did you follow me?"

"Why shouldn't I follow the most delectable woman present this evening?"

Leo's hands caressed hers as he provocatively embraced her while pulling the door closed again.

As she turned to face her foe, his hand moved easily against her hips and guided her so her back was pressed to the wall. Leo stood close, not so close they touched, but close enough that she did not mistake the flaring of his pupils for anything but ardor. She pinched her lips tighter knowing she needed to remain quiet lest they be overheard.

With one finger skimming over the side of her jaw, Leo tilted her head to the side, his hand tracing the delicate spot of her neck in a teasing gesture. Oh, he hadn't forgotten how to heighten her senses, or how to make her breath catch from the slightest of touches.

Afraid to speak too loudly and give away their position, she whispered, "What do you want?"

He grinned like the cat that ate the canary. He didn't need to respond. It was loud and quite clear to her what he would say. Simply "you" or even something more daring, such as . . . "can't you guess," or . . .

"Isn't it obvious?" he responded so quietly she barely heard him and doubted she would have had he not been two inches from her face.

Her back pressed firmly against the wall, the molding jabbed into her shoulder blades. How could she care about a little bit of pain when she knew that if she didn't sidle past Leo, he'd make his intentions of seduction more clear than he already had? And she wasn't sure she could resist him a moment longer.

"Let me pass, Barrington. If you dare stop me from

finding my cousin, I'll find a way to make you pay, and pay dearly."

"Your cousin is not doing anything you yourself haven't tried at least once."

She grasped the front lapel of his jacket between her fists, uncaring that she might wrinkle the fine material. "She is in my care, and I'll not let her be ruined as you ruined me."

He looked down to where her hand clutched at him, a perplexed expression on his face before his lip curled upward. "If inciting your ire was all I needed to do to have you touching me, I'd have tipped you over that scale last eve when I was sporting an erect—"

"Don't you dare finish that sentence!"

He only gave her that infuriatingly handsome, smug smile that made her want to simultaneously kiss and smack it away.

No, that wasn't right.

She did *not* want to kiss him.

Not at all.

All right, perhaps a little, but that wasn't something she'd ever admit to out loud, especially to him.

Pushing past him, she made for the door successfully this time and didn't hesitate at the entrance. She strode right through the doorway, uncaring of what she might be witness to because it was better than being trapped in Leo's arms, thinking illicit thoughts.

The sight that met her couldn't have shocked her more.

Sitting in opposing sage-velvet chairs, her cousin faced off with Castleigh . . .

Over a game of chess.

Lady Ariel sat on a settee four feet away, her attention focused on an open book.

Genny looked closely at her cousin's dress. Every pearl

button was perfectly lined up and in place. And not a strand of hair had moved from the upswept ringlets, nor did any wrinkles blemish her voluminous skirts. It was a picture of pure innocence.

She narrowed her gaze and placed her hands on her hips. *What sort of trickery was this?*

"Charlotte." Even though she'd been caught off guard by the wholly harmless sight, Genny managed to keep her voice stern. "Castleigh, you cannot simply abscond with my cousin as the mood takes you. Had you asked for her company, I would have been willing to escort you both from the parlor to a more private setting."

Ariel looked up from her book. "You were occupied with Lady Carleton and we did not wish to interrupt."

"And I did not think you'd be so accommodating. We've done nothing wrong, cousin. I even came with a witness." Charlotte looked at Castleigh and had the audacity to flash the man a daring grin. "Pooh, we'll have to arrange to play another game now that I've angered Genny. And I was winning."

Charlotte stood and Castleigh followed suit as etiquette dictated.

"Do escort me back to the rest of the company, my lord." With a clever flick of her hips, Charlotte realigned her skirts to perfection before gliding from the room with Ariel on her heels, book tucked beneath her arm.

How had Genny lost this small battle? It was she who should be at her cousin's side, not Charlotte's friend and certainly not *that* man.

Someone cleared their throat behind her. How had she forgotten *he* was present? The door clicked shut and the lock tumbled over as she turned to face her shadow and nemesis.

"Do you really think that wise?"

Leo glanced over his shoulder at the bolted door. "Quite."

"You're a cad, Barrington."

She picked up her skirts in a huff and barreled her way toward the exit. Gently grasping her upper arm, Barrington pulled her to a stop just before she could pass him by.

"Why the rush to quit my company?"

"You cannot be serious, my lord."

He maneuvered himself in front of her and crossed his arms over his wide chest. "You once called me by my given name."

"We will never know each other on so intimate a level again."

"I disagree."

She dropped her hold on her skirts and stamped her foot in a poor demonstration of her frustration. "Let me pass."

"Call me Leo first."

Genny shook her head, refusing him any concessions. "I have not changed my mind where you are concerned. I was once young and stupid, but I'm too old to play your games now. You act as though I don't understand your intent."

"I've noticed one great change in you," he said conversationally, as though her complaints against him were easy to ignore. Then again, he wasn't denying what she had guessed to be the truth. "Would you care to know what that is?"

"What you think of me and what respectable society thinks of me are two very opposing views. You might think to associate me with the naïve young woman I was, but you'll be sorely disappointed when you realize I grew up long ago. When you finally figure out that there is nothing between us, you'll find another young woman to fawn your attentions on."

"I'd rather not argue over something so trivial."

"Then let me pass, *Barrington*." With a beseeching tone, she said, "And please, just leave me alone."

"We should reacquaint ourselves." Leo's gaze traveled the length of her body. He wasn't referring to mere friendship but another liaison.

"You might be a cad. But I never took you for a fool."

"So you've already said. I'm still not letting you storm off. Not till this matter is settled between us."

"You are an infuriating man. If I never had to spend another minute in your company for the rest of my days, I'd be the most content woman there ever was."

"Now you wound me, princess."

Making a bold move, Genny tried shouldering him away from the door latch so she could make an exit. Instead of budging from her path, Leo clutched each of her upper arms to hold her still, giving her no choice but to face him.

"Don't tell me I'm the only one fighting this damnable attraction, Genny."

Impressed he hadn't caught her off guard, and had only put voice to the very thoughts she'd been having, she said coolly, "Whatever I felt for you four years ago was quelled the day you left to pursue your own path. Don't flatter yourself and think that I've spared you a single thought since then."

"Damn you," he said vehemently.

She gasped, giving him an open advantage of her mouth. His lips took hers in what could only be described as a rather feral and delicious kiss; his tongue plunged between her startled lips and suddenly . . . she forgot all her arguments and . . .

It became impossible to remain cool and in control.

Because she wanted this. It was the second stupidest thing she'd done in her entire life, the first being her previous affair with him. She apparently had a reckless nature about her.

She forgot that she should be making efforts to avoid Leo, not tempt him and encourage their current position. She'd craved his kiss and touch for so long now, that she just wanted to enjoy the moment for a little while longer.

When his tongue delved deep into her mouth, she tasted him back. Just as eager, just as hungry for more as apparently he was. The stroke of his tongue slowed, became less urgent as she relaxed into the kiss. It was a reacquaintance of their sensual, need-to-be-touched side.

Foolishly, she'd thought her desire for him had dulled to a slow burn, but the feel of his lips pressed to hers, his solid body beneath her spread palms pliable and so very masculine, made her realize otherwise.

She wanted to touch him in the flesh. Strip him out of his clothes so she could feel the hard muscles roped throughout his body, and let him do the most wicked things he could possibly do to her—and preferably with his tongue. She wanted to sink into his skin and indulge in the sensation of his body next to hers.

Why couldn't they forever indulge in this mutual passion? Why couldn't things have turned out differently? Why had it been so easy for him to walk away at all?

An inferno of lust burned through her veins and seared her senses. It was impossible to remain impassive or idle. Not when her body had other ideas.

Leo's, too. His hands slipped upward from her rib cage to lance the sides of her breasts, the action cutting through to her core like a sword through soft flesh.

She pulled away with sheer force of will, panting from the onslaught of his mouth hot against hers. His eyes were full of fire. Goodness, his gaze bored a hole straight through her center and pierced her fast pacing heart—but it didn't slow any from the onslaught of feelings bombarding her. It hitched into a higher gear, fervent for more.

"Tell me you can so easily walk away from that," he said.

Though she'd been flushed with desire, anger for her hasty actions outshone the passion she'd just felt and she donned her proverbial matron's hat. It wasn't easy to stand away from Leo, but she did it.

"I don't want to see you again, my lord." Her voice was cold. "I do hope you'll make a point of avoiding my cousin, or I will find a way to make your life miserable."

He remained silent and she thought her battle easily won. Until . . .

"I will take your challenge, my lady."

"There is no challenge!" She pounded her fist against the wall beside her to emphasize her point. "There is nothing except an unseemly past between us. And if you don't mind, I would like to keep that time between us buried exactly where it belongs . . . forever forgotten and easily dismissed as a past indiscretion."

There must have been something in her expression that clearly showed she would not cede this argument for he stepped aside to finally let her pass.

She didn't even glance at him as she reached for the door latch.

As she slid through the open door, Leo gently clasped her wrist in his warm hand. "We *will* see each other again."

He stated it as a simple fact. Just a fact.

Only time would tell if that would come to pass. Well, she could be just as stubborn as he. And she'd make it a personal goal to avoid him at every turn from here on out.

They looked at each other for a long, charged moment. There was a small part of her that thrilled at the prospect of him chasing after her, but the rational part of her mind knew she had to shutter off those kinds of feelings. Nothing good would come from participating in a liaison with him.

Chapter 7

This writer will certainly entertain readers today. Not only has Lord B—— attended the most coveted dinner engagement of the season, but a Miss C—— also known to my readers previously as the mysterious chaperone of one Lady C.L., has also attended this exclusive dinner party. One must wonder at her association with the revered countess.
The Mayfair Chronicles, May 29, 1846

After the Carleton dinner party, Leo hailed a hansom and headed directly for Hayden's townhouse. They had arrived in Tristan's coach, but his friend had wrapped not only Ponsley's offspring around his finger but also Mrs. Greystone, a widow he knew well, who did this thing with her tongue around a man . . . He blew out a breath in frustration. Even the thought of Mrs. Greystone caught in flagrante delicto with that wicked tongue of hers didn't rouse his ardor.

His thoughts remained on Genny. Good Lord, what in the name of heaven was wrong with him that caused his thoughts to be wholly consumed by one woman?

He had met Genny purely by accident. Some of Lady

Carleton's country party guests had daringly gone for a midsummer dip in a shallow, somewhat warm pond on her country property.

He rephrased that . . . a handful of the ladies in attendance of said summer party had doffed their heavy dresses and waded into the cooling water in only their underclothes. Of all the delectable sights he'd been privy to, that one topped the list of what he wished to see again.

He'd been enjoying an afternoon stroll away from the stuffed suits of his father's set. Genny had boldly teased him and suggested he join them in the water. He'd been tempted, *really* tempted, but had refrained, and then more houseguests had arrived.

That had been the one and only time he recalled acting the perfect gentleman, ushering off the new arrivals so the women could find their way back to the house and don their society dresses as though nothing had happened. He swore on his walk back to the manor that he'd heard the odd giggle following closely behind.

That very evening, Genny had boldly introduced herself to him and thanked him for his discretion.

He found himself offering his services any time she so requested and had insisted she walk in the gardens to take the morning air with him the following day.

She had proposed a stargazing adventure instead, and without her maid in attendance, so they could freely enjoy themselves. How was a man to refuse such a generous offer? Better yet, what sane man would argue away the opportunity to spend a few unhindered hours with a beautiful woman?

They'd definitely enjoyed themselves. So much so, that for the first time in his twenty-five years—at the time—he had halted their intimacies before he found himself buried betwixt her lovely thighs.

That was not to say that they hadn't indulged in other

things. There had been much petting and stroking. There had also been plenty of kissing and in not so obvious places. He'd left marks on her skin that night, but had put them in places that would stay hidden from anyone's prying eyes. Even then, he couldn't resist finding her the night after that.

Pulling up to the duke's townhouse, Leo pressed his hand to his straining erection, moving it to the side so he wasn't so bloody uncomfortable in his trousers. He could not go anywhere in his current state.

Closing his eyes, he rested his head back on the worn leather seat and counted to five, all the while thinking of his father lecturing him on his behavior and conduct. His father insisting that he cut off all ties to the country lass he'd fallen for since it was nothing more than a passing fancy. Leo had known from the moment he'd left Genny behind that it was the wrong step to take. But how could he go back to her when she had the perfect opportunity to marry another?

Better fit for company now that his thoughts weren't solely focused on one troublesome young woman, he stepped down from the hansom and flicked a coin up to the driver with a nod in farewell.

Hayden's footman opened the door before Leo could lift the knocker. The tall young man bowed and stepped aside to allow him entrance.

"My lord," he said, "His Grace is in his study."

Leo removed his hat and gloves, and handed them over along with his cane. The man took them, leaving Leo to find his own way to Hayden's study.

Leo strode down the hall, determined to get answers about Fallon's will.

Smart man that Hayden was, he had not partaken in the game to woo the young lady out from Mr. Warren's grasp. No one expected it of him. He had lived like a bloody monk for more than a year. Leo and Tristan thought maybe the last break-off with his mistress had done more lasting damage than anyone could guess. Hayden hadn't set his eyes on another woman since that very public split.

The door to the study was ajar. Flickering amber indicated the lamps were lit bright. Stepping into the room, Leo located his friend sitting in a wingback chair. His feet were perched on a small ottoman, spectacles rested on the edge of his nose as he stared down at an open book in his lap.

The clock on the marble-encased mantel indicated the late hour with a chime at half past one. Leo took the settee across from his friend.

"Anything?" he asked, flopping back on the cushioned seat.

Hayden raised his brows, eyes focusing on Leo instead of the book he'd been reading. "Afraid not. Everything, including his investments, is tied into the entailments and estate. It can only be accessed by the Earl of Fallon and then signed off with the official Fallon seal."

"The bastard."

Hayden tossed the leather-bound book down on the table beside him. "Would you expect anything less after the tumultuous marriage they had?"

"No, I suppose not. Is there any way she can appeal the will?"

"Not without an issue." When Leo opened his mouth to say something, Hayden raised his hand in a bid for silence. "I've already asked the delicate question. She knows she has no standing ground without an heir to succeed the father."

"Christ, it just keeps getting worse. Mr. Warren doesn't seem . . . How shall I word this?" Leo motioned with his hands as he searched for the right word. "Generous. He's known as a pit bull in Parliament."

"And with his upcoming engagement and nuptials, as Jez assures us, the chit will breed quickly. He's already got bastards stretched from one end of the country to the other from what I've been able to dig up. Not that I could find proof of the so-called bastards."

Did Jez think he and Tristan would court every marriageable young woman Mr. Warren set his sights on? While any man with a heavy hand for the fairer sex didn't deserve to marry, they couldn't stop him indefinitely from marrying. It wasn't possible for so many reasons. The main one being that Leo was interested in one particular woman at the moment.

"Jez cannot expect us to court every young woman who could potentially take on her husband's legacy. Not only is it poor sport, it'll ban us from every social event of the season. Jez, too, should it be discovered what we are doing."

Fingers drumming along the arm of the padded brocade chair, Hayden said, "Then let her assume you plan to complete the task at hand. In the meantime, I'll talk to her. Maybe convince her to invest her meager annual into something offering high interest on returns. It should appease her for the time being."

"It's a start if nothing else." Leo stood.

"I can make no promises, but I'll try to convince her to take another path to secure her future. It'll be difficult, though, because she has her sights set on her husband's fortune."

"Can you still hold up the will in court?"

"There is nothing I can do." Hayden brushed his hands through his hair. "Everyone will wait out the year to make sure she isn't increasing, then all the entailments will pass on to Mr. Warren."

"So she has some time to plan her future."

"If she doesn't do anything damaging to her reputation in the meantime, yes."

"I'll talk to Jez," he said with a nod and left Hayden's study.

It suddenly felt like Leo's reasons for continuing with Jez's charade were selfish. And they absolutely were. He'd lost sight of his purpose the moment he'd laid eyes upon Genny.

What he needed to do was help Jez. She needed to let go of the past, of the abuse she'd suffered at the hands of her husband and move on. Leo's stepmother had learned to move on with the help of Leo's father.

Leo still remembered the day the woman he loved like his own flesh and blood had come to them. One eye swollen shut from the fist she'd taken to the face, her right arm broken and hanging limp at her side, her underclothes in which she'd escaped from her house covered in mud and soaked right through from the rain. Leo's father had taken her in, helped her, and eventually married her when word came that her husband had died in a carriage accident. Though Leo was sure there had never been an accident, but a duel between rivals. He'd never know the truth now that his father had passed away.

The only question that remained was whether he would be able to help Jez as his father had helped his stepmother.

Genny sat at a writing table that faced a window overlooking the back garden. She was writing a letter to her friend Helena. She could see her cousin from the corner of her eye, sitting on the chaise and reading a letter of her own.

Charlotte folded the parchment and tucked it in the book she had been reading for the past few days. "When did you meet Lord Barrington? You seem rather knowledgeable about his character."

Genny supposed it was an innocent enough question from her cousin and one that deserved a truthful response. She turned on the stool to face her cousin directly. "I met him in my third season."

"I heard he courted you for a short time." Charlotte's brow rose marginally as though waiting for her denial. "At least that is the impression I received from Lady Hargrove."

"Charlotte Lindsey, why do you bother asking me if the rumor mill has been busy enough to inform you of my past?"

"It's obviously been years since you've seen each other and I wanted the truth from you. One can never be sure until the actual source verifies the facts."

Her cousin was astute, but Genny could never reveal just how close she'd been to Leo.

With a heavy sigh, she gave in to her cousin's curious nature. "If it appeases you in any way, and if the truth persuades you to cease this line of questioning, then I'll tell you what you are so eager to know. While Barrington and I were well acquainted, we were no more than friends."

"Well, I'm going to offer up my opinion on the matter now that you've given me enough to form one," Charlotte said.

Genny would really rather not hear her cousin's opinion. If there was one thing Charlotte excelled at, it was sorting out a puzzle before anyone else could begin to connect the pieces for themselves.

"I believe," Charlotte went on, "that you met him and became fast friends—you can be charming and witty when you aren't such a slave to my father's orders."

Genny made a face at that assessment and turned to put away her writing accessories. "Must we have your opinion at all? Barrington and I were friends *ages ago,* as you've so kindly pointed out."

"You'll have it anyway." Her cousin gave a short laugh of amusement. "I believe you started as friends . . . only you might have developed a *tendre* for the young Lord Barrington. The feeling was not returned, was it?"

"You're wrong on so many counts that I can't even think of where to start to correct your misconceptions." Was she so transparent to everyone or just her cousin? Genny wiped the nib of her pen off and put the cap back on the Indian ink.

"I'm not wrong in this. You know you wouldn't try so hard to persuade me otherwise if I were off my mark."

"Fine, Charlotte." Genny let out a frustrated sigh. "If you are correct, then tell me . . . do I still harbor feelings for the earl?"

Charlotte's forehead puckered in thought. Charlotte had seen them interact and there was no love apparent with their constant bantering, so she couldn't possibly think Genny wanted to reacquaint with Barrington.

"It remains to be seen," Charlotte finally said. "What would you do if Lord Castleigh and Lord Barrington made an appearance at the theater tonight?"

"Why should it matter?" She refused to believe it would happen. "We will be in Lady Carleton's box, and I imagine both gentlemen have their own family boxes." She turned to her cousin once again.

Charlotte tapped her chin and narrowed her eyes as she assessed Genny.

"I know that look." Genny put her elbows on her knees and leaned forward. "It is as though you've a bit of the devil in your eyes. There will be no mischief on your part."

"You really do try to take the fun out of everything." Charlotte pouted, tossed her book next to her on the chaise, and crossed her arms over her chest. "When Papa announced that you would escort me around for my debut instead of Grandmamma, I was beyond thrilled to have a confidante. But you play too close to the rules instead of having fun with life. Have some fun with me—I feel as though the opportunity for any excitement is about to run out."

Genny stood from the stool and made her way to her cousin. She gave her a hug of reassurance before releasing her.

"You can have all the fun you desire once you are married."

"Oh, I intend to. But at the same time, I will not allow my pending marriage to stop me from enjoying the attentions I am receiving now. Castleigh understands my position and he does not shelter me nearly as much as you. It's nice to be courted by a man not of my father's choosing."

"It is my duty not only as your chaperone but as a member of your family to keep you away from men of his character."

Charlotte leaned back on the cushions with a discontented sigh.

"Castleigh has ruined more than a few good ladies' reputations with his antics. Have you told him of your upcoming nuptials?"

Charlotte shook her head. "I haven't, but it'll be obvious to everyone soon enough if Mr. Warren continues to call on me and take me around the park in his barouche. Then again, with the marquess seeking me out, it might look as though I have a few contenders for my hand."

Could it be that Lord Castleigh liked Charlotte in more a capacity than friendship? Did he wish to court her cousin? That didn't seem likely. Leo had asked quite pointedly who the girl was to Genny. There was trickery at play with both gentlemen. And she would not let her guard down, no matter how innocent a scene she'd walked in on with Charlotte and the marquess.

Her experience had been much different with Leo, and

it had happened so many years ago now that she couldn't be sure if she had instigated the seduction or if he had simply made her believe that.

"Do you have feelings for the marquess?"

Charlotte's grin was everything but innocent. "Castleigh and I are no more than *friends.*"

The butler entered the parlor, cutting off Genny's reply—not that she was sure what her rebuttal would be. He bowed and presented a silver platter on which sat a small vellum box with a brown satin ribbon tied in a neat bow around it.

"A present arrived moments ago. A messenger awaits your reply," the butler said.

The box was small and unremarkable. A neatly folded, unmarked envelope was tucked just beneath the top of the ribbon. Charlotte clapped her hands together excitedly and stood to retrieve the card. Genny could not make out the words on the heavy parchment from where she sat.

Her cousin's eyes widened and her mouth formed a little O of surprise as she turned her gaze in Genny's direction.

"Who is it from?" In all likelihood—and judging by the size of the box, which she guessed housed jewelry of some sort—they'd be returning the gift.

"*Friends,* you say?" Charlotte's tone was teasing as she passed over the opened notecard.

Genny took it reluctantly. *He wouldn't.* He wouldn't *dare* send her a present for all to take note of.

Her hand shook slightly as she read the neat cursive message:

My Dearest Miss Camden,
    Something to catch the fire in your eyes.
                                        Your
                                        L

Her fingers itched to free the ribbon and see what lay inside the box. Of course, she could never open it. She would have to send it back to Leo immediately. Why did he have to do this to her? Why should Charlotte have to witness this? It negated everything she'd said earlier about her past association with Lord Barrington.

Genny made her way toward the settee, needing to be out of reach of the present Leo had sent. She arranged her skirts into something altogether neater as she perched herself on the edge of the seat, glaring back at the box, which was nothing more than a bribe and a declaration of Leo's challenge to win her over.

It would not work.

"Please have it returned from whence it came." She regretted having to send it back at all and wished that the present could be considered a spoil of their war.

The butler didn't so much as blink an eye. "Instructions for the carrier, madam?"

She busied herself with a wrinkled frill on her bodice. "No message is required."

Which was a lie. There was a lot to be said about Leo's boldness. How dare he endanger her position by doing something so . . . so *obvious*. How dare he express his attraction toward her in such a public way. She sincerely hoped this wouldn't become the talk of Town.

As the butler left the room, Charlotte sat beside her on the settee.

"You should have at least taken a peek before sending it off. I'm desperate to know what he bought for you."

That small bit of camaraderie with her cousin brought a smile to her lips and a little pitter-patter to her heart. Genny found herself responding honestly. "It was too neatly put together to do such a thing. Yes, I wish to know what the box contained, but it simply wasn't meant to be. You know why I couldn't open it. It's wholly inappropriate for Lord Barrington to send such a thing. Let this be a lesson in life."

"There you go again . . ." Charlotte shook her head. "There is no lesson other then self-torture. Why would you subject yourself to that? You're going to forever wonder which hair comb he purchased for you. And now you'll never know."

"It was necessary." Genny's gaze slipped to the door, almost wishing the butler would come back with the box she desperately wanted to open. "Why is that so hard for you to accept?"

"Because I don't. You'll never convince me now that your association with the earl is only as deep as friendship. He likes you, and I think that scares you."

"He does not scare me." Her voice sounded too defensive even to her own ears.

Charlotte laughed as she stood and made her way from the room. "You can keep telling yourself that if it makes you feel better."

Chapter 8

*It appears that Lord B—— has taken to courting.
That is not something this writer thought would
ever be put down in ink. Perhaps all he has in mind
is another discreet affair that will be surrounded
with speculation but buried in secrecy like his past
relationships.*

*Also, a notable blush stole over the mysterious
Miss C——'s cheeks as she was escorted about the
opera house on her admirer's arm. Yes, I believe
courting to be too tame a word for what Lord B——
has in mind. Perhaps this is a most illicit liaison in
the works and hopefully one that will be exposed
this time.*

The Mayfair Chronicles, June 1, 1846

As Genny and her cousin entered the private box, the
glow of the gaslights behind them flashed orange tendrils
of light across the richly carpeted floor. The box went
dark as the red velvet curtains fell back in place, and they
slowly wound their way around the chairs and toward two
unoccupied seats in the front row next to Lady Carleton.

Charlotte sat beside their host and Genny took the

chair on the end. Even if Castleigh did come, there would be no available seat near her cousin. And that was all that mattered at the moment. Leo was another matter entirely. Not that he'd be able to sit with them in the front of the box, since the chairs could not be arranged any differently to accommodate more seats per row.

The wall fixtures set around the stage gave little light to see by; most had been lowered or snuffed completely as the orchestra set up for the opening act.

Patrons were still finding their seats, conversing with the people they sat next to, and gawking at other guests around and above them. The opera was set to start momentarily, and there was no sign of Barrington or Castleigh this evening. That brought a smile to Genny's face.

What a perfect evening this was turning out to be.

"Here, Miss Camden," Lady Carleton said. "Take my opera glasses. Squinting at the surrounding company is unbecoming for a lady."

Genny felt a blush infuse her cheeks. "My apologies. I didn't even realize I was doing that."

"No need to apologize. But you should know that Barrington is with my husband, and they will be joining us when their matters at Parliament wrap up this evening." Lady Carleton tapped her white satin glove to her chin. "They do seem to be running later than usual."

Equal measures of desire and irritation filled Genny on hearing the announcement. She should be thankful Castleigh wasn't attending but was too annoyed to put much thought to that welcome fact.

"What matters are keeping them in Parliament if I might be so bold to ask?"

"A tax is being levied on sugar imports coming in from the West Indies and more specifically Barbados. Did you know my husband has fifty acres next to Lord Barrington's property?"

So this was how he so easily secured a seat at Lady Carleton's dinners and summer house parties. "I wasn't aware. I suppose you've known Lord Barrington for as long as you've been married to your husband."

"I have, and his father when he was alive, too."

"And what of Lord Castleigh, my lady?" Charlotte interjected.

Lady Carleton turned her sharp assessing gaze on Charlotte and cocked one eyebrow. "Don't think I haven't noticed your regard for the marquess. And though he declined our invitation tonight, you should know he's not the kind of gentleman for you, dear Charlotte."

"He's kind to me, my lady. I count him as a friend." Charlotte gave an ineffectual pout.

Lady Carleton squeezed Charlotte's hand with a cluck of her tongue. "I'm sorry to tell you this, but allowing a man like Castleigh to court you, as charming and sweet as he is, would have you shunned from good society and make you a mother before you are ready to take it to task."

"I don't understand."

Genny had to tell her cousin the truth about the scandal that man would bring to Charlotte's name should she pursue more than friendship with the man.

"What she means, Charlotte, is that Lord Castleigh has two children out of wedlock living *with* him." Her cousin gasped. "No one even knows who the mother is. Rumor has it that they were dropped off on his front steps the day they were born. The worst of it is that he allows them to live openly with him in his own home. So any woman he does marry will come under the scrutiny of society for allowing such a thing to continue."

"Oh, I hadn't any idea. H—he never told me that he had . . . children."

"That is exactly as it should be. Believe it or not, he was

doing you a great favor by not telling you. One doesn't talk about these things in polite company," Genny said.

Maybe now her cousin would take her advice and avoid the marquess.

"Enough with all this speculative talk. I hear my husband." Lady Carleton turned her back to the stage and faced the closed curtain.

Genny took a deep breath and focused on a stain on the wall as all three of them stood in anticipation of the men's arrival. She heard Leo talking quietly to Lord Carleton as they entered.

"Lady Charlotte. Miss Camden." Leo's deep voice sent a titillating vibration right down to her toes.

And because half the opera house probably watched their exchange, Genny forced herself to meet his gaze. It wasn't as though she could avoid him for the remainder of the night.

"Lord Barrington." She dipped her head in a semblance of polite greeting.

Barrington took her hand and placed a kiss on the back of her knuckles. Though she wanted to pull her hand out of his reach, she held firm and let her displeasure be read clearly in her narrowed gaze. His dark eyes only twinkled in amusement.

After greetings were exchanged, Lord Carleton sat next to his wife, which meant Genny needed to take the seat next to Barrington behind the first row of chairs.

She would not allow Charlotte to sit beside the lout. Though there was a distance of about a foot between their chairs, Leo slid his marginally closer. Would he attempt to whisper sweet nothings in her ear? If he did that, he would leave her with no choice but to pinch him.

As delicious as their stolen kiss had been, there would be no mistaking it for anything but an awkward misunderstanding. Just because they had once been lovers did not give him license to assume anything had changed between them or that they could simply pick up where they had left off.

"I did not take a program from the usher when I arrived. Which opera is it tonight?" Leo asked of no one in particular.

Lady Charlotte turned in her chair and passed back her leaflet of paper. "Albert Lortzing's *Undine*. I'm told we will not need a handkerchief for the ending, as this particular opera is a romance."

"Really? It's a shame that I haven't more time for the opera when Parliament is in session. I do enjoy spending my evening in the company of such lovely ladies."

"So good of you to treat yourself to a night out, then," Genny said under her breath.

"I was not able to catch what you said, Miss Camden? Would you mind repeating it?" He enjoyed teasing her far too much.

"Nothing of import, my lord. Just nattering on about how good it is that no one dies in the opera tonight."

"Quite the save, Miss Camden. Quite the save."

She put her shoulders back and tilted her chin up haughtily. "I don't know what you refer to, Lord Barrington."

"Of course not." He gave her a knowing grin.

She picked up her opera glasses and looked around the opera house, deliberately ignoring him. He'd not give her the opportunity to snub him for the remainder of the night, however.

Quickly reading over the synopsis for the opera, he handed the program back to the front row. "Thank you, Lady Charlotte."

"You're welcome," she responded before turning back to the front.

Grasping the arm of Miss Camden's chair, he leaned in close to whisper in her ear. "A tale of a water nymph getting her prince. How fitting when I met you in nothing more than your chemise whilst swimming."

Without hesitation or warning, she rapped him on his hand with her closed fan. He yanked his smarting hand away and rubbed the back of his knuckles. And though he wanted to laugh, he did not want to draw eyes their way. Right now, he had her all to himself and he'd like it to stay that way for as long as possible.

"Where have you been all my life, Miss Camden? I don't think I've enjoyed anyone's company above yours. You have a miraculous way about you that keeps me in line when I most need straightening out."

"I'm afraid the sentiment will have to go unreturned."

"Touché."

She did not respond further, only glared at him, retribution clear in the perturbed pinch of her lips and the crack of wood as her hand tightened around her closed fan.

As the orchestra started the opening act, he took advantage of the noise to slide his chair nearer yet to hers.

He sat close enough that he could make out every delicate feature of her face in the dimly lit box. Her chin was slightly pointed, her cheekbones high but not overly defined in her fairylike face. Her lips weren't very generous, but had enough flesh to pull and suck on when they kissed.

He wanted to taste her lips now but forced his gaze downward to assess the rest of her ensemble.

Her collarbone and shoulders were exposed tonight in a dress that scooped down on her curvaceous frame. It looked to be another dark and drab color, but he'd not be able to confirm that till the lights were restored in the opera house.

Her skin shone luminescent like a pearl glimpsed in the murky gloom of seawater, but she was all warm flesh and blood that he craved more than ever to touch and feel for himself. Her bosom was pushed high and unfortunately covered except for the very top swell that caught the black-beaded drops of her necklace. She should have a strand of diamonds wrapped about her neck and be draped in the finest of silks, not wearing paste jewels and outdated styles.

Her hair was coiled and held in place with plain hairpins and a simple, black lacquered hair comb. A shame she hadn't accepted his gift; it would have looked lovely in her hair tonight.

He had to pry his eyes off her and physically turn in his seat so he could focus on the stage for the opening act. It felt like forever before the first intermission came upon them.

"The music is lovely," Lady Charlotte exclaimed, taking Lady Carleton's arm as they headed out of the box for refreshments.

"So glad to have joined you. I'm pleased to know the ending won't be the typical operatic bloodbath," Lord Carleton said, following his wife from the box.

Leo didn't fail to notice that Genny held back, so Leo stood aside to let the rest of their party precede them.

She grasped his wrist and pulled him out of sight from the other attendees outside their private box.

"Why are you trying so hard to unsettle me?"

Knowing they would only have a moment alone, he acted quickly. Placing his palm to the small of her back, he used his free hand to flick one of the heavy velvet curtains around their forms and pressed her gently against the recessed wall at the back of the Carleton box.

He must have caught her off guard because she didn't struggle to be free of him. They were effectively locked together in their own little realm of velvet and gilt where no one could witness what might transpire. The familiar lavender scent of her clothes clung to her like fresh spring rain. God, the woman drove him mad with lust just by being so close to her.

"I like you unsettled, Miss Camden. It allows me to take certain advantages I wouldn't have the opportunity for otherwise." He paused in his speech, his eyes dropping to her mouth. "Nothing would please me more than kissing you. Right here. Right now."

"Your behavior is uncalled for." She shoved at his chest, but it wasn't to push him away because her hands flattened and relaxed there. "We will be missed if we don't find the rest of our party."

He couldn't care less about her cousin and the Carletons when he was too busy imagining the wicked things he could do to her. Like peel her dress away and lick every inch of her skin, which he knew was as soft as the petals of a flower in bloom. He wanted to hike up her skirts and feel the litheness of her legs as they wrapped around him. Neither of those things could be accomplished here, but when he did finally have her in his bed again, he'd take his time and savor every touch, every taste, until he was drowning in her very essence.

A small taste of her would have to suffice for now.

Placing his thumb on the center of her chin, he inched it down far enough to separate her lips and see her tongue peeking out from between the pink folds. His gaze caught hers full on. He couldn't stop himself from sliding his fingers over the side of her face and slipping them lower to capture her neck in his hand. She didn't resist him, didn't pull away. Instead, she arched her body marginally forward in invitation.

She was an enthralling and fascinating creature. His very own water nymph come to life.

Fingers reaching out, she found his chest and slipped her hand higher, above his necktie, and wrapped it around the bare portion of his neck. Her palm was warm, and her touch made him more desperate than ever to whisk her away from the prying eyes around them. Steal her away so he could have her all to himself.

"Kiss me, Genny."

She shook her head. "I can't do this with you."

"You wish to do this with another?" Even though he said this in jest, the very idea sickened him. He would never allow another man to lay a finger upon her.

"You know precisely what I mean."

"Then you leave me no choice but to make the first move."

With his hand still at the small of her back, he pulled her solidly along the length of his body. When she gave in and stopped fighting the natural press of their bodies, a low sigh escaped her parted lips. He traced the seam of her mouth with his finger, building the anticipation of what was to come.

The scent of her perfume was an aphrodisiac in and of itself. Loose tendrils of her hair teased at his nose. One touch, even one taste would be stepping into dangerous territory.

What had happened to her resolve to remain distant with Barrington? No good would come of spending any time with him . . . alone.

And why was she practically throwing herself into his arms, enticing him in a way she had no right to do?

"You are making a spectacle of yourself," she said.

"We are cocooned in our own private sanctuary. Only the two of us will know that I am a fool for you."

Without warning his free hand threaded through the back of her hair to cup her head and better angle her face. The warmth of him enveloped their fused forms, making her skin feel overheated.

His lips found the heavily beating pulse at her neck

instead of her lips, which she had parted in anticipation. She had wanted to feel the press of his mouth upon hers, wanted to taste his passion upon her tongue.

Something akin to disappointment filled her heart that he did not lay claim to her mouth. But what right did she have to that feeling? She should be picking her skirts up and running as fast and as far as she could.

His mouth was firm but soft against the vein pulsing heavily at her neck. His teeth pulled lightly, teasingly. The tickle of his nose drew a line from the base of her neck to the sensitive spot behind her ear.

Why was she failing to keep a cool distance from him? Why couldn't she detach herself from her feelings of old? Opening herself up to this man would lead to heartache once he was done with her and gone again.

His teeth pulled at her earlobe, sucking it into the recess of his hot mouth. Her traitorous body molded impossibly tighter to his.

It had been so long since he had held her. She wanted more. Even if that desire was complete madness.

Drawing in a deep breath, she forced her hands between their bodies and gave a small shove against his chest. This intimacy, this need to touch each other couldn't continue. She had to take herself as far away from this man as possible.

Obligingly, he lifted his head from the sweet torture he was inflicting on her skin and senses and took a step back. It wasn't that she wanted to leave his arms. She wished she could relish in the feel of his strong body surrounding her and reigniting passions long vanquished by his leaving four years ago. To feel so utterly feminine and protected in his arms, even for an unguarded moment, made her yearn for what could never be and had never been because he hadn't wanted to marry her.

She pressed her fingers to her neck, sliding the tips over

the sensitive spot he'd nibbled at. Palms flattened over his chest, she had to fight against the craving to bask in the touch of every solid warm inch beneath. She would prefer to pull him back and have his lips descend upon hers, instead of pushing him back another step.

Allowing this concession of a second kiss had been a grave mistake.

Closing her eyes, she took in a deep breath hoping to find her equilibrium again. What had she just allowed to happen? A cool caress of air brushed her skin as the curtain was pulled aside. Leo grabbed her hand and led her out into the corridor.

"Come, before we are truly missed."

The bright lights stung her eyes for a moment but they adjusted quickly, and she could see her cousin and Lady Carleton ahead of the rush as they made their way downstairs to the refreshment table. Even though it felt as though she and Leo had delayed for a lengthy period of time, they'd only been behind the curtain for a few minutes.

Leo took her arm in his and strolled down the hall at an unhurried pace. There were enough witnesses to see them acting above reproach. But would any of them guess why her cheeks were flushed and her neck probably reddened from Leo's ministrations?

Would any of them wonder if Barrington and she were merely friends? Or would they think Leo was courting her? Genny wondered if they thought his intentions pure or devilish. Definitely the latter.

"You're a daring man," she mused aloud.

"Life wouldn't be nearly as fun if I didn't step outside society's strictures every now and again. I do have a reputation to uphold."

Only a man could say such a bold thing. Though she'd done just that once upon a time, she knew she'd spend the rest of her days trying to hide it from the world. "I still stand by what I said earlier, Lord Barrington."

"I seem to have forgotten what that was."

When she peered up at him, he gave her a knowing and pleased grin.

"You must find yourself another woman to toy with."

"Toy with?" He tsked and gave a slight shake of his head. "Such harsh words, Miss Camden. You wound me."

"I doubt that."

"Surely you'll understand my predicament better when I explain that I just can't seem to stay away."

"I'll not buy into your charm as so many others do. I know exactly what type of person you are. Now if you'll excuse me, I would like to discuss the opera with my cousin."

With that she quit his company. But not before he whispered something altogether improper, along the lines of rekindling old passions, in her ear.

Damn that man. He'd ruin her before the season was out if she didn't learn quickly how to better guard herself. She was no young debutante, easy to disarm and take advantage of. She was a grown woman with far too much experience in dealing with the opposite sex. So why couldn't she fend off Barrington? Was it because he had intimate knowledge of her? Or was it because she secretly craved his touch?

As she saw it, her main problem was that he kept showing up at every event she attended. She almost wondered if he had orchestrated their meeting at the jewelry shop.

If she couldn't find a way to avoid him, she'd have to learn to ignore him when they attended the same functions. And if she failed at doing that . . .

Well, she could only hope that she would never find out.

* * *

Leo watched Genny as she weaved her way through the crowds to make it to her cousin's side. Genny whispered something in her cousin's ear, causing the young woman to laugh. Then they turned down the wide entry stairs at the front of the opera house and headed toward the lobby.

He followed them as far as the top landing of the stairs, though he kept an eye on her from his vantage point.

Ponsley was a cheap bastard where his *servants* were concerned. Maybe the old man had dressed Genny in drab ensembles intentionally so she wouldn't draw eyes away from his daughter, who was adorned in the finest that the seamstresses in London offered. It couldn't be argued that both women were lovely in their own way but only one had managed to catch Leo's eye.

Chapter 9

Would you believe that none other than the infamous Dowager F—— has gone into a long overdue seclusion? She has not been seen for three days, not even at her usual gaming hells. Though the rumor cannot be proved as of yet, it is thought that a Mr. W—— may take his seat with the Lords sooner than anticipated.

The Mayfair Chronicles, June 3, 1846

No one answered the door after Leo's second knock. And that wasn't necessarily the most unsettling part.

If the footman or butler were not available, then the housekeeper or even a maid should have come at his knock.

What in bloody hell was going on?

The gargoyle-shaped knocker was firmly in place, so he knew Jezebel was in residence and hadn't in fact up and left for the country in the middle of the night. Besides, Hayden would have sent him a note had he successfully managed to remove Jez from London at the height of the season.

Leo rapped the heavy brass knocker against the ebony-painted door once again, and stepped away from the townhouse to glance up to the tall-paned second-story windows. As tempting as it was to shout out for Jez in the middle of Mayfair, the curtains were all closed and he didn't wish to wake her if she was indeed in residence. He also had no intention of drawing unwanted attention from Jez's neighbors. Regardless, someone should have answered his summons already.

Not wishing to stand in the street all night, he tested the latch on the door. It clicked up easily and he pushed it open.

All the lamps were snuffed in the anteroom and not a sound could be heard from any direction. If Mr. Warren had so much as put a hair out of place on Jezebel's head, he'd murder the blighter on sight.

Catching up his cane, he pressed in the tiny silver nob that would release the blade hidden within.

"Jezebel," he called out, his voice echoing around the marble foyer.

Impatiently, he waited for a response. Not necessarily from Jez, but from one of the multitude of servants she kept on hand at all times.

So why was no one answering?

"Jez," he called out again, taking the stairs two at a time, making his way to the double doors at the far end of the hall. He'd been here many times and had attended to her in her boudoir when they planned their evenings, her maids readying her for whatever event they chose to crash.

He didn't bother knocking when he reached the heavy oak door of her private chamber but threw it open so hard that it only stopped when the latch lodged into the wall.

He stormed through the sitting room and into her bedroom where four startled sets of eyes jolted up and stared at him in openmouthed astonishment. The housekeeper's mouth flapped like a landed fish, the butler—an aged and frail man—was hunched over, attempting to help his mistress up from the floor where she lay rumpled and twisted in her bedding. Two maids stood by, one twisting and wringing a wet towel between nervous hands, the other kneeling on the floor with Jez resting her feverish-looking head in her lap.

Leo rushed to Jez's side and lifted her in his arms to place her back atop the bed. He froze at the sight of the dark stain that covered her bedding.

What in hell?

Goddamn it.

Was it possible she carried the next Earl of Fallon in her womb? Hell yes, it was possible. The blighter had only died a week ago.

"I'll send for the surgeon."

How had he been so bloody daft as to not realize she'd been with child sooner?

"Please don't." She pressed her cold, feverish palm to his face. "He can't be here." Her voice was cracked and dry.

Her frame felt slight and delicate as he lifted her easily from the floor. Why hadn't he noticed her evident weight loss before now?

"You are unwell, Jez. A medical professional needs to have a look at you."

"They'll bleed me." Her eyes slid shut as he took her into her sitting room and settled her on the red velvet divan she used for mid-afternoon naps. A place where he had lain down so many times while her maids dressed her behind the Chinese screen set in the farthest corner of the room. He grabbed the yellow bolstered pillow at the end of the divan and stuck it behind her back when she rolled onto her side.

A hiss of what could only be described as painful agony

pressed out from between her parted lips. Her brow was beaded in a cold sweat, her teeth chattered as she sucked in another pained breath.

"Bleeding might be your best option," he said. The only certainty he had about the situation was that anything was better than nothing.

"I've bled enough today," she grunted out and then pinched her lips together before sobbing out her pain. She grasped his arm; her hold was painfully firm. "You can't fix this. Call on Hayden if you want to send for someone."

What did Hayden know that he did not?

Leo turned to the maid who had been nervously standing by. "You." He pointed at her. "My house is four doors down, knock on the front door and ask for Frederick. Tell him to take you straight to the Duke of Alsborough's."

She nodded and ran out of the room with all due haste.

He flicked a coin at the butler and the man caught it surprisingly quick. "Rouse the surgeon and get him here without delay."

Jez pulled at his arm that she still held on to. "No, Leo."

"I'm not giving you a choice in the matter. We'll wait for Hayden to arrive before we decide anything, all right? But the surgeon will be standing by if he's needed."

Jez nodded her head and furrowed her brows together as another wave of pain visibly hit her. She brought her knees up to her chest, curling into fetal position. Leo scratched at the side of his prickly face in thought. There had to be something he could do to make this better.

"I'm so tired, Leo. I just want it all to end."

"Stop with that nonsense. Do you really want your dead husband to win?" He held out his hand for a cloth to wipe her sweat-dampened brow. The housekeeper handed him a cool cloth. "Carry on, Jez. Be bold and strong as you always have been."

"I don't feel very strong at the moment," was her weak response.

"We'll get you healthy again. Now tell me why you were resting on the floor as opposed to your comfortable bed?"

"I—I fell," she responded.

Sobs overtook her for a moment and she couldn't seem to say more. She bit her bottom lip so fiercely he thought she'd pierce it if she didn't let up.

"You should have sent for someone to assist you."

"Isn't it obvious that I don't want anyone to see me at present?"

Yes, it was. And he was a cad for saying otherwise. God, he could be such an insensitive ass at the oddest of times.

The housekeeper stepped close to the head of the divan and leaned over the arm to whisper something in Jez's ear. Leo held his friend's hand in his as the maid wrung out the towel and mopped Jez's forehead again. What should he do? What could he even say?

When Hayden came running through the door like a barreling bull, Leo stood and moved away from Jez to perch himself on the back of an upholstered chair.

Hayden's expression was grim. He only nodded to Leo before making his way to Jez's side. Taking her outstretched hand, he leaned over her and whispered something privately in her ear.

Despite the urgency of the situation, it seemed Leo was the only one not to be informed of Jez's condition.

Hayden gave directions to the maid to ready her ladyship's bed. The young woman was off before Hayden completed his request, as though she knew exactly what needed to be done.

Leo stepped closer to Jez and Hayden. "I'll do whatever is needed. Just tell me what to do."

Hayden turned to him, an oddly saddened expression clouding his eyes. "I can handle this."

"Tell me she will fare well, Hayden." He roughly put his hands through his hair, which he was sure stood on end from doing that repeatedly over the past half hour.

"Let me settle her in her room." Without further explanation Hayden leaned directly over Jez and asked her to put her arms around his shoulders. She weakly complied and her arms shook as she raised them.

Carefully, Hayden lifted her in his arms and made his way to the adjacent room. Leo spied the maid stripping the bedding and putting down wide pieces of linen with the help of the housekeeper.

There was nothing left for him to do here, so he made his way downstairs.

His open palm slammed against the wall when he hit the bottom landing. Hayden didn't need to tell him what was going on. It suddenly came to him why the surgeon couldn't see Jez; the reason was like a bloody banshee screaming in his ear till he was going deaf from the truth.

If the surgeon knew or so much as guessed that she had miscarried the last issue for the previous Earl of Fallon then everyone else would find out. If it was known that the babe hadn't lasted in her womb, then Mr. Warren would move faster on securing the title and remove Jez from the house.

Son of a bitch.

After Leo sent the doctor away with a purse full of coins, explaining that everything was fine since it was a bad dish at dinner that had bothered Jezebel, the man had left in a sour mood.

An hour later Leo made his way back upstairs, still digesting the truth. How could he mention anything about their *friendly* wager to court the Ponsley girl now? Quite simply he couldn't. What a bloody mess everything had turned out to be.

Hayden looked up from Jez's prone, sleeping form when Leo entered the bedchamber. He came out of the room Jez rested in and shut the door behind him.

"She finally sleeps," he said.

Leo nodded, understanding he would have to let his anger simmer over not knowing the truth sooner. He did not wish to wake his ailing friend.

Hayden was down to his shirtsleeves, which were rolled up to his elbows and damp at the edges. He must have helped with washing the sweat from Jez's brow.

"How long have you known?" Leo felt betrayed that no one had confided the truth to him before now.

"I only found out."

"You told me it was impossible."

"I did not misguide you. Her husband knew of her condition and took it upon himself to lace her food and tea with blue cohosh."

Leo crossed his arms and leaned against the wall. "Blue cohosh?"

"An herb to purge the babe from her body. He made a point of telling her before he passed."

Leo swore red filled his vision. He'd never been so infuriated in his whole life. Never had he wanted to seek retribution on behalf of his friend so much. Nothing but sinking the pointed end of his rapier into the heart of his foe would make this marginally better. But this particular enemy was already dead.

"How did that bastard accomplish it?"

"His loyal valet, whom I have dispatched only this morning on a ship to Australia. Though he actively took part in aborting the baby, he did not know that the poisoning had succeeded."

"I presume your reasoning for sending him off is that he can tell no one."

"Precisely."

"Has Jez sought help?"

Hayden swept his hand through his golden locks and scratched the back of his head. "When she found out what her husband had done, she saw a midwife outside of Town. She had hoped that the damage could be reversed, but it was too late to save the babe. The pains for her miscarriage, from what she told me, started just after her husband's funeral."

Hence her immediate retaliation against the man who stood to inherit it all, and her need to lose herself in a bottle of rum with her friends who were not aware of her situation.

"How long will she be away from society?" The unasked question was how long would the miscarriage last. How long before others noticed something to be unusually off with Jez?

"It's hard to say. She was maybe four months into the pregnancy. She said the sickness at the beginning made her body too weak to withstand the herb Fallon had laced her food and drink with. I think she'll be on her feet again in a week or so."

Leo paced the room, rubbing his hand over his eyes and face as exhaustion from the long day settled over him.

While he empathized with Jez's reasons to stop Mr. Warren from marrying, he better understood where the revenge stemmed from. Who was to say the man was as bad as she made him out to be? This had, in the course of a couple of hours, become an incredibly delicate situation.

He paused and then turned on his heel to face Hayden. "Does Tristan know?"

Leo wasn't upset that Jez had chosen to confide in

Hayden. She was closer to him, just as he was closer to Tristan in their friendship.

"He does not."

Leo took to pacing the floor. "How is it you came by this information?"

"She was forced to reveal the truth when I had my solicitor start looking over the will. He asked if she was sure there was no possibility she was in a delicate way. She asked to speak to me privately at that point. She was very specific in her wish that I tell no one and to find some other wording that would let her contest the will." The underlying meaning was that the fewer people who knew the better. "I'm sorry that included you and Tristan."

"There is no need to apologize. I understand."

Leo also assumed that he wasn't to reveal any of tonight's events to Tristan. And had he not come to talk to Jez, he probably never would have found out the truth, either.

"About the business with the girl," Hayden said. "I suggest you give Tristan some excuse not to carry through. Mr. Warren has caught himself in the middle of a feud with Jez and her dead husband. Jez will regret her decision to ruin the girl's hopes for a decent marriage when the melancholy of her loss subsides."

"Tristan's eyes are set firmly on the young lady. He'll not be easily persuaded to leave the task unfinished."

"If Tristan succeeds in this, I'm positive Jez will feel immense guilt when she is back to her old self."

Would she? She had more reason than any to seek vengeance in a form that was satisfying and equal to that of her own loss.

"I hope you're right. I'll head over to Tristan's house in the next few days. His sister arrived with his brats only yesterday, so he'll be occupied with them."

Hayden reached out and clasped his arm. "I know it's difficult to keep this to ourselves, but we must do so for Jez's sake. I worry she won't pull through this and emerge as the woman we count as our dearest friend."

"She's not been herself since the funeral preparations were made." He plucked his jacket from the chair he'd tossed it on earlier. "I'll find a way to convince Tristan that this isn't right."

"I know you will," Hayden said before Leo left for home.

Chapter 10

Though this writer did not receive an invite to the most talked-about house party of every summer, nor, would it seem, did the most ostensible Marquess of C——. Dear readers, can you guess which friend of the marquess's did receive an invite?

Another noteworthy event is that Lady of G—— birthed the duke's heir only three months after nuptials. The question remains as to who sired the love child since rumor has it that the duke dueled at an undisclosed location two days after the birth of his son.

The Mayfair Chronicles, June 14, 1846

Not telling Tristan what had transpired at Jez's townhouse had been more difficult than it should have been. But he had kept his word and would continue to remain silent.

Today, while he convinced his friend to abandon the Ponsley girl, he wouldn't whisper a word of what he knew. Would Jezebel ever confide the truth in Tristan? Was she ashamed of what had happened? That would be outlandish considering she had had no control over the situation.

He'd been to visit her last evening but she'd been in too

much pain to enjoy his company. Not that he was sure she even wanted his company when she was still out of sorts. It had been an uncomfortably short visit. He'd given her time to open up the gift he'd purchased—the fan that Hayden had told him about—and left without whispering a word of his concerns. She had put the present down without a second glance and given him a lackluster smile of gratitude.

Of course, he'd not been able to broach the subject of Lord Ponsley's daughter, so he resolved to discuss it directly with Tristan.

"What brings you to my neck of the woods?" Tristan asked.

They rarely convened any business of a professional or personal nature at Tristan's home. Mainly because of the brats his friend let rule his life like wild animals. Though Leo admitted he was fond of the children. They were well behaved and intelligent enough to have a conversation with now that they'd outgrown the awkward babbling toddler years.

And really, they were as bad as their father with their pranks, trickery, and charming wit.

Rowan, the youngest at seven, was as sharp as a sword. Veronica, or Ronnie as everyone addressed her, was a match in intelligence to anyone who dared to challenge her inquisitive ten-year-old mind. While Rowan was the very image of his father, Ronnie was a blue-eyed blonde— and a beauty in the making.

Chin resting on her folded hands atop the luncheon table, she scrunched up her nose as though she were trying to put together a long-unsolved puzzle.

Why hadn't he thought to come later in the day? Sometimes it was easy to forget that when Tristan was in residence with his children, he turned into a doting, caring father, who actually enjoyed time with the little devils. The only thing missing was a mother for Ronnie and Rowan and a wife for Tristan. Though his friend swore that another person in his life was the last thing he wanted.

Oddly enough, Tristan shed this dutiful, fatherly appearance the moment he stepped out into society. Perhaps he only wanted to be a good role model? He had come into fatherhood at a young age—nineteen to be precise.

Leo narrowed his gaze from one child to the next. Tristan took his meaning.

"It's off with you lot now, isn't it?" Tristan ran his hand through his son's hair and tugged gently on a long lock of Ronnie's hair. "Up to see your aunt you go."

"But Papa, we have a guest," Ronnie protested.

"There will be plenty of guests another time, angel. Right now, I need to discuss business with Leo. So do me a favor and run up and see Beatrice. If you finish your lessons early and to her satisfaction, you can have one of those chocolate tarts Cook makes."

Ronnie pouted out her lower lip and reached for her brother's hand. "Come on, Rowan. Papa thinks we're intruding."

"Don't be mean to Papa, Ronnie. Aunt Beat will make you write out lines if you say bad things."

Their voices faded as they left the room. The last thing Leo heard was, "Not if you don't tell her." It brought a smile to his face. They were a mischievous set, and he was glad they weren't his children.

"As I was saying, what brings you here?"

Leo leaned back in his chair and crossed his arms over his chest. "We need to discuss Ponsley's daughter."

"Ah, I see." Tristan turned to the waiting attendants. "We can serve ourselves, you are dismissed." To Leo he said, "Coffee? Cook always works some sort of magic with that vacuum pot of hers; I wish I could figure out how to get the grinds out. She manages to make it taste better than any of the coffeehouses about Town."

"Coffee without grinds sounds perfect. I don't have anywhere to be this early in the day, anyway."

Tristan handed over the carafe with a grin. "I suppose not. Can't imagine why you'd come so early to discuss Lady Charlotte."

After pouring himself a coffee and adding a generous helping of milk, Leo made himself comfortable in his chair. "I would like to call off our wager in courting and winning the girl to our favor."

"Poor sportsmanship of you, isn't it? We did bet that fine filly of yours."

"How about I offer breeding rights?"

Tristan leaned back in his chair and gave him a scrutinizing look. "Have you managed to steal the chit right out from under my nose?"

"I'm glad to say that I have not. Nor do I wish to pursue this mission of Jezebel's."

"Have you told her?"

"Once she stops mourning her old life I'll find the time to tell her."

Tristan gave him a look that said he didn't believe him. "You can't be serious."

"Oh, I am. Think on it, Tristan, Jez is in a rough patch right now. Mr. Warren has never shown an inclination toward brutishness. I've never heard a bad word about him." Leo paused deliberately and let his words sink in. "Besides, once you gain favor with the Ponsley girl, I guarantee you there will be another . . . and another after that to keep away from Mr. Warren. In fact, I don't see an end in sight."

Tristan took a long sip of his coffee and set the empty cup on the table to pour himself out more of the dark brew. "But this is *Ponsley's* daughter. Have you forgotten that?"

"I haven't."

"It's that woman, isn't it? Miss Camden has your balls in a noose."

Genny.

Of course this was partially about Genny. "I assure you, I came to my senses long before seeing Miss Camden again."

"Precisely how did you come to know her before?"

"Tristan, you're not focusing on the topic at hand."

"Oh, indeed I am. You have a *tendre* for Miss Camden and you don't want to upset that if I move on the Ponsley chit." Tristan actually guffawed like some old biddy might do at the latest joke and smacked the flat of his hand on the table. "This is brilliantly hilarious! I didn't believe I would ever see a day when you actually cared for someone more than you care for yourself."

Leo gave him a droll, unimpressed look and ignored the jab at his character. "Think of your daughter, if you won't think of the damage you will do to this young woman."

"I assure you, that young woman is nothing like my daughter."

"And what if someone wanted to ruin Ronnie's chances to marry into a decent title and fortune?"

"I think you are mistaking my children for someone else's. Unless you have forgotten their roots, let me remind you that their mothers dropped them off on my doorstep without so much as shouting out a hallo."

"I do not mistake their origins. But that isn't to say that young men won't chase after your daughter as we have chased after so many women. I hate to admit this but the Ponsley girl seems decent. A hell of a lot more decent than her father."

"Decent?" His friend snorted at that and took another sip of his coffee. "That is not a word I would associate with Lady Charlotte."

"You think you have a better understanding of her character than I do?"

"I have spent time with her, so yes, I like to think I have a good understanding of her disposition."

"Is your mind set on garnering her favor and ruining her chance at marrying Mr. Warren?"

"I didn't say that precisely."

"Then stop beating around the truth and spit it out, man." Leo sat back in his chair, quite frustrated that this conversation was going nowhere.

"Look, I can't make any promises where Lady Charlotte is concerned. She's become a problem for us both, eh? Not only through Jez but by her own scheming tactics."

"She's fresh into society and you claim her to be cunning? This I need to know the details of."

"It is probably better you don't. Let it alone. Well, not the bit about giving me breeding rights on that equine you managed to get your hands on."

Leo wasn't sure if this meant Tristan agreed that they needed to leave the young lady alone or not.

He wasn't sure he had accomplished anything in coming here. Should he warn Genny of someone's—not specifically Tristan's, because he'd not inform on his friend—intent to ruin Lady Charlotte's upcoming nuptials? Or would the girl be able to fend off Tristan on her own? It was unlikely she would have the defenses needed to steer someone of Tristan's reputation in a different direction.

This whole scenario put him in a damnable position. Where should his loyalties lie in all this? With Jez who stood to lose everything and already had in a sense? With Tristan whom he'd known all his life, or with Genny, the woman he wanted back in his life if she would accept him?

*   *   *

Was it possible she was in the clear? She hadn't laid eyes upon Leo since the night of the opera. Nor were any more inappropriate gifts sent to the Ponsley residence. He must realize bribery would not sway her assessment of his character.

Over the past week Castleigh hadn't tried absconding with her cousin once. They hadn't seen the marquess since the Carleton party. Was he already bored with the idea of chasing a young debutante?

Clasping the vellum envelope between her hands, Genny broke the wax seal and removed the heavy parchment. After reading it over quickly, she looked across the breakfast table to her cousin.

"Have we been invited to the house party or not?" her cousin asked impatiently.

Charlotte's father looked up from his paper and picked up his cup of tea to take a sip of the dark liquid. "I don't see why you would want to attend, poppet. It's not as though you will be finding a prospective match."

"Must you constantly remind me? I know you don't approve of our friendship with Lady Carleton, but she has treated us fabulously and we wouldn't have been invited to half the get-togethers this season if not for her."

"Miss Camden should be the one reminding you, not I."

Charlotte put down the marmalade-covered biscuit she'd been about to bite into.

"Everyone else will be leaving for the country in the next week if this heat doesn't let up. I don't see why we wouldn't be thrilled at the prospect of attending the most exclusive summer house party, one that affords us the opportunity to get some much needed fresh air, Papa."

"Rusticate if you must, but remember your responsibility to this family."

"You know I will," Charlotte said sweetly to her father. When Lord Ponsley picked up his morning paper, Charlotte focused on Genny.

"We are invited," Genny confirmed. "But we must think of your grandmother's health in this heat. It would be unwise to leave her here without a companion."

Charlotte pushed her chair out from the table and folded her napkin over her place. "I must speak to Grandmamma at once."

At Genny's raised eyebrow, her cousin rounded the table and kissed her father on the cheek. "Please excuse me from breakfast."

Her father made a noncommittal grunt on the heels of Charlotte's exit from the room.

Genny looked across the table at Lord Ponsley. She really disliked being left alone with him. He wasn't an easy man to talk to, at least not for her. He doted upon his daughter, which was part of the reason her cousin acted spoiled at times. When he did lower himself to address Genny—which was a rare event—it was clear that she was no more than the help; a poor relation who would never rise to a higher position than the servitude she found herself in at present.

She cut into her poached egg and focused on her breakfast plate. If Charlotte didn't return soon, Genny would excuse herself before Lord Ponsley remembered that she was even there.

"Miss Camden?" She flinched at her spoken name and swallowed the lump of egg that was only half chewed in her mouth. It wouldn't do to keep his lordship waiting for a response.

"Yes, my lord?"

Everything about Lord Ponsley was firmly above reproach and so she never addressed him informally. There were no lost feelings between them, even though Lord Ponsley was her uncle.

"Has Lord Castleigh attempted to *court* my daughter?"

How had he come by that information? And was the exaggeration about courting his own, or the observation of another? She didn't think it wise to lie in this instance.

"Very briefly. It seems he found another distraction once I made my displeasure known when he befriended Charlotte."

Lord Ponsley grunted at her response. "You are paid—generously I might add—to ensure that my daughter is ready for her upcoming nuptials. She does not need new friends, nor does she need men with the reputation Castleigh has approaching her. How he ever had the opportunity to be introduced to my daughter makes me question your capability as a chaperone."

"Charlotte is aware that Lord Castleigh is not welcome to join us at any mutually attended events in the future." Of course she'd not tell him that she had been clear and honest with her cousin about the man being nothing more than a libertine.

"There should never be a need to warn my daughter of the unseemly characters that lurk in wait for an easy victim during the season. Do what you were hired to do, and make sure you are close to my daughter at all times. I'll not have her compromised."

Genny lowered her head and stared at her half-eaten egg. She was no longer hungry and wished she could simply leave the breakfast room. "Yes, my lord."

The crinkle and flick of the newspaper told Genny that Lord Ponsley no longer wished to converse with her. When he was well focused on his reading, she folded her napkin and placed it on the lace tablecloth and excused herself from Lord Ponsley's company. As usual he took no notice of her.

It should not surprise Genny that the gossips had been busy speculating about the marquess's attention toward Charlotte.

"Before you leave, Miss Camden," Lord Ponsley said, looking over the edge of his paper at her.

"Yes, my lord?"

"Make sure that you cut your ties with Lord Barrington, too. You'll turn me into a laughingstock should it get out that someone in my employ would dare to be so defiant as to allow herself to be courted by my opponent."

She lowered her head. "I didn't mean—"

"Save your speech. Just make sure no one else has a reason to whisper in my ear that you are visibly going behind my back to engage in some wickedly inappropriate liaison."

"I've done nothing wrong." She really should have just left the room instead of defending herself. Once Lord Ponsley made up his mind about something, there was no changing what he thought.

"If you are seen consorting with him again, you'll be removed from this house, Miss Camden. Endeavor to keep that in mind."

He turned the page in his paper and gave it a violent flick to straighten it out.

She didn't say anything else, just stood near the door, keeping her eyes downcast from Lord Ponsley and the two footmen who gave her a brief pitying glance.

He waved her off. "You're dismissed."

She made her way slowly toward the parlor. How was she going to avoid Leo? He was the one always searching her out, not the other way around. Maybe if they ran into each other again, she'd speak plainly and make sure that

Leo understood that her position didn't allow for any sort of friendship or rivalry between them. It might be a better idea to send him a note.

Now was not the time to worry about it, however, for she had to arrange her afternoon with her cousin. They were taking a ride through Hyde Park with Mr. Warren. The past few months had gone by faster than Genny had anticipated. Before she knew it, her cousin would be a married woman and Genny's role in life once again uncertain.

A piano piece by Bach filled the corridor as she approached the parlor. It was a small but comfortable room, and a favorite place for both her and Charlotte to retreat to when they stayed in.

As Genny pushed the white-paneled door open, Charlotte said, "Grandmamma insists we take advantage of the invite and enjoy the summer reprieve."

"She does?" Oddly enough, this tidbit of news surprised Genny. She never thought the woman could be without someone close by to harangue at all hours of the day.

Charlotte closed the lid on the piano keys and pushed out the bench so she could turn to look at her. Genny made herself comfortable on the cushioned window seat that overlooked the street below, which was bustling with activity this late in the morning.

Folding her legs under her, she asked, "Who will keep her company while we are away?"

"Grandmamma said she will send a note to Aunt Alice today and summon her to Town with all due haste."

Genny was silently relieved that they would be able to escape the heat and stench of the city and spend the hottest time of year in Hertfordshire. Not to mention being away from Barrington and Castleigh for the better part of the summer season. She didn't wish to test her luck avoiding Barrington under the public eye any time soon.

They had an hour to ready for their long afternoon. Genny glanced at Charlotte's pale yellow walking dress. She looked lovely as always. "Is this what you wish to wear for your afternoon out with Mr. Warren?"

Charlotte shut the music book she'd been reading from. "Do you disapprove of my ensemble?" She fanned out her stylish skirts, and pressed her palms to her torso as she looked down at her dress.

"Not at all. It rained early this morning and we will be in an open carriage."

"Then I will instruct Mr. Warren to stay on the dry paths."

"Charlotte." Genny sighed. She really didn't want the day to be a trial with her cousin.

"If I don't stand up for myself now, his soon-to-be lordship will take advantage of me at every opportunity."

"You judge others too harshly."

Charlotte crossed her arms and emitted a huff of annoyance. "It's necessary when you aren't given a choice as to whom you marry."

"You aren't in any different a position than half the young ladies who debuted this season," Genny said.

"Yes, but if this man is a friend of my father's, I can only imagine them to be two peas in a pod."

Genny barely concealed her laugh. "Is that where all your dissonance comes from? You're afraid you will be marrying a man like your father."

Charlotte nodded as she walked toward the window seat. "Wouldn't *that* prospect have scared you when you debuted?"

"My father was much different from yours. Calm, patient, loving, and doting to my mother and me. If I had met a man like my father, I would have counted myself lucky. That's not to say I wouldn't be horrified to marry someone with a briskly calculating and cool demeanor."

"You understand me perfectly, then."

Charlotte came over and sat opposite her, stretching out her legs on the bench.

"I do." Genny reached for her cousin's hand and gave it a light squeeze. "But take note that Mr. Warren is a great deal younger than your father. He's done well to secure a very comfortable future for you. You'll want for nothing."

"Some things are worth sacrificing, including comfort, when you want more than a marriage of convenience."

"And what would you sacrifice all the comfort in the world for?"

"Love," her cousin said on a wistful breath.

"Charlotte . . ." Had Genny been blind to her cousin's feelings for another? "Do you hold a *tendre* for someone else?"

Please let it not be Castleigh, she thought.

"Not precisely."

Genny exhaled a relieved breath, though she wasn't completely convinced that her cousin was telling the truth.

"Don't you think I should be given a fair opportunity to experience that feeling at least once before tying myself to a man I don't love for all eternity?" Charlotte asked.

"Give it time. Love can grow between the two of you."

"Easy enough for you to say when you aren't being told you must marry someone you wish you didn't have to."

"You only have to put a little effort into building a strong relationship with your future husband. I know a great number of people who have married out of duty, but have found love by working toward friendship and family."

"And why should I have to have children at all, when I'm still young?" Charlotte let out a distressed huff of air and rested her head back against the wall. "I just wish Papa would have let me travel the Continent—or at least have given me a few more years before *doing my duty for the family*," Charlotte said, mocking her father's words.

"That is not for young ladies to do before they wed. But your future husband may take you anywhere in the world that you want to visit."

Charlotte snorted. "Don't be obtuse. You have met Mr. Warren."

"You have sat with him but a few times a week this past month. That is certainly not enough time to form a lasting opinion of anyone's character."

"It is for me," Charlotte assured her.

Genny took in a deep breath, hoping for patience because she might need it this afternoon. If Charlotte was contradictory with Mr. Warren, she didn't know what she would do to smooth things over.

"If he didn't want this marriage to work, he wouldn't pay you the kindness of publicly courting you."

Charlotte met her gaze and rolled her eyes. "Yes, because my fifty-thousand-pound dowry has nothing to do with this kindness of his."

"Mr. Warren stands to inherit a great fortune. And when he does, your dowry will be nothing but a drop in the bucket," Genny pointed out.

"That's *if* he inherits."

"There is no question in my mind that the earldom will be his, Charlotte. These matters take time to sort out, and once everything is resolved, he'll take you as his wife."

Charlotte swung her legs back to the ground. She must have had enough of Genny lecturing her on this topic. "You needn't remind me."

"I suggest you take the opportunity to better acquaint

yourself with him over the next week. Endear him to your favor before we leave for the Carleton house party."

"Only because you are forcing me to do so."

"If that's as close to acquiescence as I can get with you, then I'll take it."

Chapter 11

It is unfortunate that nothing ever seems to happen during the summer. Mind you, Lord P—— was seen visiting with Mr. W—— yesterday past at a gentlemen's club . . . one that shall remain unnamed. With the current showing of P——'s daughter this season, and her recent outings with Mr. W——, one can only imagine where this will be leading near the end of the year. Is a spring wedding on the horizon? Hmm, I think not.

I make a prediction, dear readers, and that is that P——'s daughter cannot be so easily tamed.
The Mayfair Chronicles, July 5, 1846

Genny tried to concentrate on the book she'd borrowed from the Carleton library last night. It was a gothic novel she had no interest in reading, but thought it might help her forget about one guest in particular. It was a useless task. She couldn't focus on anything except the man sitting ten feet away from her.

Lord Ponsley must have been aware that Lord Barrington would be here. Maybe the warning he'd given her was intended to make her extra vigilant in her dealings with Lord Barrington over the next few weeks?

Why hadn't she realized sooner that Leo could easily secure an invite to Lady Carleton's annual house party? After all, this was where they had first met.

The heat wasn't helping with the distraction, either. While she'd forgone the heavy underlayers beneath her dress today due to the scorching temperature, it only made her realize how underdressed she was in the presence of Lord Barrington. How silly it was for her to worry about her lack of underthings when there were ten others in the parlor. But mulling on that thought fired her imagination to go in directions it had no right venturing.

The interior, sheer curtains had been drawn in the room to help keep it cool, though that wasn't really helping.

It seemed she wasn't the only one affected. Aside from Leo playing chess near a shaded window with Lady Hargrove, Genny sat across from Lady Carleton. There were two gentlemen and two ladies sitting with them on the opposing settees. Charlotte and Ariel reclined on a sofa perpendicular to Genny, their fans slowly flicking back and forth to cool their flushed faces.

"I propose," the countess said, "that we spend the rest of this dreadfully hot afternoon al fresco."

Charlotte and Ariel both sat up, their fans slowing with the welcome idea.

Fresh air would do everyone in the room a world of good. And Genny would be able to put a great deal more distance between her and Leo.

"What a fantastic idea," Genny said.

So long as there was an elm to sit beneath and lemonade in hand, she'd be content. Agreement went all around the room. Lady Carleton made arrangements with her butler and everyone fanned out of the parlor to retrieve their hats, bonnets, and parasols.

Leo held back with his chess partner, making a final play before standing from the unfinished board. Genny waited for Charlotte and Ariel to exit the room. She wasn't sure how it happened, but she was suddenly standing in the entrance of the room with only Barrington for company.

"After you, Miss Camden." One of his hands fell possessively to the small of her back to guide her through the door.

Had anyone else been there, she knew he wouldn't have taken the liberty to touch her. The intimate touch had her freezing momentarily to the spot. Moving meant losing the feel of his hand against her and, admittedly, she'd been thinking about his hands on her all morning. Her thoughts must be all jumbled from the heat. She did not want Barrington to actually touch her.

Only moments ago she had wanted nothing more than to escape his presence. And hadn't she promised to pinch herself if she thought of Barrington in too fond a fashion ever again?

She pointed her finger accusingly at him. "Don't think because you were invited to this house party that you are also invited into my bed."

She might as well put that on the table for discussion.

Leo's arm extended above her head to rest on the door frame. The move brought him within kissing distance. "I'm flattered that you think of me often enough to conclude that that was the reason I came."

Genny brushed a strand of hair from her forehead as she glared at him. What was he about? He could not deny that he had designs on her. Why else would he have held back to speak with her? Why would he attempt to catch her eye when he thought no one was looking?

"You barely register in my thoughts." She nearly

flinched at those words. It was a terribly cruel thing to say, but she needed to set boundaries with this man.

He leaned so close to her that their faces were level.

"Really?"

She didn't blink or lower her gaze.

"There were great times between us, but if you want more honorable relations then I will do as you wish."

Then she did blink, not sure that she'd heard him correctly. Folding her arms over her chest, she said, "Ah, so that's the way of it? You'll be spending your time here on another *task*."

Had he intended to seduce another all along, and right under her very nose? How in the world had she ever seen any decency in him? Or been charmed by his flattering words, and pseudo-chivalric ways?

"I'd hate to disappoint you, princess, but you are sorely mistaken."

She tapped her slippered foot, suddenly uncomfortable with the direction of their conversation. "Surely you jest."

"Is it so hard to believe that I don't have designs on anyone else?" He held up his hands as though in surrender.

She chose not to respond and instead stepped through the door intent on leaving him there alone. But she stopped and turned back to him, needing to know one thing: "Is no one to your liking?"

"Only one lady, and she's made it clear that I am to refrain from any advances."

"Oh," was the only intelligible response she could muster.

He meant her, didn't he? She mentally kicked herself for the little flutter in her stomach at the thought of having his undivided attention. She would *not* allow herself to be charmed by his flattering words.

"You should retrieve your bonnet before anyone wonders where we have disappeared to," he reminded her.

Yes, she should. Nothing short of a good mile separating them would do. To keep her wits about her, she'd need to remain in the company of the other houseguests *at all times*. She could not find herself alone in his company again.

She sped off to her room without looking back, unable to bear seeing his smiling face, for he most certainly understood her discomfiture. Worse, he knew exactly how to put her out of sorts. She would gather her courage to stand up to him after she had a moment to calm her frayed nerves in her room. He would not turn her into a blushing, stammering, speechless fool.

Leo wasn't precisely sure what he was doing. All he knew was that he'd craved Genny's company since his arrival yesterday morning. She had managed to avoid him at every turn, always surrounding herself with other houseguests.

Did she really think warning him off would make him leave? Well, he'd not give her a chance to avoid him for much longer. He waited for her at the bottom of the grand staircase that led up to the bedchambers. He was already dressed to go. Everyone else had a head start toward the afternoon spot. He was the last one who could keep Genny company on the walk and he was glad she would have to take his arm as they made their way outside to their impromptu luncheon.

He smiled up at her as she came down the stairs, face flushed from her exertions to ready herself quickly. Her hair was tucked away in a beige bonnet, and she carried a matching lace parasol. Disappointment flashed in her eyes as her gaze slipped past his shoulder in search of any others. He wouldn't let her escape him so easily.

"Have they all left?"

He ignored the disappointment in her voice and gave

her his most charming smile. "Everyone has a five-minute head start on us. I said we'd be out in a trice."

"We'll have to hurry to catch them." Genny practically skipped down the stairs in her rush to be away from him.

"There is no rush, Miss Camden. I promised Lady Carleton I would take good care of you. We can get to know each other better on our walk."

She pinched her lips together as she glided past him. "I can't imagine what it is you wish to know."

"Everything, Miss Camden. Including your darkest secrets—though I daresay I already know a few, hmm?"

She glared back at him.

He held out his arm for her to take. While they'd been friends and had spent time together four years ago, they'd never touched in public, afraid they might give away just how well they knew each other. Things were different now. They were both older and more mature, and he liked to think wiser.

Instead of taking his arm, she brushed past him and headed for the exit. She opened her parasol and weaved down the stone path in front of him without so much as a glance back in his direction.

When he caught up to her, she gave him a curious glance over her shoulder. "And will you in turn share your deepest and darkest secrets, my lord?"

"Only those decent enough for a lady's ear."

"That hardly seems fair."

He chuckled and caught up to her so they were walking side by side. Their party was a quarter of a mile ahead, already sitting in the shade of an ancient elm tree. He didn't offer his arm again; instead, he clasped his hands behind his back as he walked leisurely by her side. At least she let him match her pace.

"Have you been a paid companion since we parted ways?"

"I have."

"What decided your path?"

So many things, including you, she wanted to admit but wouldn't dare. Why should he care to know?

"My aunt—the one who sponsored me—took a terrible fall the summer we met. She was confined to her bed for six months. Naturally, I stayed with her. It was the least I could do after everything she'd done for me. Both my parents had passed when I was eighteen of fever, so I had nowhere else to go. And by that point in my life I had already turned down my only prospects for marriage."

There had also been a very brief time in her life when she'd wanted Leo to come after her, profess his undying love and beg her hand in marriage. Thank Providence she'd come to her senses and had shaken off the sentiments two weeks after those thoughts had snared and consumed her mind.

"So you never attended any balls after your aunt's injury?"

"I couldn't when Aunt Hilda was unable to make an appearance with me. And I could never leave her to care for herself after everything she'd done for me." She sighed. Her aunt had been a genuinely wonderful person, and she missed her a great deal. "Her health declined rapidly after her fall."

Every so often Barrington's arm would brush against hers. She chose to ignore it and continued on as if he weren't doing something to put her off balance.

"It's a lot of responsibility for someone so young."

"Most of my friends had already married and started families at that point in my life. Don't insult me, Barrington."

"I didn't intend to. It would have been too much to take

to task for me at that age. You did a commendable thing for your aunt."

"There was nothing commendable about it. I did it because I loved my aunt, not because it was my duty."

Finally, they came upon their party, who were all seated on a small periwinkle blanket spread out on the grass. It wouldn't surprise Genny if Lady Carleton had chosen such a tiny scrap of material intentionally. It made luncheon rather cozy and more intimate than Genny liked.

No one said anything about her and Leo's late arrival. Though it wasn't as though the rest of the company hadn't watched them as they approached.

Ignoring Leo, Genny carefully picked her way around to a solitary seat between Mr. Torrance and Lady Hargrove. To her everlasting dismay Barrington squeezed in next to her.

"Do allow me to finish my conversation with Miss Camden."

Mr. Torrance obliged by pressing closer to Ariel and Charlotte.

"What is it you discussed?" Lady Carleton asked.

Genny opened her mouth to say they were finished talking, when Barrington cut her off. "I wished to know more about the life of a chaperone and companion. I never thought to ask one about the position, and I admit I am curious to know what would make a lady seek such a life."

"There are many reasons involved for a lady to choose such a path." Lady Carleton took a sip of her lemonade and picked up a few cherries from a bowl set between them.

"I'm only just understanding this from my conversation with Miss Camden. It's enlightening and I never knew her to be such an esteemed woman. It's quite the task to take on, looking after an ailing relative."

"Perhaps you don't give women enough credit? We are

hardier than most gentlemen like to think," Genny said as she pushed her elbow out to move him over a few inches.

It wasn't as though she were some simpering miss, and he did make it sound as though women in general didn't amount to much in his eyes. Or maybe she was just so annoyed with him for sitting beside her that she couldn't give him the benefit of the doubt in this instance.

Leo's palm clasped at his chest in shock. "I don't know where I would be in life without the guidance of women in general. I adore them at any age and in every form."

"We tend to choose more honorable paths than some pleasure-seeking men," Genny said.

Of all the things to blurt out. Genny felt her cheeks heat. Mr. Torrance guffawed, and started a chorus of laughter among their group, saving her further embarrassment.

Genny glanced in the direction of her cousin, begging silently for her to take over the conversation, but she was too busy laughing with the rest of them.

"My approach on life has always been that it is too short to not enjoy all it has to offer," Leo said.

"How philosophical an approach, but more typical of a man's prerogative," Lady Hargrove said.

"While I have never thought to define the roles between the sexes, you are right." Leo stretched his hands above his head and leaned against the tree behind him. "It's a shame women cannot enjoy themselves as freely as men."

"You sound like a suffragist, Lord Barrington," was Charlotte's observation.

"Hardly. I only trouble myself with politics that directly involve me." He winked at Charlotte. "Life is also too short to discriminate between beliefs and whatnot. Everyone should enjoy life as they see fit. Before you know it, you'll be hobbling around on a cane, too angry with yourself for not doing the one thing you always thought you ought to try."

Was that comment directed at Genny, or was it just a general observation?

"Lord Barrington," Mr. Torrance interjected, "has the typical belief of most men who appreciate the finer company of women."

"I certainly wouldn't want to spend the rest of my days with the stuffed shirts found in Parliament," Barrington joked.

"I'd have to agree with you, Lord Barrington," Lady Carleton said. "Though my husband has always been an exception."

"Ah, yes, he was never one of those stuffed turkeys."

Genny nibbled on the fruits set out before them so that she wouldn't make any other verbal gaffes, letting the conversation flow around her.

Leo caught her gaze once and gave her a slow smile. There was nothing innocent in the look he gave her. He purposely brushed against her arm or leg every time he reached for something else to eat in the array of food on display. There was nowhere to escape, so she did her best to pretend he simply wasn't sitting next to her.

The next three weeks might prove to be the longest in all her life.

Chapter 12

The Countess of F—— has made an appearance after a lengthy absence, looking slightly thinner than she has previously. She entered a club—which shall remain nameless in these chronicles—and didn't exit said club for a good three hours. Upon her exit, notably on the Duke of A——'s arm, there was a slight miss in her steps. Perhaps melancholy can strike even the most jaded, coldhearted person in the haute ton?
The Mayfair Chronicles, July 18, 1846

It was a late and rather warm starry night. Leo was pleased to have figured out Genny's evening habit only two days into the house party. Tonight wasn't her first excursion out of doors past the setting of the sun, but her third straight night in a row.

She wore a white nightgown, all spread out over the grass like gossamer silk. Her peignoir was sprigged with little pink flowers and lay open at her midriff. Her hair was down and bound in a long braid that hung over one shoulder, and her fingers played with the tufted ends tied with a pink silk ribbon.

The only reason he'd known she'd come out to stargaze to begin with was because his room was conveniently situated next to hers. It was the last pair of rooms that unfortunately didn't have an adjoining door.

Genny's room was beside his and Lady Charlotte's on the far end of the hall with the other young, unattached ladies and their mothers.

Leo walked across the lawn, hands in his pockets. He was down to his shirtsleeves and vest this evening because the weather demanded it and there was no one else awake to see him in a state of undress.

He stopped by the top of her head and looked down into her blinking eyes. A frown marred her pretty face at his appearance.

"I guess it was too much to ask that I could be left alone for even a short while?"

"I heard your door open, so I came to investigate . . ."

Not that he'd tell her he'd witnessed this very sight last night, but had stayed at a distance, feeling as though he needed to give her more time before he approached.

"So you followed me outside. You could have turned around at any point and gone back to your own room." She glared at him. "How long have you been watching me?"

"Not long." He moved to stand beside her, hitched up his trousers at the knee, and made himself comfortable on the grass next to her. He lay back, resting his head in his threaded fingers, and stared up at the stars with her.

He felt her eyes on him before she let out a resigned sigh and did as he did—stargazed. A smile touched his lips. Was this acquiescence? Had he known she'd give in to him so easily he would have joined her last night.

"What are we looking at tonight?" he asked.

"Argo Navis."

"Ah, the great Greek ship. I've never been able to connect the dots in the night sky." Which was the truth; he'd read about them but that was where his interest stopped.

"It's simple really." Her finger pointed into the air at some of the larger stars. He sidled closer to her so their shoulders touched, and he could clearly see her drawing the outline of the ship with her finger. "You can't really make out the stern of the ship. It's as though it's coming toward you at a forty-five-degree angle." She tapped at the sky, indicating a small cluster of stars. "These smaller stars are the bow of the ship."

"I still don't see it."

She placed her open palm above his midsection. "Give me your hand, I will draw it with you. Maybe then you will understand what I am looking at."

Without question, he gave her his hand. Any excuse to touch her was reason enough to do as she commanded. His arm was longer than hers so she kept his bent and stretched hers full out using her fingers atop his to draw the front of the ship. They started at the top bow she'd already pointed out and drew a curved line down the front stem of the imaginary vessel.

"These scattered stars mark the side of the boat." She blotted out some more dots in quick succession. "And these stars shooting up through the middle make up the mast. Do you see it now?"

"Not at all." He laughed more at his inability than anything.

"Then we will draw an easier one." She seemed determined to teach him some simple astronomy.

She raised their joined hands to a squiggled line above her illusory ship. "This here is the Hydra. Its movement is serpentine and you will feel the slithery shape of her body as you trace it. It's smooth like a snake when the stars are joined." This one he *saw* as she drew the curved line of the mythical creature with him.

"You are quite marvelous, Genny."

She turned her head to look at him. They were nose to nose and only three inches separated them. "Charming words from a rogue should never be trusted."

"Well, I still mean it regardless of your ill thoughts toward me."

"Actually, I have no thoughts at all where you are concerned."

He ignored the sting of her words. She had every right to be angry with him over their past. "Where did you learn the stars?"

"My father and I used to sit and stare at the night sky for hours on end. He taught me to see the pictures." An exasperated sigh fell from her lips. "Why did you follow me out here, Lord Barrington?"

"Like Orpheus to Eurydice's silent steps, I could not help myself and leave you to your own devices this evening."

"Have you become a poet these past few years?"

"Apparently not." He gave her a cheeky grin. "Though I do hope you find my ability to wax poetic somewhat charming."

"It is nearly as bad as asking a woman to visit your study to see your etchings."

She let go of him and folded her hands over her midsection.

"Something I never asked of you."

"That is true."

She grew silent beside him. He took advantage of their time alone and asked, "I have been dying to know why you never married."

"I did not come out here to chat. I wanted to be *alone* before returning to my duties in the morning."

She remained silent for some time.

"This could hardly be considered small talk when it is a serious issue for any young marriage-minded woman."

"If you must know, I *chose* not to marry."

"And I'm sure it was my doing."

"You weren't alone in our *indiscretion*. I played my part well." He heard the thread of disappointment in her response.

"But I knew better. And as a friend of the Carletons I should have shown you the respect you deserved. I knew you were here to find your match, yet I wanted you all to myself."

"As I recall it, it wasn't you taking advantage of me. There is no sense in dissecting our past. Nothing can be changed about our prior association, and I really wish it could be forgotten altogether."

"Confound you. Do you truly think me so callous a man that I could simply forget the time we spent together? Tell me you didn't want more."

When she remained quiet he closed his eyes and damned his stupidity once again. Why hadn't she said something? Why couldn't she have given him some indication that her feelings ran deeper than he believed?

"I wanted more, too, you know," he said, hoping she'd return the sentiment.

"It's too late," was her response. So she wasn't open to this line of conversation. He would pursue the truth from her lips another time.

Leo shook his head, at a loss for what to say. "Genny, Genny, Genny. What am I to do with you?"

"Peace and quiet would be lovely, but probably too much to ask for at the moment."

"Definitely too much to ask for. I'm afraid you're stuck with me for the time being. I have absolutely no intention of getting up. In fact, I might just have to sleep here in the grass, staring at the starry night. It is a lovely night."

She let out an annoyed rush of air and sat up. "Fine. I will leave."

Standing now, she dusted loose bits of grass from her nightclothes. He caught her hand before she could storm off.

"I have no desire to argue or make you uncomfortable in my presence. I want only to spend the evening out here with you."

"You know very well we can't be caught this way."

"Then walk with me during the day as you used to. We both know how lovely the gardens are during the summer months."

"I have other duties to attend to while you spend your summer rusticating, my lord. I cannot simply leave Charlotte to her own devices."

"An excuse."

"It is a great reason to avoid you for the remainder of my stay." She shook his hand off.

"Why fight this?"

"Because you insist on making everything so difficult for me."

He stood and walked back to the house with her. "Only because you are too stubborn to admit you might like spending time with me."

"Don't flatter yourself." She increased her pace. Did she really think she could outrun him?

"Will you stop and listen to me for a moment?"

She turned on him suddenly and marched up to him with a finger pointed accusingly at his chest. "Must you shout out to all in residence that you are in the gardens with someone? Haven't you thought of the damage you'll do to me by exposing our evening liaison?"

"I have something entirely different in mind for an evening tryst, my dearest Miss Camden. This hardly counts as a liaison." He tried to take her hand, but she sidestepped his reach.

"Of course you do. You are so . . . so *you!*" She threw her hands up in exasperation, walked away, then stormed back toward him. "I'm not sure what I ever saw in you. You couldn't charm the curl out of a pig's tail."

He quirked his brow and had a hell of a time keeping the laughter from his voice. "Really?"

"Yes, that is the best I can come up with. Had you not caught me unawares, I wouldn't be this flustered."

"Then I will be sure to sneak up on you more often. I quite enjoy how you are just now."

When he reached out this time, he snagged her around the waist and pulled her nearer. She didn't resist him now.

"This is no joke," she said.

His smile was gone in the next moment. "No. It certainly isn't. We were doing so well out on the grass. What changed your mind on spending a quiet evening with me?"

"It's not as though you had any intention of keeping this simple." She pointed that damnable finger at him again, only this time she pressed it into his chest. "And I never agreed to spend the night with you in any shape or form. You invited yourself."

"I can't seem to stay away from you. Where you go, I most certainly will follow; and I'll continue to follow you, especially if you go on very many of these midnight excursions where I can have you all to myself."

"You are impossible."

"It's what endeared me to you all those years ago."

She made a sound of disbelief in her throat. The more Leo pressed her, the more her true self showed. The Genny he remembered from four years ago who was tenacious, willful, and more fun than any woman he'd ever spent time with. "Will you trust me to be the perfect gentlemen in your company? I only want for us to become reacquainted."

"Do you think it gentlemanly to address me by my given name?" She tilted her head inquisitively to the side.

"There is a long past between us. I've earned it just as you have earned the right to address me in the same way."

With a roll of her eyes, she spun out of his grasp. "Yes, that is a brilliant plan, because no one would notice us addressing each other by our Christian names."

"Only in private," he amended.

She turned back to him, a look of calm pensiveness weighing down her brow. "What do I have to do to be rid of you permanently?"

"I will prove you want otherwise, Genny. I was a bloody fool when we first met. I should never have left, and there really isn't an excuse adequate enough for the way things turned out between us."

"You won't let this drop, will you?"

He shook his head.

"Not only are you impossible, but as thickheaded as a mule."

"I'll take that as a compliment, since we've moved on from swine."

She gave him a look of pure annoyance, then finally let out a defeated exhalation. He would prove their time together could rekindle old feelings. He'd also show her that he wouldn't run at the first opportunity for something longer lasting this time. And while he would honor his word to treat her with the great respect she deserved, he was still a man and would find his way into her bed before long. It simply couldn't be helped and it was inevitable between them.

"I'm sorry I can't trust you. No, I take that back. I have nothing to be sorry about. You are untrustworthy."

Leo sighed, knowing his argument would not be won tonight, and perhaps not tomorrow night, either. But he could and would be patient with Genny.

"All I am asking for is time. It's not as if either of us has somewhere else to be over the next few weeks."

"I don't suppose you are going to give me a choice in the matter."

He smiled. She read him well.

"Men are unreasonable beasts. Do you realize that?"

"I wouldn't know since I am one of those beasts you are talking about."

"I'm going to bed." She pressed her hand to his chest to stall his forward momentum. *"Alone."*

He gave her his most charming grin and a gallant bow. "As the lady wishes."

How had her quiet night of solitude turned into a debate over courting? No, that wasn't the right term for what Leo had in mind. More like a seduction to keep him amused over their summer holiday. She'd be lying if she said she didn't want a resumption of their old intimacies, but that was the difference between being young and foolish and being seasoned and *firmly* on the shelf.

While she recognized the things she wanted, she knew how to hold herself back from temptation.

She turned the corner on the top landing and headed in the direction of her room. The lights in the hallway were dim, so she ran her finger along the wall, counting the doors till she reached her room.

She bumped into someone quite forcefully and let out a little yelp as her limbs tangled with the other late-night wanderer.

"Shush," her cousin whispered. "You'll have everyone coming out of their room to see what the commotion is and they'll find us wandering the halls at this hour."

Charlotte placed her forearm under Genny's and hauled her to her feet.

"What are you doing out here? It's past midnight."

"I should ask you the same thing, Genny. I couldn't sleep and when I went to your room you weren't there."

"I went to the kitchen for a snack. And since when do you have trouble sleeping?"

"We can't stand out in the corridor." Charlotte dragged her farther down the hall and pulled them both into Genny's room.

Genny looked her cousin over. She wore her nightclothes and a light wrapper. A cap was pulled over her hair, and a few of the rag-tied curls fell around her shoulders becomingly. Of course her cousin looked lovely even when in her bedclothes.

Charlotte appeared to be all right, so why had she come looking for Genny in the middle of the night, when she'd never done so before?

"Are you ill?"

"I'm well enough. I needed to talk to you."

Genny took her cousin's hand and led her into her bedchamber. She drew back the coverlet on her bed. "Did you want to stay the night?"

Charlotte nodded her head.

"What's wrong?"

"I was thinking about Mr. Warren. And it put me in such a tizzy that I just couldn't bear to be alone." Charlotte crossed her arms over her middle and rubbed both arms as though she were cold. Her cousin was truly upset. "I don't want to marry him, Genny. I don't know if there is something you can say to convince my father that this isn't the right match for me, but I am begging for your help."

When Charlotte stepped into the light of the freshly lit candle, Genny noticed her cousin's tear-streaked face and the dark circles under her eyes.

She opened her arms and gathered Charlotte close. "What brought this on?"

"Papa sent a note to say that my engagement will be announced on our return home, and I kept thinking how I didn't want to marry Mr. Warren. I really can't bring myself to say yes."

"He's a fine man, Charlotte, and he's been very kind to you throughout your courtship."

Charlotte's hands stopped moving for a moment and a look of unhappiness fell over her face. "And what if I've fallen in love with someone else?"

Genny felt her heart stop in her chest. This was the second time Charlotte had mentioned love.

"How could you possibly—" If this had anything to do with Castleigh, she'd personally strangle the man, or at least find someone to do it for her.

"I don't know what I feel, I just know I don't love Mr. Warren." Charlotte's tone was plaintive.

Was it possible her cousin had fallen in love with another? If it wasn't Castleigh, who else could it be?

"How do you know you won't feel that with Mr. Warren?"

"He won't be any fun if I marry him." Charlotte frowned. "He'll probably send me to the country and keep me hidden from the world so I don't cause any trouble."

"Because you aren't the type to cause trouble," Genny teased, in the hope that she could lighten the mood and cheer up her cousin's spirits.

Charlotte's laugh was weak and lifeless. "I can't help it. And I feel all sick inside when I think of becoming his wife."

"You won't know what Mr. Warren is like until you marry him."

"And isn't that the problem? Because by then it'll be

too late." Charlotte wiped her damp eyes on the sleeve of her night wrap. Genny reached for a fresh handkerchief on her night table and handed it to her cousin. "Sometimes I want nothing more than to run away."

"Stop with this nonsense." Genny put her arms around her cousin, hugging her and rubbing her back soothingly. "You wouldn't like life nearly as much as you think if you weren't part of all the balls and glamor."

"I think I might like it well enough if it meant I didn't have to marry a man I can't picture myself living with for the rest of my life."

"Oh, Charlotte. Do you know how many young ladies would like to wear your slippers for even one night?"

Charlotte's forehead puckered. "Why should they want that?"

"Because you have so much that so many don't. Your dowry is exceptional; your upcoming nuptials will be the talk of Town."

"I don't want any of it." Charlotte flopped down on the bed, and lay on her side. "I just want to be happy. And the thought of marrying Mr. Warren makes me incredibly unhappy."

"You can find happiness in marriage." Genny curled her feet up on the bed so she lay face-to-face with her cousin. "If you are miserable going into a marriage, then you will make both your lives a trial. But if you go in with an open heart and a willingness to try, then life will treat you both kindly."

Charlotte closed her eyes and wiped what seemed like the last of her tears away. They lay oddly in her bed for a few minutes before Charlotte opened her eyes again, appearing much calmer.

"Can I ask you something deeply personal?"

"I will answer to the best of my ability." What remained unsaid was that if the question was too personal or the answer too risqué, she might very well be forced to defer her response to another day.

"Do you regret not marrying?" Charlotte asked softly.

A sad smile touched Genny's lips. "I suppose that would be burning most in your mind."

Charlotte nodded.

"You have to understand that I was not in the same position as you."

"But you had offers. Lady Carleton told Ariel and me that you were a diamond even without your dowry and that gentlemen once fawned their attentions on you."

Yes, they had, but none of them had been as interesting to her as Barrington had.

"Why would you turn down offers of marriage at all to become a companion?"

It would be hypocritical to say that she had wanted to marry for love. It would also give away the true feelings she once harbored for a man who never wanted something of a permanent nature with her.

"While I was fine to dine and dance with, I was not necessarily considered good marriage material. Many lords are looking for a large dowry for their titles and estates. I had nothing to offer to a marriage."

"So I'm only marrying because of my dowry?"

Genny reached out and squeezed her cousin's hand. "That's not what I meant."

"Even with my dowry, I do not have many suitors."

"If you had another season, you would. But you are still quite young in some gentlemen's eyes."

"Well, pooh."

Charlotte's spirit seemed to be back up. Actually, it was odd that this upset her cousin at all since nothing generally overwhelmed her.

"You haven't answered my question," Charlotte pointed out.

Could the truth do any damage? The truth hadn't done Genny any favors in the long run, and maybe Charlotte would understand that and realize she had no choice but to do her father's bidding.

"I know you might not believe this, and it seems even a bit cruel to tell you when I've told you not to marry for this reason, but I thought myself in love with someone."

Charlotte sat up and stared at her with that curious gaze of hers. She was assessing Genny and figuring out another damnable piece to the puzzle she wanted to solve.

"It was Barrington, wasn't it?" Charlotte asked.

Oh, dear. Genny shouldn't have said anything. She didn't need her past feelings analyzed by her cousin. "As you can see, I did not marry for love. And while I enjoy nothing more than spending time with family and having had the opportunity to get to know my aunt as well as I did, I still crave marriage and a family of my own. This is not a life for you, Charlotte. I came from few prospects. It was a miracle that I had one season, let alone three."

"You're evading my question."

"It's best that way."

"Did he know?"

It was a fact that she'd never shared her true feelings with him, but she'd been unsure how to do it and there was no one who could give her advice when she was having an illicit affair with the man.

Telling Charlotte the truth no longer seemed like an ideal plan. "He didn't notice me enough to care at the time. It was a foolish fancy on my part. And I daresay, it may not have been love at all, but an infatuation with a handsome young lord who had more charm than all the gentlemen I knew put together. He did not return my feelings." Not that he had ever confided in her what he felt.

"He certainly lavishes his attention on you now." Charlotte scrutinized Genny for a long quiet moment. "What information are you intentionally holding back from me, cousin?"

"You are reading too much into this. Barrington and I had an easy friendship, and he is only being kind to me because we do know each other. Although his reputation might leave something to be desired, he has a kind heart."

"So, you loved Barrington, and because you were friends, and only friends, he never thought to offer for you."

"I never expected him to offer."

"Something doesn't fit in your story. You could save yourself the trouble and tell me what you are leaving out."

"I have given you an answer, Charlotte. There are very few people in our circle of family and friends that have married for love."

"Lady Carleton did."

Genny pressed her fingers to her eyes in frustration. Her cousin was impossible. Genny stood from the bed and held out her hand. "It's time to get you to bed, don't you think?"

Her cousin looked vulnerable and alone when she glanced back at Genny.

"Can I stay in here for a while longer?"

Genny turned down the rest of the bedding. "I'm told I'm a dreadful snorer, so if you can put up with that, you are welcome to stay the night."

Charlotte gave her a warm smile and climbed under the covers with her. "Thank you, Genny. You've given me more tonight than anyone has ever offered on this topic."

"You're welcome," she said, snuffing the light, not sure that she'd done any such thing. What insight could her cousin take from this? Was it possible Charlotte would be happy playing the same role Genny played in life? She didn't think so.

Chapter 13

*Rumor has it that an illicit affair has started be-
tween a lady of notable peerage and a much younger
man below such distinction. What would happen if
the lady's husband were made aware of this noted
indiscretion? She seems to have made it her lifelong
goal to see to the ruin of no less than half a dozen
ladies of good breeding, who did no more than fall
victim to the charm of men better ignored. It is on
days like these that this writer has the strong urge to
no longer protect those carefully mentioned within
these rags. Why shouldn't it be my choice to print
their full, true names?*
The Mayfair Chronicles, July 23, 1846

Charlotte and Ariel walked up ahead of her with Mr. Torrance between them. Genny followed at a slower pace.
They'd been planning this morning's jaunt to the creek
since last evening over sherry in the parlor. Genny had a
feeling that the young man had taken a liking to Ariel.
She wondered if Ariel was free to marry whomever she
desired. While Lady Ariel's dowry was decent, it did not
bring as much to a marriage as Charlotte's.

The three of them were a good twenty paces ahead of her, wholly focused on their surroundings and not her. They were far enough away that she could not hear or intrude on their conversation.

The life of a chaperone was a little lonely. But at the same time, she had the perfect opportunity to think over her conversation with Barrington last night.

When they stopped to admire a patch of wildflowers, Genny stilled, too, wanting to give them as much privacy as possible.

Reaching into her pocket for her book, she backed up a few steps to find a bench while Charlotte and Ariel perched themselves on the edge of a similar stone bench near the streambed that ran through the property.

She bumped into a solid, steady figure. Turning around, she almost lost her footing, but Leo caught her around the arms and kept her from teetering over.

His hands trailed the length of her arms in a caress that was anything but innocent, and then he released her to stand on her own.

She pressed her hand to her heart. "You scared me half to death, Barrington. It's not polite to approach someone without making your presence known."

"I merely wanted to surprise you." He gave her a cocky grin. "And to get my hands on you at least once this morning."

"You've definitely done both."

When she sat on the bench, he indicated the empty seat next to her. "Might I join you for a spell?"

"By all means. It's not as if you'll leave me alone if I say otherwise."

"Too true, princess."

He plucked the small leather-bound book from her hands and read the spine.

"The Mysteries of Udolpho," he read aloud with interest. "I never took you for a reader of gothic novels."

"What should I be reading?"

"Perhaps a book on proper decorum for young ladies? You seem intent on being above reproach where your cousin is concerned . . . and about our past."

She grabbed at her book, but he pulled it away before she could get her hands on it. "If you continue to insult and mock me, I will have to ask you to leave my company immediately."

"You should take pity on me, Miss Camden, I am after all an unfortunate beast that needs your gentle guidance."

"Unreasonable, not unfortunate."

"Is that what I am, then." He laughed. "What would I do if you weren't around to keep my head on straight?"

"You'd suffer from stupidity, as most men do."

"You are a never-ending source of amusement."

"I'm glad you think so." She held out her hand. "May I please have my book back?"

"You haven't answered why you are reading it. Is it for the romance?"

"I do not read it for the romance." A very strong urge to stamp her foot on his instep nearly overtook her. She managed to pull back her irritation before she acted rashly. "There wasn't a great deal of fiction in the library to choose from. Why are you bothering me?"

"I asked if we could walk together this morning and took your silence as an invitation."

He was very persistent. "I specifically told you I had duties where my cousin is concerned."

"Yes, and I see your concern not twenty feet away." He pointed the book in the direction of Charlotte. "You don't suppose she should be my concern now, too, since I intend to spend my mornings out walking with you?"

She gave him a long, annoyed look, then snatched the small book from his hands, and slid it back into the wide deep pocket hidden in her skirts.

"At least pretend you are enjoying my company." His voice was low and held a measure of hurt.

She hadn't meant to be cruel, only to make him seek amusement elsewhere.

She turned to face him and stared into his searching eyes. She cleared her throat before saying, "I think I owe you an apology."

"You owe me no such thing. It was probably as awkward for you to see me again as it was for me. Though 'awkward' doesn't seem like the proper word."

"Strange?" she offered.

"Astonished? Or even surprised?" he countered.

She smiled. She couldn't help herself when his good humor got the better of her and broke through her first layer of defense. Why had she said they couldn't spend mornings together doing no more than converse? It was a great deal safer that they see each other like this as opposed to finding each other alone in the evenings.

"I don't dislike your company per se."

His smile left her a little breathless, and she forced her attention back to Charlotte when a blush heated her neck and face. The girls paid them no mind and were raptly attuned to whatever it was Mr. Torrance said.

Genny was almost giddy with the idea that Leo had sought her out this morning so he could enjoy a simple conversation with her. Maybe he was a changed man?

Leo took the opportunity of their faux solitude to clasp his hands around the back curve of the stone bench. The hand closest to her bunched up the skirts near her rump. She could not slide forward to escape the closeness of him, as the bench was too narrow. No, he was not a changed man; he was still the rogue she remembered. And she secretly enjoyed that.

"And what exactly do you think you are about?" She turned and gave him a curious look.

"I'm making myself comfortable and watching the show closer to the creek." *Nonchalant*—only a man could act in such a fashion—he leaned closer as though sharing a private joke with her. "They are young and in love with the idea of being loved, don't you think?"

"Carefree." She'd once been like that.

Mr. Torrance was reciting some poem or play—she was too far away to hear which—and Ariel held her hands clasped together in front of her, eyes solely focused on their gentleman friend. What would it be like to be in such a position as them again? No worries, no cares in the world, only the moment as it took them. Genny wondered if she would repeat her mistakes. Not that she wished to think of her past actions as poorly made decisions—even if they were.

She didn't think she'd want to repeat her earlier years. She liked the self-sufficient woman she'd grown into. As one grew older, one understood more about human nature and more about oneself. She'd not trade her experiences for anything in the world.

Leo stared at his companion on the bench. She was lovely to stare upon, and he had to nearly tear his gaze away from her before it became clear to anyone else how taken he was by her.

Should he let her in on his plans for this evening? "I have something planned for us tonight. Nothing too risqué, though I do require your attendance . . . *alone*."

She turned her attention back to him. "I don't think that's a very good idea. Are mornings in my company not enough?"

"I imagined that would be your answer." Leo was unfazed by her response, he knew what she was going to say before she had uttered the first words. "Just give me one night of your trust and I will give you no reason to lose faith in me."

Genny frowned. "And if we are caught sneaking around like two thieves in the night, what do you suppose that will do to my reputation?"

"I promise you that we won't be found out."

"You are awfully sure of yourself. Is there any circumstance that makes you feel less . . . kingly?"

"Lady Luck has always been generous with me. Everyone in the house will be abed when we meet, and I promise to remain circumspect and the perfect gentleman for the whole evening." He leaned in close to her ear. In a seductively low voice, he said, "Unless you prefer to live dangerously . . ."

She raised her brows. "I've had enough danger over the years to last me a lifetime."

He shrugged his shoulders as he leaned back, hands still curled around the back of the bench. "Suit yourself, but I cannot take no for an answer."

"What will you do?" She laughed. "Barge into my room like a marauder, throw me over your shoulder, and take me where you please?"

He waggled his eyebrows and gave her a smug, daring look. "If I must."

She shook her head. Well, it was a fabulous idea that he might have to act out if she didn't cooperate sooner rather than later.

"At least give me a clue as to what you plan." She tilted her head back to catch some rays of sun on her face.

"But then it wouldn't be a secret. I well remember your love of a good adventure, Genny."

"You're not doing a very good job of convincing me this is worth the risk."

She gave him a sidelong look, as though trying to figure it out for herself.

"Ah, but you won't say no, not when your curiosity is irrevocably piqued. If you intended to cruelly deny me your company, you wouldn't ask to be convinced otherwise."

"Fine, you know me well enough to know that." She turned away from him again to watch her cousin. "If you do try anything not to plan and go against your word, I won't speak to you for the rest of our stay here."

"I aim to please only you." He caressed the side of her arm. "Should you initiate something . . . it will be beyond my control to stop you."

"You're too sure of your ability to seduce a woman."

"There you go tossing out tempting words like a dare to act upon. And it's not any woman I aim to seduce. You're the one driving me mad with this need to please."

She glared down at his hand where he was absently running his fingers back and forth over her arm. He had no choice but to stop. "Your flattery falls on deaf ears."

He breathed in that familiar trace of lavender and found himself shifting on the bench seat. "I don't believe you."

She made a disgruntled noise. "Are you planning on spending the whole morning with me?"

"I believe I will. This bench is comfortable and the scenery lovely. And really, we can't help but admire the youth of today, and have a few laughs at their expense."

Mr. Torrance was currently on his knees reciting something that made the ladies giggle like schoolgirls.

Leo shuddered. "I do hope I was never so desperate as that."

"You were worse."

He laughed at that. "Perhaps you are right."

She seemed to feel more at ease with him now that he'd stated his intentions as honorable.

"Will you attend to my whims this evening?" he asked again.

Genny hesitated in her response. "I intend to keep you guessing." No, she didn't intend to do any such thing. She'd join him tonight. He was sure of it.

"In that case, meet me at midnight exactly where I found you gazing at the stars."

"I've not said yes."

He leaned to the side, brushing playfully against her shoulder with his. "You will."

"You truly are unbearable," Genny said.

"I think it's what you like most about me."

They enjoyed companionable silence for the next twenty minutes, and then headed back to the main house on the tail of Genny's charge. The one thing he kept going over in his mind was Jez's demand that the Ponsley girl be swayed from the path of marriage with Mr. Warren. The young woman was safe enough at this house party since Tristan wasn't here. What would happen when they all returned to Town? Not telling Genny of his initial plans was weighing on his mind. There was time yet before he needed to reveal the truth.

Chapter 14

*My dearest, my darling, and my most faithful read-
ers, I have only the latest gossip about myself to
share today. Can you believe someone is actively
pursuing my identity and has gone to great lengths
to reveal who the writer of your cherished* Mayfair
Chronicles *really is? Herein lies a warning for my
pursuer: Whatever it is you think you'll accomplish,
I'll always be three steps ahead of you. I know who
you are. I know all your faults . . . and I must say, it
would be a great pleasure to expose you for the
person you are.*

The Mayfair Chronicles, July 25, 1846

Unable to wait outdoors, Leo stood outside his room hoping he hadn't been wrong to believe she'd take him up on
his offer. If anyone aside from Genny found him wandering the halls, he intended to make excuses about finding a
book since he was having a sleepless night.

When her door finally opened, he stepped out of the
shadows to reveal his presence, and placed a finger over
his mouth in the general motion to remain silent. He held
out his hand for her to take. She nibbled on her lower lip,

gave him a thoughtful look before stepping forward and taking his proffered hand.

Leading her away from the main staircase, he took her through a paneled wall and down the servants' stairs that led to the kitchens. Before opening the door, he whispered, "I've already been down to see if anyone was awake. We're well alone but don't speak until I give you leave to."

She nodded. "Don't lead me astray, Barrington. It would be disappointing to have trusted you thus far to have you betray me now."

Hand at the small of her back, he pulled her in closer. "I always make good on my promises, Genny."

Stepping up on the tips of her toes, one of her hands cupped his shoulder as she leaned into his ear. "Then do your best to ensure I don't regret tonight."

Quickly stepping away from her, knowing now was not the time to lay claim to her lips, he grasped her hand again and led her along the narrow path. Sliding the hidden door open, they made their way to the exit that led to the cook's herb and vegetable patches. They ran hand in hand over the fields, both knowing that they needed to be as far from sight as quickly as was possible.

When they'd made it a safe distance from the house, he pulled Genny to a stop and released her hand. He started to untie his cravat.

"What happened to playing the perfect gentlemen?" She raised her brow, her eyes full of unconcealed pleasure.

"Live dangerously with me." He leaned forward hoping she'd kiss him, but she took a step back, shaking her head.

"Just because you feel the urge to divest yourself of clothing, I will not follow suit." She crossed her arms over her bosom and glared at him.

"I only seek to remove my cravat." He tugged at the annoying strip of heavily starched material. "I can't bloody well release this knot. All this running has overheated me."

She let out a hearty laugh and bent at the waist; he joined her.

"You can't be serious," she said.

"I most certainly am."

She seemed to ponder the idea of him removing any piece of clothing for a moment. Finally, she raised her hands and brushed his away to help release the elaborate knot. She made quick work of it and pulled it from around his neck, handing the material to him once it was off. He shoved it in the pocket of his trousers.

He tugged at his collar to let the cool air brush against his skin. "Marginally better, if I do say so. Thank you."

Grabbing up her hand again—because he couldn't not touch her—he led her over the hillock that separated the Carleton property from his.

"Are you ever going to tell me where we are going? We've walked for a good quarter hour."

"I insist upon this being a surprise."

He led her down a set of stone steps and toward the greenhouse situated off his property. They'd not be found here, not unless his servants were wandering about in the middle of the night. Regardless, his servants could be trusted to remain silent about his midnight visitor.

He grasped her by the waist to lift her over an odd incline and onto one of the narrower paths flanked by a myriad of wildflowers and tall oak trees that hid the large glass structure ahead of them.

"There are only so many places you can take me within walking distance to the Carletons'."

"True enough. We are almost there, so I might as well tell you that we are at the greenhouse."

Her head tilted to the side in question. "But the Carletons don't have a greenhouse."

"They don't. But I do. Come on, we'll do the hothouse first."

This time he placed his hand to the small of her back and led her down the slate stone path.

"This isn't some sort of trick to get me alone and away from anyone who might find us, is it?"

"Would you mind so much if that was indeed my plan?"

She yanked her hand away from his. "Lord Barrington." There was no mistaking her tone for anything but a firm reprimand.

"Don't go pulling away from me." He tugged her close once again and smiled when she didn't resist. He would have gotten her off the Carleton property days ago if he'd known she would drop her guard and allow him to touch her in any way. "I'm simply returning the favor of last evening. I might not know a star from a comet, but I spent a great deal of time with my father and stepmother in this greenhouse. I can name just about every flower that grows here."

"Oh." Her brows furrowed and she seemed baffled by this hidden facet of his character. "I assumed . . . I really shouldn't say *what* I assumed."

He pressed his forefinger to her lips. "You needn't say anything. I know my reputation is well deserved. But I did promise you could trust me."

"Then I can do no less than just that."

"Thank you." And because he liked holding her hand, he took it back and led her through the doors of the greenhouse. "I know you enjoy the flowers in the Carletons' gardens. I've seen you out there enough times picking flowers and putting together bouquets."

"I didn't realize you took notice."

"There isn't much I don't notice where you're concerned, Genny." He gave her hand a squeeze. "I thought you would enjoy seeing the little piece of heaven my parents created on the estate."

"Didn't you say it was your stepmother's garden?"

He nodded. "My mother died shortly after my birth. My stepmother came to live with us when I was five and I think I loved her from the moment she gave me that first motherly hug."

She cleared her throat. "She must have been a wonderful woman."

"She was. But enough about me, tell me what you desire to see most."

"I have a certain fondness for roses. Do you have any?"

He nearly snorted. Didn't every gardener have their fair share of roses? "More than a handful of varieties. My parents were fervent horticulturists."

"I never knew."

"It was a great hobby and passion of theirs. I keep on a large staff to maintain this place in their memory. My father might have been a bit stuffy and old-fashioned, but he loved nothing more than spending time in here, especially after my stepmother died."

"Your father passed away around the same time my aunt did. I remember someone telling me. I'm very sorry." She squeezed his hand affectionately with her condolences.

"No more sorry than I. Now, enough of this reminiscing; tonight is supposed to be about us."

"I didn't intend to stir up sad memories."

"I know. But thank you for the condolences. As I was saying, there is a whole arboretum dedicated to some forty varieties of roses. But they will come in due course. Orchids first, since they are the closest."

He twirled her around, quite taking her by surprise. When she was standing next to him again, she clutched her fist to her chest and laughed. She had the most beautiful smile he had ever seen.

"What was that for?"

He shrugged as though he'd done nothing out of the ordinary. "I like to see you laugh."

She dropped her gaze demurely, and when she looked at him again, she asked, "Why haven't you ever suggested a morning expedition from the Carletons' estate?"

He didn't miss the note of excitement in her voice.

"It's my private place. I don't want people who don't appreciate this as much as I do tromping through here, breaking flowers, and wearing down the paths."

Her hand tightened around his. "Thank you for sharing it with me."

Opening the first door, they stepped into a tropical garden filled with various orchids. He threaded his fingers through hers, enjoying the feel of her skin against his. What he really wanted was to pull her into his arms and taste her lips.

"It is warm in here," she said.

"Orchids need a stable temperature. They won't thrive in our damp cold for long, so the temperature is controlled with steam pipes."

Her gaze followed his pointed finger that indicated the piping about twelve feet up that surrounded the perimeter of the greenhouse. He led her down the stone path that rounded the small hothouse, her arm threaded tightly through his as the path narrowed and he felt the press of her bosom against his arm. He pointed to a stalky plant that was only starting to furl open.

"Those beauties are called birds-of-paradise. Not an orchid, but they enjoy the hotter temperatures in here. I've seen them grow as tall as eight feet. And the dark blue centers turn to deep shades of burgundy, orange, and red when they open up."

"I don't think I've ever seen one before."

"You'll see a lot of firsts here," he promised. "Do you hear the water trickling down the rock façade?"

"Yes, I hear it but don't see it anywhere." She turned, like a child in a confectionary for the first time, looking for the source of water. She really did have the most splendid smile. "It's just missing the sound of birds to make one feel as though we really are in a tropical paradise."

That depended on the type of paradise she referred to because she certainly played his Eve in the Garden. He could swear the serpent whispered in his ear, telling him to do wicked things to her. He shook his head and walked into an adjoining hothouse. He had promised only an evening out. That's not to say he'd stop her if she felt inclined to initiate something more.

"The odd warbler and yellow tit tend to find their way into this little haven from the outside world, but they won't be up and chirping for another few hours."

The source of the water was before them. Water cascaded down from large boulders his parents had thought to put in here to create a miniature waterfall and to keep the water in the koi ponds refreshed and clean.

She put her hand out and brushed it along the stone rail that lined the three-foot bridge and stared down at the large gold and black koi that swam and created a tide of sunshine beneath them.

Her shawl fell from her shoulders to rest in the crook of her bent arms.

"It's not too hot for you, is it?"

"No," she answered, a little breathless.

"I probably should have had you dress more appropriately for the different temperatures."

He hoped the heat in the arboretum would have her removing her shawl to reveal the gentle scoop of her evening dress and the nip of her laced-in waist. Hell, he wanted her to take off more than her shawl. But not here. Well, maybe he did want her to take it all off here.

Damnation, what was wrong with him?

He needed a hell of a lot more focus than he currently had.

"Come along." He took her hand again and led her down the shale path. "The orchids come in every color and size; flowers ranging from tiny bulbs to palm-sized petals. Some stems are taller than you or I."

Her gaze was everywhere, taking in the rainbow of beauty around them. "It's all so wonderful."

A broken pink flower head lay below the bloom it looked to have been accidentally torn from. He picked it up and ran it down the side of her face. She stopped walking and faced him, bringing them both to a standstill.

Water misted down on the cocooned world they created in their orchid realm. She gave a cheerful laugh and tilted her head back to catch the mist full on her face as it fell. Her tongue reached for the water that lightly sprayed them both. Glancing up to the piping that ran the length of the ceiling he, too, tasted the fresh water on his tongue.

"What a glorious surprise tonight has been. I can't thank you enough for bringing me here." She dropped her shawl, obviously uncaring that it landed in a heap in the dirt-trodden path as she stretched out her arms, catching the cool water on the tips of her fingers as it sprayed down on them.

All the beauty in the world didn't compare to the expression on her face in that moment. He wanted to taste the liquid building on her eyelids, her lips, her pale dew-covered skin. He wanted to lick at her neck and dip his tongue into the swell of her breasts above the tight-laced corset.

But he would not allow temptation to overwhelm his better judgment. He settled for taking only the slightest of liberties, and lowered his knuckles to skim the damp exposed skin at her collar. She turned her head to the side in invitation, but because the words to invite him closer did not fall from her lips he released her instead of curling his hand around her delicate neck to pull her to him.

The mist stopped just as suddenly as it had started, piercing the privately shared fantasy they'd indulged too briefly in. He pulled away reluctantly, pushed the orchid low between her breasts, and picked the shawl up to drape it back around her shoulders. She said nothing, just pressed her fingers to her heart, though the smile on her face told him exactly how she felt.

She wanted more, and she had enjoyed the moment just as much as he had.

He tucked her arm through his and they walked on. He clenched his jaw and focused on breathing deeply. Focused on the blooms, beauty, and the sights around them. He tried unsuccessfully to shift his thoughts away from only her.

He brought her outside and down the path that led toward the rose room. He'd lost his control and his sanity back in the orchid house and hoped to gain some of it back before they found themselves in a similar situation.

When they reached the door for the rose arboretum, and pushed it open, her expression lightened as the scent of the flowers tenderly surrounded them.

She took a step away from him, closed her eyes, and breathed deeply.

When she opened them again, she turned to him and said, "It's spectacular."

She reached her hand out to touch one of the multitudes of soft-petaled flowers surrounding them. Clasping his hand tightly around her wrist, he pulled her hand back too late; a thorn caught the side of her finger. She hissed in a sharp breath and jerked away from the smarting.

A small well of blood beaded where the thorn had stuck her. "Damn," she muttered.

He took his necktie from his pocket and blotted away the evidence of her injury without a word.

"Thank you," she whispered, as though afraid of being heard by anyone who might be nearby.

"Don't thank me." His voice didn't come easy and he was sure she'd be able to tell just how aroused he was by the rusty quality. "Here . . ." He plucked a pink rose by pinching the bottom of its head at the stem, and pressed it into her hand. "I have a feeling these are your favorite flower."

"Hard not to guess when my first inclination was to ask if you kept roses. My mum used to call me her little rose because the slightest exertion would turn my face pink. They are like a namesake to me."

She spun in a small circle, head back, as she breathed in the scent of the gardens and took in the sight of the rose-bushes from the stone-cobbled dirt floor to the glass-covered ceiling. That damned smile she wore so naturally was doing something to him. He wanted to always see that expression on her face—day and night . . . for an eternity if he could.

When she turned back to him she reached for his hand this time. He didn't hesitate to clasp her hands in return and pull her nearer; knowing he was going against his word but unable to stop himself. Only a few inches separated them and it wouldn't be hard to pull her in the remaining distance.

He threaded his fingers through her hair and clasped the back of her head lightly to draw her face closer as he lowered his mouth. He gave her all the time in the world to object, but the only thing to fall past her lips was a soft sigh.

She relaxed into him when their mouths fused and he took her lips between his in a gentle persuading kiss. Her head angled back to give him better access to her open mouth and he licked his tongue inside, sucking on her upper lip as he pulled back. When she still didn't protest his taking advantage of her, he did it again. This time, her tongue met his in the middle and danced around his as she went up on the tips of her toes and wrapped her arms around his shoulders.

One of his hands lowered to the top of her buttocks and rested at the small of her back. He edged her closer, pressing her belly against his arousal, letting her feel just how much he wanted her.

She moaned into his mouth and rubbed the front of her body tightly against his before she slowly pulled away, inching back a step but looking reluctant as she did so.

"We should go," she said.

"Stay a while longer. I'll do no more or less than you ask."

"We can't."

The enthusiastic smile slipped from her face. In its place was something more alluring and seductive. There was dew left on her cheeks and lips from the mist that had showered down on them. It was hard to suppress his desire to lick it all away.

"You've barely gone around the room."

"I think it wise we stop everything that we are doing, Barrington. My reputation cannot withstand whatever it is you have in mind."

He spread his arms wide. "Look around you, Genny. It's only the two of us here. There is no one to offer censure or tell you what you can or cannot do—least of all me."

"I can't do these outings with you and not involve my feelings."

Her words stung. "Do you think I'm so coldhearted that I feel nothing? So carefree that I don't feel some of the same things you do?"

"No . . . I didn't mean it in that sense."

"Then what did you mean? Aside from telling me repeatedly that I am a bad sort and not worthy of your company, you insist that I have every intention of ruining you. Why won't you let me prove myself otherwise?"

"And why should I believe you when you have yet to tell me why you sought out my cousin all those weeks ago? I know you have no prior association with her. What was it you planned?"

That he couldn't tell her. Not yet. Not when he was trying to convince her that he was a decent man. But, really, was he decent when he was lying to her about his original purpose in pursuing, however briefly, Lady Charlotte that first evening they had run into each other?

Eventually he would tell her the truth but that time was not now. Not when she didn't completely trust him. Not when she would turn her back on him and not think to give him another chance. He knew he was being selfish, but he wanted it to be harder for her to walk away from him.

"Let us get back to the main house." He tugged her down the cobbled path, intent on going back the same way they'd entered since it was the shortest way back to the Carleton Estate.

"Don't think I haven't noticed your desire to keep your secrets."

"For now, they must and will remain my secrets, Genny."

Before they exited the indoor rose garden, he picked up the gardening shears and cut two pink roses high on the stem and scraped off the thorns before he pressed them into Genny's hands.

She looked down to the flowers that were half in bloom and brought them up to her nose to smell their intoxicating scent. "Thank you for tonight."

"You can come here any time you so wish it. Let it be my gift to you."

"It's very kind of you."

"I mean it. The flowers are meant to be enjoyed, not to languish here without someone to admire them. Feel free to wander over here any time of the day . . . or night. I'll alert my staff that a young woman may be around to take in the beauty of the gardens."

"You know I can do no such thing."

"Yes you can. You just don't want to live dangerously at the moment. If the urge should ever take you, my offer is open-ended." He gave her a gallant bow before offering her his arm. "Now, let us get you tucked into the relative safety of your room."

"Thank you for making good on your word."

"Why you thought I wouldn't baffles me." He gave her a smile and simply enjoyed their proximity on the walk back to the Carleton Estate.

Chapter 15

It has come to this writer's attention that the soon-to-be-appointed Earl of F—— was seen shopping at a jeweler's known to provide the most delicate and precious of gems for those with deep enough pockets for such lavish finery. Though he did not leave with a box in hand, he did spend a great deal of time inside conversing with the proprietor.

Being the type of gentleman he is, and setting aside his most recent accounts of courting, who's to say this gift isn't yet another bauble for the plethora of women it is rumored he keeps on hand in Town like a harem for a Turkish Bey?

The Mayfair Chronicles, July 28, 1846

Delirious. That was the precise feeling that bombarded her very being. He'd played his games of seduction these past few days, charmed her at every opportunity, and he made her feel . . . smitten and drunk on a familiar sensation of anticipation, desire, and rekindled love.

All he had to do was glance at her from across the room to make her quiver with eagerness. It was difficult to keep her gaze from constantly straying in his direction, difficult to keep from brushing up against him when they were alone even for the briefest of moments. Every surreptitious touch made her crave him all the more.

He made her feel alive.

And because of *that* she couldn't stay away.

They were acting as circumspect as they had four years ago, or, at least, she hoped that to be true because the *inevitable* was bound to happen. And soon. It wouldn't do for their affair to be revealed to anyone currently in residence at the Carleton Estate.

While Leo had kept his word and done no more than spend time with her, she didn't think she could stick to the rules she had demanded for much longer. There was an unfulfilled yearning so palpable between them that the very air they breathed was filled with sexual tension.

Could she be so bold as to steal into his room tonight? Or should she ask that he meet her somewhere less conspicuous? Perhaps they could find a place where they could let go of all their inhibitions and indulge in their every sense without fear of being caught by another houseguest.

She felt very wicked and decided to retire early from the parlor that evening with Charlotte. Tonight she would be bold and . . . adventurous.

Putting her evening dress in the wardrobe, she donned her nightclothes. She chose a simple white linen nightgown with a matching robe with a Chantilly lace and satin frill at the hem. Her nipples puckered as the cool material slipped over her skin like a lover's touch. The very thought of Leo's hands skimming and molding her naked body had her heart racing.

Carefully removing all her hairpins, she dropped them in a crystal tray on her vanity and uncoiled her hair, letting the locks fall loose about her shoulders and down the length of her back. She took up the tresses, split them into sections, and weaved the pieces together in a thick braid.

How much longer should she delay? Would Leo be in his room? Surely he was, it was past eleven.

She stared at her reflection above her vanity and pinched her cheeks to bring some color to them. Without doubt, he wanted her. And she'd not lie to herself, she wanted him and had secretly wanted to go to him since he'd found her stargazing and done no more than have an intelligent conversation with her.

In spite of the fact that she should refrain from doing her heart's desire, because that was the right thing to do, she was doing something for herself, and only herself since the last time she'd seen Leo.

She was really going to do this.

Not questioning the oddly freeing sensation she felt, she went over to her door and stood in the little anteroom with her ear pressed tightly against the wood. The only thing she heard was the mantel clock ticking out the minutes back in her room.

As she turned the oval brass knob on the door, it clicked loudly open. She paused and held her breath, hand still clasped tightly around the cool handle. She was not so alarmed by the sound as to close the door and retreat to the safety of her room and lonely bed. Tonight, she didn't want to be alone—not now that her mind was decided.

Peeking her head out the door, she glanced left and then right. A sigh of relief escaped her as she quickly closed the door behind her and ran to Barrington's room. The design of the house was a wonderful aid to clandestine affairs; each bedchamber was equipped with two doors. There was only about three feet of space between the two, but it was enough to close herself quietly between them and stay hidden from anyone wandering the halls at this late hour. Not that she saw anyone else.

Rapping her knuckles very lightly against Barrington's

chamber door, she waited with a thrill of excitement skipping her heart along. Her knuckles fell heavier against the paneled door when he didn't immediately answer.

She chewed nervously at her lip and dropped her hand when she heard another voice—not Leo's—emanating from Barrington's private room. Before her mind could come up with a number of scenarios that had her cursing silently at her stupidity, the door flew open.

Barrington stood before her in his shirtsleeves, one hand holding the door open, the other braced on the door frame.

His smile softened to something more sensual when he saw that it was she standing on the other side. "Lady Luck has brought me a treasure this evening."

She opened her mouth to ask him who had been in the room with him but couldn't speak once his mouth descended upon hers.

It took every bit of her will to push her fists between them and break the delicious press of their mouths.

"I heard someone else," she said breathlessly.

"Are you jealous?"

"No. But . . ." She was but she'd sound like a ninny admitting that. "You enjoy tormenting me far too much. I should go." The disappointment was palpable in her tone as she backed up a few steps.

"Princess." Leo shook his head and cupped his hands over her arms. "Marks, my valet, was attending to me."

He spread his arms wide, drawing her attention back to his lack of attire. He wore only his shirtsleeves, suspenders, and dark trousers. Suddenly embarrassed that she'd questioned who was in his room, her gaze veered away from him and to the surrounding room. Similarly appointed as hers, the room varied only in the color scheme, his being darker and more masculine. The bed looked slightly larger than hers, the coverlet a deep brown to match the burgundy walls. There was a writing desk and couch whereas she had a vanity and a chair by the fire grate in her room.

"I'm sorry," she murmured. "You must think me juvenile and foolish."

"Never foolish. And my thoughts are far from juvenile. So much so, I believe you need to let me kiss you again to prove it."

An impish grin curved her mouth upward as she took his offered hand so he could lure her fully into his room.

"We'll have to be very quiet," she whispered.

"I look forward to smothering your cries with my mouth, and my hands if necessary." He waggled his eyebrows suggestively as he took her hands in his and drew her nearer. His breath fanned out over the shell of her ear seconds before he nibbled on the sensitive lobe.

"What changed your mind about coming to me, princess?"

"I really can't say." She cocked one eyebrow. "Why would you question that right now?"

In response, he gave her a deep chuckle as he released the tie on her robe. "If you change your mind at any point, you'll need to tell me."

"Had I any reservations, I would not have come."

Leo pushed the satiny material from her shoulders and let it pool on the ground around her feet. His breath hitched. It wasn't that she wore anything out of the ordinary. Beneath her cover was a simple shift, and her stays were still bound tightly around her waist. Though she had thought to step out of her slippers on entering his room.

"Do you think we'll be safe enough from discovery in here?"

Leo left her side and headed back toward the door. He

turned the key in the lock and placed it on a rectangular oak table flush to the wall.

"Trust me to protect your reputation, Genny." His voice was sincere. "I won't fail you."

"Tall words, my lord."

"I like you. Isn't that enough to see that my words and actions are genuine?"

He liked her. And she liked him, too. Her desire for a fairy-tale happy-ever-after ending had skipped in her heart before it was crushed by his simple but truthful words.

Like.

"Like" was the henchman's noose. The executioner's ax. The guillotine's screeching, sharp end.

Why couldn't he love her?

And why were her thoughts turning maudlin? She focused on the present—on the reason she had come here. On the man she'd come to in the dead of night with only one purpose in mind.

He gave her a wide berth as he walked toward the sofa that filled the small sitting area. Was he so attuned to her that he sensed her sudden unease and wanted to give her space?

"Do you want me to send Marks for some refreshments or a late-night snack?"

She shook her head. "While I trust you, I don't want anyone else to know I'm here."

"You needn't fear. I've promised to protect you from discovery."

He had.

Walking slowly around the room, Genny felt completely comfortable in what little clothes she wore—it was almost reminiscent of old times. Leo followed her, eating her up with that rapt, intent gaze of his. It was clear that she held a great deal of power over this man right now.

Had she always had this kind of control over him? It was possible she had been too young and inexperienced in life to have ever noticed it before now.

The thought gave her renewed courage in her seduction.

Genny sauntered over to the back of the sofa and beckoned Leo over with a single nod of her head. "Won't you sit?"

The black fire blazing in his eyes told her everything she needed to know about his thoughts. "What do you have planned, my lady?"

"It's better to keep you guessing. Besides, you'll know soon enough." She patted the back of the dark-upholstered sofa with the palm of her hand.

"I aim to please you." And with that, he complied.

It had been so long since she'd touched him intimately that she wanted to savor every moment tonight. Though she was thankful they would have other nights since the house party went on for two more weeks.

She whispered huskily in his ear, "Lie back, my lord."

He made a noise of contentment as the flats of her hands ran over the planes of his heavily muscled chest. Her palms slid beneath the open vee of his shirt to press against his warm skin.

Pulling her hands free, she yanked on the suspenders. "I like this look on you. The change in fashion and move away from corsets on men is an improvement."

"Since when did I ever wear such a thing?"

"Never, but so many do. It would be a shame to hide your brawny, masculine frame."

Leo tugged at her braid, which had fallen over his chest when she leaned over him. He untied the satin ribbon on the end so her hair could be easily unraveled. "I like it when your hair is unbound. Now come closer so that I can assault your mouth a while longer."

As she stood on the tips of her toes, their noses brushed

together before their lips met. His arms reached up to cradle her head closer as their lips meshed, parted, and tasted. Their tongues tangled in a familiar dance of eroticism. Not caught off guard by this kiss, she enjoyed every nip and lick.

Leo pulled her over the back of the sofa and onto his lap. He maneuvered them so he lay stretched out beneath her, head resting on one of the gold-tasseled velvet bolsters decorating either end. Hitching up the long frilly skirt of her nightgown, he settled her body over his.

He broke their kiss for a second. "Will you come to me every night?"

"Possibly." She liked being in control of their affair. She also liked to tease him. Of course she had every intention of coming to him every night, but she also liked the note of desperation in his voice.

"I'd like it if you did." He brushed away a stray lock of hair that had fallen down the side of her face.

"I'm sure you would."

His hands slid down her back next, running along the corset laces, plucking at them as if they were the strings of a cello. He loosened her stays at a painstakingly slow pace. She just wanted it off.

The hard ridge of his arousal pressed into her belly. She craved to touch him and wanted to rub her body along his without clothes to hinder them, but she wanted to savor every moment of removing each other's clothes first.

Slowly releasing the strings that bound the corset around her waist, Leo tugged at the contraption till it was loose. All that was left was to unclasp the front busk. He left it alone to push the material of her shift aside.

"Your skin is as soft as I remember," he said as he pressed his lips against her exposed shoulder. Her fingers threaded through the longish locks of his dark hair, luxuriating in the soft texture. His kisses were slow and exploring. He was moving too unhurriedly for her liking. She was hungry for so much more of him.

"We need to reacquaint faster, Leo."

"I like it when you call me Leo." He cupped her face in his hands and pulled her mouth closer to lay tender bites to her lips before releasing her. "We have all night, princess. And we have a lot of time to make up for."

She put her hands down around his shoulders to keep from toppling completely onto him. One of his hands went around her back and gripped one buttock cheek tightly. He shifted her so her pelvis cradled his, and the jut of his manhood pressed firmly against her core. She rubbed against him, loving the titillating sensation of their position.

Removing his hand from her rear, he undid her corset and tossed it aside. It landed with a soft thud somewhere on the floor.

"Leo . . ."

She lost her train of thought when his hungry gaze snared hers. Though she saw desire etched in his handsome face, she also saw a fount of emotion that had been previously pent up and hidden from her before now. He really had missed her. Missed this. Her hand traced the strong line of his jaw and the soft plushness of his lips. He nibbled on the tip of her finger.

"Genny?"

"I wanted to stay away," she confessed.

Resist him.

Avoid him.

Anything but fall into his arms and his bed again.

But it felt as though she belonged here. Society strictures aside, this was exactly where she wanted to be. Because she far more than *liked* this man.

The back of his fingers gently ran over the side of her face, returning the gentle caress she'd given him. "I'm glad you didn't."

"What if I had?" she asked.

"Then I would have had no choice but to respect your decision and carry on as I have been and will continue to do."

"You wouldn't have stopped courting me?" How she loved the attention he lavished on her.

"Is that what you're worried about?" His hands caressed the length of her back. "That once I have you in my bed again, I'll not want to spend time with you outside of my private chambers?"

She nodded.

"Silly girl." He kissed her fiercely, his tongue delving hard between her lips in silent demand that she savor the moment with him. "Have you forgotten what our last affair was like? I cannot keep myself from you, princess."

"Do you give all your lovers that moniker?"

"Only you, Genny. I've never wanted a woman more than I want you."

"You left me, though." The hurt was palpable in her tone.

"I shouldn't have walked away from you four years ago. I won't walk away a second time." Leo sat up so he could lean against the curved arm of the sofa. He took her with him, settling her comfortably in his lap. "It was an odd situation, and I was too stupid to realize I was walking away from the one thing I truly enjoyed in life."

"Yet you didn't come back."

"The truth is, I didn't think you'd have me, Genny." His thumb rubbed the side of her face affectionately. "Leaving you is the only regret I have in my life."

"Do you mean to . . . to marry me, Leo?"

He brushed his hand through his hair roughly, disheveling it more than she had. "I know that what we have won't end here in my bed tonight. Nor will it end the night after or the night after that."

The possibility of marriage sent a deep thrill of happiness through every part of her body. She pressed her mouth to his, slipped her tongue between his lips, and let the feelings of love guide her actions.

Her tongue wound around his as she busied herself with removing his clothes. Sliding her fingers beneath his suspenders once again, she pushed them off his shoulders and tugged at his shirt, wanting to be rid of it.

"Genny?"

More determined than ever not to ruin the night they were finally sharing, she shook her head. "Don't say another word, Leo. Just help me remove your clothes."

He complied with her wishes, yanking the long tails of his shirt free from his trousers. When he pulled his shirt over his head, she took a moment to appreciate his strong physique. His body was strong, thickly roped with muscles. She traced the tight lines of his torso. There was a small patch of coarse hair at the center of his chest that she brushed her fingers through.

His hands caressed the length of her back in soft strokes. Her legs straddled around his hips as they both sat facing each other. She well remembered the feel of his body but wanted to retrace every line she had etched to memory four years ago. He seemed bigger, as though age had made him larger than life. And perhaps it had in her mind.

"I've missed this," she found herself saying.

"So have I." His hand lazily stroked the outside of her thighs, pushing the material of her shift closer to her waist. "Can I remove this?"

How could she ever mind? She'd do anything he asked of her. "Yes."

She raised her arms so he could lift the soft material over her head. Her hair was still half-braided and fell with a light thump against her back when she was unhindered by the material of her nightclothes.

Leo's hands lightly grazed her bare breasts before lifting their weight and squeezing both together. "I love that you don't shy away from me, Genny. You never have, and I hope you never will."

Was she supposed to hide herself, pretend to be ashamed of her body instead of sharing it freely with him? He always made her feel like the most beautiful woman to walk the face of the earth. It felt like a sin to not share and indulge her body as he did with his.

"You make me feel so much more like a woman when I'm with you. So much more worthy of . . . you."

"Kiss me, Genny."

And she did. Her tongue was slow and exploring, but it dove deep within the cavern of his mouth. His hands skimmed over her breasts one final time, brushing over the firm peaks of her nipples before moving with calm tenderness over her ribs and around to her back. He drew long lines up and down her spine, swirling little circles with his fingers every time he reached the swell of her buttocks.

"I will indulge your every sense tonight. This is a promise."

"I like your promises." Her voice was husky and full of desire.

"I aim to please you."

Her hands cupped either side of his face so she could stare directly into his eyes. "And I am glad for it."

He pressed his hot lips against the arch of her neck and tongued and nibbled a line of kisses and love bites over the pulsing vein there. "What time do you think we should get you back to your room?"

"Never," she admitted, and was offered a chuckle in response. The vibration tickled against her over-sensitized flesh and had her arching her back so that she could feel the heat of his body tightly pressed against hers.

"I understand the sentiment completely. Let us aim for

four. I'm afraid you'll be dreadfully tired tomorrow but this is the price of passion, hmm?"

His fingers worked at loosening the rest of her braid. His fingertips massaged her scalp once he reached the top.

"Yes, it is."

He tipped her back till she was lying down on the sofa and adjusted his position so he could lie atop her. "Wrap your legs around my hips."

She complied and pulled her pelvis up so she could grind herself against his erection. He groaned loudly in her ear. "Hell, woman, I won't last an hour if you keep at that."

"I need to feel you, Leo."

"In due course," he promised. "Are you comfortable here?"

She gently wrapped her hands around his shoulders, threading her fingers lightly together behind his neck. "Comfort is far from my mind right now."

"You never fail to amuse me in any given circumstance." He lifted her from the sofa, holding her easily around his waist by gripping her thighs. Her ankles were still locked together at the small of his back.

His strong fingers kneaded into the flesh of her thighs as he walked toward the high bed. He set her down on the satiny coverlet.

He leaned over her, kissing a path down her stomach as he removed her pantalettes. It took one hard yank to relieve her of the last of her clothing. She didn't try and cover her nakedness. He'd always appreciated her in the flesh, and the expression on his face said he still did. His eyes roamed over her form, eating up her naked body. A mere look from him had her panting in need of his touch. She felt wetness dampen her core, and make her thighs slick. She was ready for him. She needed him all over her, licking and kissing every part of her body.

Seeing that he was fully entranced with her form, she

pointed to one breast. "It aches for your touch . . . will you kiss it?"

He ripped at the buttons that held his trousers up and shed them quickly. His manhood jutted out, long and heavy with a need of its own. He pressed her thighs wide open and stared down at her spread out on the bed. His breath came a little quicker as he grasped her by her waist and lifted her with ease toward the middle of the bed before he joined her. Genny put her arms above her head and stretched like a supple feline.

He stared down at her as if she were a great banquet dinner, and he was currently eating up all the appetizers at once. "It's been too long."

"Then you should love me thoroughly."

"I intend to just as soon as my eyes are drunk from the view you make, gloriously naked in *my* bed."

He did no more than touch her. Tracing the backs of his knuckles and then his fingers over her curves, he molded his hands to her form . . .

A host of conflicting feelings bombarded her, making her feel vulnerable yet safe, desired yet cherished. Leo would never harm her. He would always protect her. She felt safe in his arms.

"Leo."

"Patience. I have an unfulfilled desire to taste every inch of you tonight."

She closed her eyes as his lips fell upon her breast, tracing little kisses over the roundness, flicking his tongue out over the firm peak of her nipple.

"You make me feel at home here. We belong together, princess."

She arched her back off the bed in supplication.

"Promise me you won't leave me again."

"You have my word."

She wanted him to trace his mouth lower. His hands

kneaded at her breasts, her ribs, and her hips. When he gripped her buttocks, he pulled her body closer so they lay facing each other on their sides. His manhood pressed intimately against her belly. There was a bead of his fluid at the tip, so she reached between them and rubbed her thumb around the velvet-soft head, spreading the wetness. That earned her another groan and a thrust against her stomach.

Hitching one of her legs over his hip, he reached between their bodies to touch her. When his fingers slicked through the evidence of her desire, he broke away from their kiss.

Placing a palm on either side of his hair-roughened jaw, she brought his mouth flush to hers and licked teasingly at his lips.

"There is much to be discussed about our future," he said between heated kisses.

"And there is plenty of time for us to talk about it later. The night grows late."

"And the morning early," he responded.

It wasn't as though she would refuse marriage, and if given the opportunity, she'd marry him tomorrow. There was no question in her mind about that.

Thoughts ceased when his fingers found her wet core again, and he flicked the flat of his thumb over the bud between the lips of her sex. The sensations he caused with his fingers alone heightened her pleasure to a fever pitch. She pressed closer to assuage the need for more running rampant in her blood.

His mouth lowered to her breast, laying gentle open-mouthed kisses against her heated flesh. Her fingers threaded through his hair, and she held him close as he suckled the firm tip of her breast into his mouth.

He pushed one of her thighs out and caressed her as he positioned himself above her. One hand grasped her rear and the other rested by her shoulder as he tilted her pelvis toward his and eased slowly inside.

They both groaned with the intimate contact and joining of their bodies. Their eyes connected, enraptured, and did not veer off for a single moment as Leo took her.

Once fully seated, he pulled himself nearly all the way out before thrusting back at full hilt. Genny traced the strong, smooth lines of his back, savoring the workings of sinew beneath her fingers with each of his forward thrusts. She pressed her mouth against his shoulder, nipping at his heated, sweat-dampened skin as her hands lowered to trace his firm buttocks.

He flipped their positions, putting her on top. "I want to watch you taking me inside your body."

Her hair tumbled around her shoulders, over her breasts, and tickled at his chest and torso. Brushing it back with her hands, she did exactly as Leo asked. While his hands gripped and guided her by the hips, she stroked the heavy pulsating length that was buried deep inside her body. The walls of her sheath flexed and pulled at him.

Leo didn't remain idle to her ministrations for long. Once she found an even rhythm, he caressed the length of her legs, the lower portion of her back and spine, even her forearms where they were stretched out over his chest.

The first tingling of her orgasm tightened the muscles of her stomach. "Leo," she moaned, grinding her body down hard on his.

He claimed her mouth with his as the first spasm of pleasure tore through her body like a wild storm.

Her voice was high-pitched and mewling with the onslaught of pleasure. Leo held her tight against him and thrust hard, milking the last of her orgasm from her until she slumped over on top of him like a lifeless rag doll.

His kisses gentled and showered over her chin, her jaw, even the tip of her nose.

"Princess," he whispered.

"I don't think my legs work anymore. I need a minute to catch my breath."

"How about I do everything?"

Genny laughed. "I can't just lie here as you finish yourself."

"I don't intend for you to do any such thing."

Unseating himself, he tossed her back into the middle of his overly large bed and worked a trail of kisses down the center of her body.

She pushed at his head, realizing his intent. "You can't be serious."

"Oh, but I am. I did promise to taste every part of you."

"Yes, but that was no more than a figure of speech." She feebly gripped him around his thick arms and attempted to haul him back up the length of her body.

He didn't budge. With one last droll look and raised brow, he spread the lips of her private area and blew a cool stream of air on the sensitive bundle of nerves at her center.

"Leo," she protested, but as his tongue flicked out, her head fell back on the pillows in surrender. Her legs cradled his wide shoulders as he went to work tasting every part of her.

Her fingers tangled and tightened in his hair the longer his tongue swirled around the swollen bud of pleasure at her core.

"Don't ever stop," she said.

His chuckle vibrated around the bud of her sex, sending a fresh wave of carnal awareness through her body and causing every nerve ending to reel with desire. Bringing her to the sweet precipice that would catapult her into another orgasm, Leo pulled away a moment shy of that apex and slid his cock deep inside her body again.

His pace was more frantic now than it had been before but no less delicious. His mouth devoured hers, tongue thrusting deep and matching the tempo of his body pounding inside her.

His hand reached between them so his thumb could flick against the nub of her sex. When another wave of pure ecstasy washed through her body, Leo pulled out with a soft curse and took his cock in hand. She folded her hand over his, pumping with him until his seed spurted out from between their entwined fingers.

When their hands stilled, he pecked her lips with his as he stood from the bed. He disappeared behind a door for a moment.

After a short rush of water, he returned to the bed with a dampened towel. She hadn't the energy to move as he took her hands and wiped them clean then let him press the warm cloth between her legs to wash away the stickiness from their lovemaking.

Tossing the cloth in the general direction of the room he'd retrieved it from, he joined her on the bed and gathered her up in his arms with his chest to her back and his arm snaked around her front.

"You can sleep for a while." He tucked her head between his chest and shoulder.

"I couldn't possibly risk it," she said.

"We have some hours left. I won't sleep."

She arched her back, stretching contentedly with a yawn. "How can you not sleep after that?"

He caressed her from stomach to breast and squeezed her hip to draw her back into his groin. His revived arousal pressed against her backside.

"Oh." She turned to face him on the bed. "I can't possibly sleep with you being in such a state."

His smile was ten kinds of wicked as he suckled her lip into his mouth.

"I did tell you that ambrosia was hard to resist after taking the first sip."

Genny wrapped her arms around his shoulders and gave him a smile she hoped matched his in sensuality. "And I never disagreed."

After Leo helped Genny put her clothes back on, she sat on the edge of his bed brushing out her long hair with her fingers and trying to put it back in order. When she reached the end of the long braid she'd put it in, she looked around his disheveled bed for the tie. It was currently tucked in his trouser pocket as a token of their night together, but he wouldn't tell her that.

"I think it's well and truly lost," he said.

She shrugged. "I have more in my room. I just hope the maids don't find it. You know how they talk."

"I wouldn't worry about it."

"I'm not. I just don't want anyone to find us out."

"They won't. I promised you they wouldn't." He held his hand out to her. "We have to get you off to your own room, princess. The servants will be up and about before we know it."

"It's half past three in the morning. Who in their right mind would get up at this hour?"

He gave her an amused laugh. "The maids to light the braziers for one."

"It's summer; there is no need."

"Yes, but you never know who else might be wandering the halls after a late-night assignation." He waggled his brows suggestively.

"You mean aside from us?"

"Absolutely. I can think of a few guests who might be otherwise engaged with someone who is not their spouse."

"You're incorrigible."

"It's one of my better traits."

He patted her rear, wishing they could stay here all night and the next morning. But for now, she really did need to return to the safety of her own room.

Leo walked her to the door, wearing only his trousers. She pressed both her palms against his chest and brushed up against him with a sultriness that had him hardening in an instant, despite their many exertions already. If only it were possible for her to stay the night.

It was late, and they would both be tired in the morning, but every part of tonight made it worth the long day to follow. He grasped her around the waist to tug her closer and lowered his mouth to hers, just sipping at her lips instead of consuming as he wanted to. Because if he did that he'd haul her back into his bed and stay there for the remainder of the week.

"What of tomorrow night?" he asked.

"We have all of the day to get through first." She yawned in perfect demonstration of just how tired she was.

"Do you want to meet in the maze tomorrow night? It'll offer more privacy. And you can be as loud as you like. It'll be a bit like old times, too."

"What if we are far too exhausted to even contemplate another night awake?"

He raised one brow in disbelief. "You're as insatiable as I. I'll make it worth your while." He held her hands, not wanting her to escape without committing to spending another evening with him.

"Let us see what the day brings us first."

"Perfect. I'll spend the day convincing you that you want nothing more than to repeat everything we did tonight."

And because he couldn't resist, he tapped her bottom once again as he opened the first door of his chamber. "I'll see you at the breakfast table." Opening the second door, he peered down the hall to make sure it was empty. "It's clear. Go."

She gave him one last kiss before looking down the hall as he had and running with all the grace of a dancer to her room and shuttering herself quickly inside.

He did one more look up and down the hall to make sure no one was hiding in the shadows. No one was around. Quietly shutting the door behind him, he fell into bed and didn't even bother to undress. Marks would wake him up in time for breakfast. He had to make an appearance in case Genny didn't make it down.

Still, he'd not spend the morning in his room trying to catch up on sleep; he had to go over his strategy and numbers with Carleton tomorrow for the upcoming vote.

They would be heading back to Town for summer Parliament meetings on the sugar import act come August. But before then, they were set to meet with a number of undecided voters at his club, to see if they could be convinced to stand up against Ponsley and his majority in the House of Lords. He also needed to figure out what to do about Jez, but that issue could be taken care of when he returned to London.

Chapter 16

The one thing to keep my pen surely scribbling is to offer up a scandal to my readers. Two weeks into the C——s' house party, and not a whisper of rumor about the guests has been offered to date. Something will surely come my way soon. And the moment it does, I know my readers will be giddy with excitement to read the gossip here first.
The Mayfair Chronicles, July 31, 1846

Genny had been sitting at her vanity for more than an hour now. To say she was tired was an understatement. Though she and Leo had been up the majority of the night, they had also slept for a short time. Well, she had slept for a while, and Leo had awakened her to make love one more time before she had to return to her room. Her heart beat faster in her chest recalling to memory the things they'd indulged in. She didn't regret her choice in going to him for one moment.

A soft rap on the door to her room helped to refocus her thoughts. It was most likely Charlotte, ready to start breakfast, and see what the day ahead held for them.

Charlotte's smile was bright as she opened the door,

but her obvious giddiness slipped as she assessed Genny's face. "You look as though you didn't sleep a wink."

"Last night was fitful, I'm afraid." She ran her fingers over her face. "Do I look as dreadful as your expression hints?"

Charlotte grabbed her hand and pulled her out of her room and down the corridor. "I'll fix it for you."

Genny laughed. "How can you possibly fix it?"

"You promise not to be angry or to so much as whisper a word about what I'm going to share with you?"

Genny covered her mouth in shock, eyes wide, as she considered the possibility that her cousin did such a thing. "You don't."

"Shush." Charlotte looked quite perturbed. "You'll inform the whole household with the way you're going on about it."

"I'd never tell anyone. No one else knows, I hope."

Charlotte shook her head. "Not a soul."

How was it that she'd never known Charlotte's propensity for maquillage? She'd lived with her for nearly eight months, and at some point, one would think that a secret such as this would be revealed. Especially since Genny spent the greater portion of her day in Charlotte's company.

"The best way to make someone keep a secret is to make them an accomplice. I plan to disguise your sleepless night so no one but us need know that you're a ragged mess without a proper night of rest."

Her cousin clicked the lock over once they entered her room. Charlotte rushed over to the white vanity, painted to match the light decor of the room. Tiny pink roses and green vines were patterned in the wallpaper and in the canopy above the bed. It was a beautiful, cheery room and perfect for any young lady.

Her cousin slid out the drawer and retrieved something wrapped and tied tight in pale linen.

"Well, why are you standing over there?"

Genny hadn't moved from the door.

"I'm not sure about this. We aren't even of the same complexion." Genny brushed her fingers over one of her cheeks.

"Posh. Now, come and sit in front of the mirror so I can have a good turn at painting your face."

Genny sat on the cushioned, tasseled stool. She was still quite shocked that her cousin—her beautiful, younger cousin—painted her face.

"And what if someone should notice what I've done?"

"Then you'll promise not to say how you came to have such an item in your possession."

"Why do you use paint, Charlotte? You are such a pretty young lady."

"A pretty girl with freckles from sitting out in the back portico at the townhouse. No one goes out there but me, it seems, and so the necessities of hat, gloves, and even shoes are unheeded."

"How did you ever learn about it?"

"How do you imagine?" At Genny's shrug, Charlotte clarified, "Grandmamma, of course. She only wants the best for me and my being beautiful is what makes her happy, so I even out my complexion during the summer months."

Her cousin pulled out a circular tin that contained a heavy whitish powder.

"You can't mean to put that on my face. It must be four shades lighter than my complexion." Genny screwed up her eyebrows, unsure that this was the wisest course to take.

"It's not opaque, silly. And I do have every intention of putting it on you."

"I'm not sure I'm convinced."

Charlotte laughed at her hesitancy. "It won't matter. We'll cover the whole of your face and no one will be the wiser."

"What if I should perspire?"

"Then you blot your face. Never rub it, even if a drop of rain were to fall upon it, you must dab it, and it will blend in with the powder."

Her cousin dabbed on the heavy powder beneath her eyes using a small flat puff.

"This is pure insanity." Charlotte distributed the powder evenly and took her time to cover the dark circles beneath Genny's eyes. When that was done, she took out a small brush with soft bristles and removed the excess powder.

"Perhaps, but we are supposed to always look our best, even if we feel ill. Covering the flaws so that only I know they exist makes passing the day a whole lot easier for you and invites far fewer questions about your tiredness when you look perfectly fine."

"I swear, Charlotte, you sometimes sound like a wise lady beyond her years, and it tends to put me out of sorts."

"You'd be bored if I didn't keep you on your toes."

Genny smiled at the reflection of her cousin in the mirror. Maybe her cousin did know her very well and Genny hadn't bothered to give Charlotte any reason to prove that she was a capable young lady.

"You still have this incredible proclivity for surprising me. And in the oddest of ways." Genny turned her face from side to side marveling at how the powder blended in and looked natural.

"I told you no one would be the wiser." Charlotte perched herself on the edge of the vanity with a sigh.

Genny reached out to touch her slightly improved reflection. The powder was barely perceptible. "My face feels a little stiff." Before she could press the backs of her fingers lightly against her cheek, her cousin pulled her hand away.

"You cannot touch it. Even a small rub or brushing of your gloves might displace the powder."

Genny didn't need coaxing to lower her hand. To be caught wearing a beauty product like this would label her as having the morals of a stage actress. "I promise to ignore the slightest itch."

"Keep a handkerchief in your reticule in case it rains."

"And then excuse myself to your room should I need to reapply it." Everything made a little more sense now. Genny could recall the many times that had happened over the course of the season.

"You know you are quite beautiful without the artifice?"

"So I've been told. I don't wear a great deal of it, only enough to cover my dreadful freckles."

"You'll have to show them to me now so I can tell you how undreadful they really are."

"You wouldn't dare say so on seeing them. That you'll have to trust me on."

"You can trust me with your secrets. But if you wish to keep your freckles hidden, then that is fine as well." Standing from the stool, she leaned in closer to the mirror to see if the powder was detectable. If someone were to stand six inches from her face, they might see a hint of the makeup, but it was well placed and nearly invisible otherwise.

"Thank you," Genny said. "Now, we had better find our way down to breakfast before everyone wonders where we are this morning."

"If the sun comes out, do you think we'll play a game out of doors?"

"It would be a great deal more fun than watching the

gentlemen fishing in the stream. You would think after three hours that someone would catch at least one fish."

They went arm in arm out the door and down to the breakfast parlor. "Yes, but I do believe Mr. Torrance was appalled at the very thought of baiting his line when he was handed the jar of worms. He said if the hook couldn't snag something, then he was fine with not having a successful outcome."

They were both laughing as they entered the parlor.

The morning sun peeked through the clouds outside and filled the whole room with its cheery appearance. The gentlemen, including Leo, stood on their entry. Genny gave him a brief smile before greeting the rest of the company at the table. She didn't want to be too obvious in her attention to Leo. What if someone should notice that they were on much friendlier terms than when the house party had started?

Not that anyone would think to watch for changes in their relationship—which had been at the very least friendly, but then so had everyone else's. Such things tended to happen when so many people were tossed together for an extended period.

A grand buffet was set up on the far right of the room, against the west-facing wall. Tiered silver platters, dishes, and large porcelain bowls were filled with kedgeree, poached eggs, and sausage. There was also a wide selection of fried tomatoes and mushrooms, scones and jellies, creams and syrups, fresh picked strawberries, and raspberries all enticing her closer. Not surprisingly she was famished this morning. But with a full room, it would be unseemly to fill her plate. Perhaps she could sneak away some scones in the deep pockets at the sides of her skirts. She couldn't believe she even contemplated such a thing.

She took three eggs, knowing they would best fill her up and then a selection of everything else. There were three spaces left at the table once Charlotte took her usual spot next to Ariel. Genny definitely didn't want to sit at the head of the table where Lord Carleton sat when he came down to breakfast, and she didn't want banal morning conversation with Mr. Torrance. So she took the seat at the end of the long table next to Leo.

He was better at being unobtrusive than she was, for he continued his conversation with Lady Hargrove about their day ahead. He even allowed Genny to pull out her own chair, only offering her a droll, "How remiss of me not to assist," as she tucked herself neatly under the table.

"We don't follow all the formalities whilst here, and I must say, it's a nice break from dinning around Town when you are expected to do everything by the book," Genny said.

"I couldn't agree more," Lady Hargrove said, taking an indelicate bite of her eggs.

Everyone at the table laughed and tucked into their own meal. Genny focused on eating and tried to ignore the nearness of Leo, who didn't seem to care for rules as long as no one could see that his leg kept bumping hers under the table.

When he pushed his plate away and set a cup of tea in front of him, a lemon floating on top, one of his hands disappeared under the table and found its way to her lap.

Genny froze, fork halfway to her mouth. He couldn't be serious.

She moved her leg, attempting to shake him off, and make him understand that she did not want to do *this* here. Instead of her plan working, he hiked up her skirt, and settled his hand over her kneecap. He simply let it rest there, without attempting any more liberties.

She turned to him, raised one brow, gave an indiscernible shake of her head and turned back to focus on her food. Thankfully, he made no further attempt to put her out of sorts, nor did he lower her skirts again to let her resume the meal in false innocence. She'd have to find a way to get back at him for this. And she would. He had another think coming if he thought he could unsettle her and tease her at any given opportunity. Even if she did enjoy the clandestine attentions he heaped upon her.

Lady Carleton entered the parlor. "My steward has consulted his ever trustworthy farmer's almanac and suggests it will rain later this afternoon. I think we should have our game of blind man's buff sooner rather than later."

Everyone put their utensils down with the announcement of a morning excursion. Breakfast would be rushed, since everyone was anxious to head out of doors into the beautiful, much cooler weather this morning.

"We could always play blind man's buff indoors and use the whole lower level to hide from the one blinded," Lady Hargrove suggested.

"I love the mazes here. I think we should have a go out of doors before we are trapped inside for the remainder of the day," Charlotte responded.

"Who will be the blind man, Lady Carleton?" Mr. Torrance asked.

"An excellent question," she said, sitting down at the head of the table in the chair her husband usually occupied. She poured herself a cup of black tea and took a small sip to test the temperature. "We can pick our names from a hat or pick straws. Shortest straw will have to be blindfolded. Now eat up everyone, we must get started."

Since most had finished their meal already, they filed out of the room to retrieve their hats and shawls. Seeing that Charlotte was finished and ready to leave, Genny carefully dabbed her mouth with her napkin. Placing the cloth on the table, she reached for Leo's hand clasped around her knee and tried to dislodge it as she commended Lady Carleton on the fine selection of breakfast food.

Genny had to fix her skirts before pushing her chair out. Now that most everyone had left, Leo took it upon himself to assist her. "Shall I escort you and your lovely cousin to the mazes?"

"It would be an honor," Charlotte chimed in but stalled before exiting the breakfast parlor. "Oh, dear. I promised to meet Ariel. Genny, take my shawl since I am feeling a little warm. You can head to the mazes straightaway. I will follow you out shortly."

No, she could absolutely not go alone with Leo, even if she wanted to. What would everyone think of such a bold action that was very much like courting? Worse, everyone might think his intentions impure, which, yes, they were, but she didn't want anyone to so much as guess what they did when they were alone.

"I'm more than happy to escort Miss Camden to the mazes."

"That is perfect. I will be out in a moment, too," Lady Carleton said. "I need to consult with Cook on luncheon arrangements."

Leo steered Genny in the direction of the door before she could provide a reason not to leave with him alone.

When they were well out of range of the house, she said, "Have you gone completely mad?"

"Have I not been on your heels every moment of every day for the past week?"

"Well, yes. But—" She paused on seeing his teasing grin.

"There can be no buts. If I don't continue to act as I have done, and you don't continue to resist me—and you have done a lovely job so far this morning—then we'll be caught out."

She realized he was right. "You've thought this through."

"Yes, I've been thinking about this since you left this morning. About how we should carry on without drawing attention our way."

"You didn't go to bed after I left?"

"How could I?"

"You'll be exhausted today."

"It was well worth it." He waggled his brows at her. "Besides, I can always disappear for a few hours after lunch. I will need to freshen up for this evening."

"We have to be careful, Leo." Her tone turned serious.

"I'm well aware of that." His forefinger and thumb rubbed at his chin in thought. "I still think we should meet in the maze tonight."

"It's supposed to rain."

"Then I will take you back to the greenhouse where we can be *completely* alone."

She bumped into his shoulder, wanting so much to have his arm wrapped around her but knowing they couldn't show such intimacy publicly. "I don't even remember how we accomplished our affair all those years ago. I am beginning to wonder how we weren't caught."

"I was careful for both of us. You have nothing to fear, we seem to be able to keep a little more distance between us during the day now that we've matured."

Leo threaded her arm through his. It seemed he wanted to touch her as much as she did him.

"That reminds me," he said. "Who was that friend of yours? The one that beat out all the men in the archery competition four years ago?"

What an odd question. "You mean Helena?" She sighed. "How I miss Helena. We still write back and forth. She married well."

"I recall. Wasn't it to the . . ." He snapped his fingers

as he tried to place the name. "Ah, yes, now I recall. It was to the Duke of Beaumont."

"Yes, your memory serves you well. She has just had her first child. A little girl they named Maisie."

"Of course I remember her. She was your friend. And I did spend a great deal of time with the two of you. So in a sense, I had a vested interest in her as well. Didn't she meet Beaumont at this very house?"

What was he getting at? "How observant of you."

"No, no. Hear me out in this. I think there were three marriages after that particular party. Your friend's being the first to come to mind. I think there was also an older gent and lady."

"I haven't a clue who you might be referring to. There was Lord Grovestead's eldest son who ran off to Gretna Green with one of the young ladies' chaperones." Reminiscing was actually quite fun to do with Leo.

Leo clapped his hands together and let out a raucous laugh that had her joining in. "What a scandal that was. I hadn't forgotten that. That put the house in such an uproar. I think it was written about in every rag by the time I returned to London. My acquaintances were shocked to find me so well behaved."

"There doesn't seem to be as much scandal afoot this time around."

"Another reason for us to be ever so vigilant," he said.

They were thick into the maze, and almost at the center. Feeling safe in the cover of hedges, Genny pressed closer to Leo, feeling his gait through the length of her body, and matching it. Or was he matching her smaller strides? Regardless, it was nice to relish the momentary closeness they had while alone.

"Which of my suitors did you think I would marry?"

"I had personally hoped that you would choose neither. Though the baron's son . . . can't recall his name—"

"Mr. Ewan," she supplied.

"Ah, yes, how remiss of me. Did you have any tender feelings for the young, fresh-faced Mr. Ewan?"

Genny tsked. "I think that tone in your voice is very close to jealousy, my lord."

"And if it is?" Leo's hand clasped around her waist and rested firmly on her hip.

"Well, it ought not to be. It wasn't as though you offered for my hand in marriage."

"No, I didn't."

"The one thing I wanted in a husband was to share the type of connection that we had." Genny wasn't sure she should admit even that much, but what did she have to lose? "We got on well, but I could not marry a man I only saw as a friend. It was almost what I imagined having a brother to be like had I had one."

"I daresay, the marriage bed would have been a trifle uncomfortable if the man felt like a brother to you."

Genny clucked her tongue. "Don't tease me so."

"I enjoy it too much to quit now." Leo tugged her closer. "Though now that I've had you in my bed, you don't seem to blush nearly as much."

Genny felt her cheeks heat under his regard, but she knew the face powder hid the telltale signs of any blush. Perhaps she should invest in her own powders? She never thought it could be so handy, and she liked the idea of covering the blushes she was prone to.

"You tease me so often that I'm growing immune to it."

"You've just challenged me, my lady. I will prove you wrong before the day is through. And I'll prove it to you before our game is complete this morning."

She dropped his arm and let him chase her down the hedged path, giggling as she made her way to the center.

He seemed to stay a few feet behind, never actually catching her. She could hear the heavy panting of his breath, and she thought she might have unintentionally aroused him. Good. He had a habit of putting her out of sorts whenever he could manage it, and she was glad to turn the tables on him for once.

She knew her way through the maze very well, having mastered the odd twists and turns her first summer here. Some of the hedges grew right over the path, making you feel locked out from the rest of the world. They occasionally broke open at the top to let the sunlight through, but before long, you'd find yourself covered by more greenery.

When she reached the center, she had every intention of pulling Leo into her arms and kissing him thoroughly before anyone else arrived. How would they explain their exertions? Perhaps no one would care.

Oh, she was acting careless.

Today was the first time she'd ventured into the maze since her arrival and everything was just as she remembered. Six double-flanked hedged paths led to the middle attraction. A large tiered fountain was the showcase here, with its naiad at the top with her breasts exposed. She held a tilted ewer that spouted water down into the basin of the fountain.

Turning in the wide round opening at the center of the maze, she stopped when she was facing Leo. He didn't say a word. He only looked at her with dark, dilated eyes before pulling her into his arms and lowering his mouth to hers. She went to him willingly, anxious to have his taste upon her tongue again. Anxious to feel the hardness of his body against her softer one.

Why did they have to be in the presence of anyone at all? Had they been alone, she didn't think she would ever stop kissing him. His mouth did very wicked things. So wicked and titillating that she felt the tips of her breasts peak beneath the light muslin of her dress. She wanted to appease the need to be touched by rubbing up against him, but settled for putting her arms around his shoulders and holding him tighter to her.

He lifted his mouth away from her but didn't pull away completely. His cheek rested atop her head as he stroked her back. "I want you now."

"The feeling is mutual," she whispered.

"We have to stop or everyone will think that I'm carrying something in my pocket."

She was feeling especially naughty after his morning's teasing, so she lifted herself up on her toes, rubbing her breasts against his chest and her belly against his arousal.

Leo groaned and hugged her tight along his body. "You're my little minx."

Laughter from the rest of their party wasn't far off, so she pulled away hurriedly and made sure her dress wasn't wrinkled.

She pressed her fingers to her mouth. "Are my lips swollen?"

Leo stepped closer, like a lion stalking his mate.

"Delightfully so." He rubbed his thumb over her parted mouth. "But don't fret, no one will notice in a moment."

There was a smidge of her face powder on his chin. Quickly, she reached for his face and tried to wipe the evidence away. She had to pull away too soon when Lady Hargrove came through one of the entrances. There was a tiny smear left that she hoped no one would notice. Not that they would inspect him as closely as she might.

Everyone gathered around the fountain and waited for Lady Carleton to come forward with her stack of sticks. Hiding the bottom half of them in a pouch, she held them out in front of her. "The person who draws the shortest will be blindfolded, though, I'm going to outline the changed rules for this game."

There were oohs and ahs around their circle.

"I propose," she said, opening a large stringed bag hanging over her arm, "that we all be blindfolded."

"How will we find each other at all?" Lady Hargrove pointed out.

"I've played a version similar to this before," Mr. Torrance said. "But how will we ensure no one goes outside of the maze."

"I've stationed a footman at each exit. Should anyone accidently exit the maze, they will be guided back in the correct direction."

"What will happen if we are caught by the person who has to find us?" Genny wasn't sure she liked these rules. All sorts of things could go wrong, yet . . . yet, she could also search out Leo and no one would be the wiser.

"Then that person will sit out the rest of the game. So if you are going to hide, try to find a decent place, and be quiet. When there is one person left, the butler will call out to everyone who the winner is and the last person can remove their blindfold and make their way back to the center."

"An ingenious idea," Mr. Torrance said.

"The straws." Lady Carleton stuck out the pouch that held the sticks they would pick from. "I think we should let the gentlemen choose theirs first, if no one picks the shortest stick, then the ladies can draw them out all at once."

The gentlemen all picked long sticks from the pouch.

"And now for the ladies." Lady Carleton had them each choose a stick without pulling it out. "Are you ready?" They all nodded their head in unison. "Pull them out then."

They did as asked. Genny was pleased to see that she had a long stick and let out a sigh of relief.

Charlotte laughed. "Well, I'm glad I'm very familiar with this maze, because I plan to find you all within an hour." With a coquettish smile on her face, Charlotte held up the stick half as long as anyone else's.

"You are a wonderful sport, Lady Charlotte. Now turn about so I can fasten your blindfold." Charlotte did as asked. "If everyone will come over here, I'll blindfold you and walk you toward one of the paths so you can try and make your escape. You will have no more than the count of fifteen to hide."

How had he ever thought he couldn't get away with an afternoon tryst with the lady of his desires? Leo was glad that Genny hadn't pulled the shorter straw. All that remained was finding her once they were given leave to hide. Though he didn't like the idea of cheating by removing his blindfold in this superbly put together game, he might have to do just that if he wanted to sequester and completely isolate Genny somewhere along the path. He'd have another taste of her sweet lips before the morning was through.

Once everyone was blindfolded, he felt the gentle guidance of Lady Carleton as she led him toward the path he would take. Before she left him, she said in a hushed tone, "There is a smidgen of face powder on your chin. It looks like the sort of evidence you would generally take great care to hide."

Leo rubbed at his chin and brought his hand away to look at the evidence, realizing too late that he couldn't see what she referred to.

"That's better," Lady Carleton said. "Now take care to be more circumspect when you find yourself in a similar position in a few minutes."

He opened his mouth to say something, but to say what? Had Lady Carleton found out about last night? If Marks had said anything to the maids, he'd wring his neck and make him walk back to London.

Lady Carleton patted his arm. "Don't worry yourself overmuch. Your secret is safe with me."

"How . . . ?"

"Never you worry about that. After all, this is my house. And I know everything that happens in it." She gave him a little shove. "Now go, I've given everyone a head start of the counting. Miss Camden isn't that far ahead of you."

"I wouldn't ever hurt Genny."

"Yet you have done so in the past. Be careful with her. I do adore everything about her. I always have."

Leo headed down his path, arms stretched out on either side of him, feeling the way. If Lady Carleton knew what he and Genny were about, was it possible she knew about their past affair? He'd think about the possibilities of that and what it meant after he found Genny.

Which way would she have gone? He daren't call out her name; that might have them caught out rather quickly. Even if he did remove his blindfold he'd have to pick and choose between turns.

He hurried his pace, knowing the stones were relatively flat and the path had only one way to turn before it broke off into more forked options. He turned his ear toward the wind, catching the brief sound of rustling hedges.

Anxious to find her, he tore off his blindfold so he didn't stumble right over her should he catch up to her. A soft curse came from up ahead, a clear indication of her direction.

He came upon her quickly, spun her around, and covered her mouth with his when she gasped out a protest. She warmed to the kiss quickly, wrapping her arms around his shoulders and rubbing those delectable breasts of hers against his chest.

"We have to keep moving," he whispered. "We aren't far enough into the maze to not be found by your cousin."

She raised her hands to untie the material about her eyes, but he stopped her.

"Right now, I'm the only one cheating at this game," he said. "I'll find us a safe, quiet place and take care not to lead you too far astray in the gardens of this paradise."

She pushed at his chest playfully and stepped out of his arms.

"Isn't there a hidden alcove in here?"

"There are three dead ends," she confirmed.

"Can you tell me where they are? Or how we find them?"

"If you turn right at every fork, you'll eventually find one."

"Then that is exactly what we'll do." He took her hand and led her down the path. He came to a sudden halt on hearing a rustling just beyond their side of the hedged wall. He placed his fingers over Genny's mouth so she wouldn't say anything and they both listened. He leaned in and whispered, "Someone is close."

She nodded, letting him know she had heard a slight rustling, too. They waited for some minutes before quietly walking farther into the maze. Another swish sounded, but it was followed by a soft moan.

Genny covered her own mouth this time. He thought it was an action derived not from shock but to smother a startled laugh. So, they weren't the only couple meeting clandestinely.

Whispering in her ear, he asked, "Should we find out who it is?"

She shook her head. "They would see us together and assume . . ."

The rest didn't need to be said. Yes, she was right. But the need to know tugged him in the direction of the other houseguests.

"Don't make any noise till I tell you it's safe to do so." He didn't want them to risk getting caught. She complied, not knowing that he planned to find out who was around the hedge before finding another place to hide.

Carefully, Leo spied around the corner he was positive the lovers had ensconced themselves in, and sure enough, he was correct. The lady's skirts were tossed back, concealing her face. Her lover thrust up between her semi-exposed thighs, with his trousers loose about his hips, his blindfold still tightly tied at the back of his head. He would never have guessed that these two would be involved. Very interesting.

Turning back the way he'd come, he nudged Genny in a different direction. When they were far enough out of earshot, he said, "Our private alcove was occupied."

"Did you see who it was?"

"I thought you didn't want to know?"

"I don't. But did you see them?"

"I did. And what a fine gossip column this would make."

Genny's mouth dropped open. She covered her expression of surprise with her gloved hand. "Say no more, I really don't want to have that kind of incriminating knowledge. What if someone should somehow finagle the truth from me?"

"Then their secret will be safe with me. Unless I should need to use it against either party involved."

"Leo, you're terrible."

"True, but sometimes the best defense against society is what you know and what information you've been privy to. How do you think my friends and I traverse society so easily with our reputations?"

"I never thought of it that way. Do you know something terrible about everyone?"

"Just about."

She was silent a moment before saying, "Never tell me. I don't want to be a part of anyone's downfall."

They walked for another five minutes before Leo came back to the center of the maze. Charlotte was nowhere in sight, and since every entrance to the center was connected one way or another, he led Genny to another path and made all the right turns she'd told him to make.

He untied her blindfold and pulled it away from her eyes when they reached their private little corner.

"Do you think we'll be safe from discovery?" she asked.

He placed his hand on the back of her head and pulled her close so her face rested against his tan-colored jacket. "We'll be extra careful. Will you meet me here later tonight when we don't have to worry overmuch about being caught?"

She raised her head suddenly when the wind rustled up branches around them.

"There is no one about," he assured her.

Her gaze clashed with his. "How can you possibly know that?"

He shrugged his shoulders. "I just do."

"How long do you think it's safe to stay here? Before either Charlotte or someone else manages to find us?"

"Everyone, aside from the couple currently enjoying their afternoon tryst, will be quietly hidden somewhere in the maze."

She worried her lower lip. "So you mean we'll be found together?"

"I doubt it. But to play it safe, we'll only stay here together for a short time. I'll leave just as soon as I've had my fill of you."

He pulled her down so she was sitting atop his lap on the small rounded bench that filled the dead end. "How is it that you know your way around this maze better than I do? I grew up next door, spent my younger years causing all sorts of havoc around town, yet I never ventured over here to figure out the secrets of this maze."

"I spent two summers here," Genny said. "The first time was the year before I met you. I tend to wander about at odd hours of the night to look at the stars. Not all the time, just when it's too hot to sleep comfortably."

"Any time you are feeling restless, you need but knock on my door."

She shook her head, but was smiling at him. "Only you would say such a thing."

"I mean that in more than one way. If you want to go for a walk, Genny, I think I've proven to you that I'm happy with simply spending time in your company."

"Yes, you have." She placed her palm against the side of his face and leaned in to give him a sweet kiss on the lips. "But I like kissing you no matter where we are or what we are doing."

"I couldn't agree more with that sentiment." Placing his hands against her face, he noticed a residual powder. "Genny, since when have you worn cosmetics?"

"I don't." She pulled back, shock in her expression at being discovered. "I'll endeavor to never wear it again if it's so noticeable. But I looked dreadful this morning."

"Well tumbled, I imagine." He grinned, happy to have been the cause of it. "And that reminds me . . . it seems we have an ally."

Abruptly, she stood from his lap and looked around them nervously.

"There are no allies for what we are engaging in." Her agitation was clear in the animated way she spoke with her hands. "People will use information about our affair against us should it be of benefit to them. You said yourself that that is what you do when needed."

"She wouldn't share this information with anyone, Genny. And I haven't had to use the gossip I know for any betterment."

"And what of your friends? Have they?"

His silence must have been answer enough to that question.

"I thought so. Who is it that you consider an ally? No, wait." She waved her hands in front of her, closed her eyes as though it could block the truth. "I don't think I could bear to know. I'd blush like a naïve virgin every time I looked at them. Don't say another word."

"I'll say no more, but you should know that she is a friend who is above gossip."

Genny pressed her fingers lightly to his mouth.

"My lips are sealed, then." He kissed her lace-gloved hands, and nibbled the tip of one finger before she pulled slowly away.

"You should go," she said in a hushed voice.

"Soon. I'm not done with you yet." He took her hand in his and pulled her back onto his lap, letting her feel his arousal. She grinded down on him and moved his hand to cover one of her breasts.

"What I'd give to take you here," he said.

"I want you to touch me."

He hiked up her skirts and burrowed his hands between her thighs searching for the slit in her drawers. When he found it, his finger slicked through the fluids that had built up in her excitement.

She pressed her mouth to his, and wrapped her slender arms around his shoulders in acceptance when he inserted his middle finger into her tight quim. Goddamn, he wanted to be inside her in a completely different way. He settled for rubbing her clitoris simultaneously with quick thrusts of his fingers inside her velvety sheath. He bit her lip gently to remind her that she needed to remain quiet.

He adjusted himself as best he could in his trousers, thrusting up into her heavy skirts with every forward jerk of her pelvis as she rode out her pleasure on his hand. It would be so easy to slip open his trousers and take her here. He needed her.

"Let me have you." He nibbled at her earlobe hoping she wouldn't say no. He so badly needed to be inside her. The danger of their actions, of the possibility of being caught, spurred them both on and heightened their appetites for something more titillating and dangerous.

When she nodded, he tossed her skirts forward more fiercely in his need to have her, released the ties on his trousers, and took his cock in hand. Fuck, he'd never needed her so bad as he did now. He settled her on his lap so her back was to his chest and pulled her hips down hard on his aching cock.

One hand guided her hip, the other wrapped around her front and pressed and rubbed at her bound breasts.

For leverage, she put both her feet on the ground and rode him as hard as he pounded up into her. When she made those sounds again that drove him mad with lust, he put his fingers in her mouth and said, "Bite down on them."

When she did, he knew it was because her orgasm took hold of her. He took her as hard as he could in this position, letting her sheath milk him for all his worth. He yanked her down on him as his come spurted out into the sweet haven between her thighs.

Shit. He hadn't meant to come in her. "I'm sorry."

She leaned her head back onto his shoulder. "For what?"

"I didn't pull out."

"It's okay. I'm not near . . ."

He wasn't sure if she stalled because she had to catch her breath or because she didn't know how to word what she was going to say.

"No harm will come of it," she finished. "We are safe right now."

He nodded against her and kissed the side of her neck. "I'll not forget myself again."

"I like it when you forget yourself." She reached her arm around and cradled his head in the crook of her neck.

They sat on the bench like that for some time. There was no way he'd ever get enough of her, so he stood her up on wobbly feet and put himself back together. Genny dabbed a handkerchief over her perspiring face and flattened out the wrinkles in her skirts.

The shush of slippered feet headed in their direction. They both looked toward the opening in the maze. Not knowing where the sound came from, he held out Genny's blindfold and she obligingly turned her back to him so he could secure it behind her head. He went around the corner first, wondering if he'd step directly into someone's path. There was no one there, so he led Genny quietly away from the noise they had heard in order to whisper in her ear.

"I know you haven't said yes to tonight, but give it some thought. I would love to see you again, Genny." He brushed the back of his hand lightly over the side of her face. "I'm going to leave you here, and it'll be your choice if you want to find another spot to hide. I'm going to tie my blindfold back in place and head in another direction."

"Thank you for finding me, Leo. I am glad I could spend even this short amount of time with you."

He gave her a quick peck on the lips. "I will see you at luncheon, when the game has concluded." He gave her one more kiss for good luck. This time he slipped his tongue gently between her lips and tangled it with hers before pulling away. "Good luck."

Then he headed down the path, away from the lady who was not only driving him mad with lust, but with a much deeper feeling of affection than he'd previously felt for her.

Chapter 17

I ponder the reason for Lord B——'s current de-
votion. Could he be slipping in his normally cir-
cumspect manner? To date, there are only rumors
surrounding his scandalous proclivities. That is
not to say that what is whispered isn't true, just yet
to be proven. Does he intend to publicly ruin a
woman who by all accounts has no prospects and
offers no political gain? How incredibly out of
character this current behavior is.

I am still awaiting news of any illicit behavior at
the most talked-about house party of every season.
Having already mentioned oddities, I find it rather
peculiar that no stories have emerged after nearly
two weeks. Never fear, this writer will dig up some
tale before the week concludes.

The Mayfair Chronicles, August 2, 1846

There must be something about being reckless that ap-
pealed to her. Could it be an inherited malady that made
her act so impulsively and scandalously? Whatever it was,
it had her up past the witching hour and searching for her
lover under the cover of night once again.

She'd contemplated sleep as opposed to what she was about to commit to. But after tossing in her bed for the past two hours with a frenzied mind on what she should do, she'd been unable to resist the lure as the midnight hour approached.

As she slipped around another corner of the tall-hedged maze, she worked her way toward the fountain. She could just hear the trickling sound of water at the center.

She knew perfectly well that Leo had suggested they meet here because of its total seclusion and privacy from the main house. And unless someone else was meeting for an assignation out of doors, the night was theirs alone. Rounding the last corner, she came to a sudden halt on reaching her destination.

The overhead sky was clear and dotted with millions of little stars, bringing light to the dark enshrouded path around them.

Leo stood up from one of the granite benches that flanked the fountain, reminiscent of a powerful predator stalking his mate. She swallowed against the sudden dryness in her throat and dropped both hands anxiously at her sides. She almost couldn't believe she was here, willing and ready to be seduced by him.

He wore dark trousers and loose shirtsleeves. She could see the dip at his throat and the hair sprinkled on his chest at the open vee. She wanted to press her face into all the strength and listen to the steady beat of his heart. The thought brought back memories of their past times, and of last night.

The closer he came, the more real the moment felt. She could make out the laugh lines around his eyes, the softness of his hair now that the pomade taming his loose curls had been washed away.

Her gaze slipped past his shoulder for a moment where she spied a basket and blanket. The very idea that he came well prepared for an evening of seduction made her smile.

"I wasn't sure you would come after all your teasing and hinting otherwise." The backs of his fingers caressed the underside of her jaw and cheek, drawing her attention solely to him.

"I almost didn't." Her voice was throaty, seductive even to her own ears. "This feels more dangerous than last time. I'm more afraid of being caught."

His thumb stroked over her lower lip and his fingers lightly grazed over her cheek. "What made you change your mind?"

"I'm not precisely sure."

His smile was magnetic and wicked and she found herself leaning closer so she could have a nibble at his lips.

"I'll make this worth your having to sneak around and the sleeplessness to come." He took her hand and led her farther into the lion's den. "How do you feel about a nightcap?"

"What have you pilfered from the kitchen?"

"Only some strawberries." That dashing smile of his was like a flash of welcome light in the pitch-black night. "The champagne I purloined from the wine cellar."

"Was it your plan all along to make me tipsy so you could properly take advantage of me?" Not that she had any objections to this mad plan of his.

He released her hand and bid her to sit on the blanket-shrouded bench. The dribble of water from the fountain was calming and added a pleasant ambiance to the setting.

"Though I don't think we need to imbibe in anything to go down the path we're headed." He popped the cork smoothly on the champagne bottle and poured out two glasses. Removing a bowl full of tiny field strawberries, he plucked the green ends off two and dropped them into each of their bubbling, fizzy drinks.

Taking a seat next to her on the bench, he tipped one glass to her lips and bid her to drink. "Does this meet with your approval?"

The coolness of the drink infused her mouth as the bubbles trickled down her throat. The strawberry added just the right amount of zest to the dry beverage.

He eyed her intently as he waited for her answer. All the while he swirled the strawberry in his champagne flute round and round.

She licked at her top lip suggestively before finally saying, "There can't be anything more delicious."

"I can think of a few things." His gaze dropped to her mouth and trailed a hot path down the front of her peignoir. She felt his gaze like a heavy petting touch, and it heated her skin and had her heart pounding in her breast.

Oh, God, she craved his touch like never before. These last two nights felt so much different than all those years ago when they'd been young and in too much of a rush for a slow seduction. Much like wine, time seemed to make some things better.

Leo tipped his head back and took a sip from his glass, catching the little red berry on his tongue. She shamelessly watched his throat work as he swallowed the champagne.

Setting the glass down on the edge of the fountain, he wrapped one big hand around the nape of her neck and inched her forward on the bench. His mouth descended upon her parted lips, the berry from his drink he held tenderly between his teeth. Her eyes slid shut as their lips met and the strawberry was pushed into her mouth. She didn't bite into it right away, but let it slide over her tongue and around his as though it were a game to capture the sweet morsel of fruit. As he pulled away, her teeth sank into the soft flesh of the berry.

Tongue sweeping out to lick off her lips, Leo swooped back in for another taste. Though gentle and still playful, this kiss felt more demanding as their tongues tangled.

She wanted to wrap her arms around his neck, pull him closer, and never let him go. He must have had the same thoughts for he plucked the glass from between her lax fingers and settled it next to his on the edge of the fountain.

"I want to taste every inch of you again, Genny."

Too afraid to express just how much she desired him in equal measure, she pulled loose the satin ribbon that cinched her peignoir tightly at her rib cage. Leo watched the material separate, and when it caught at the top swell of her breast, he pulled at the strands and slipped the soft muslin from her shoulders.

She shivered as the night air brushed the fine hair along her forearms. Leo ran the palms of his hands down them as if to warm her, but she was shivering for an entirely different reason than the cool breeze that wrapped around them.

Unable to resist any longer, she reached forward to pull the tails of his shirt free from his trousers. Though they'd been intimate yesterday, this still felt new. A lot had changed over the years for them. They were essentially the same people . . . yet different. And so much remained to be explored of each other.

Leo pulled away before she could hike the obtrusive material of his shirt over his head. "We have all evening, and I promised to take this slowly."

"Not to me, you didn't."

His chuckled before standing from the bench to retrieve their drinks. Was he attempting to keep a safe distance? Trying to tamp down his attraction so he wouldn't pounce like she thought he would have done only a moment ago? Oh, she really wanted him to seize and lay claim to her, body and soul.

"I asked you to come here not only to spend the night

with me, but so we could talk privately without being overheard."

"What is it you wish to discuss?" She held out her hand to him in invitation. "Leo, come back and keep me warm."

He handed her glass back to her and topped up both flutes. "What happens after this?"

Genny tipped back the rest of the contents in her glass and held it out for Leo to top it up with more. "Why the champagne and strawberries if you don't wish to seduce me? Is this part of your plan . . . your game? Do you want to lead on the hapless chaperone? Ruin me in society's eyes for some sort of wager?"

"God, no." He swept his hand through his hair in agitation. "Don't be ridiculous, Genny. I only want to discuss what the outcome of the house party will be. I want to know your expectations. It was wrong of me to not ask you the first time after we made love, and I'll not repeat that mistake."

Was he rethinking his earlier sentiments of a more permanent attachment? Had she read him wrong last night, or had she misunderstood his meaning? "I'm a little savvier than I used to be and understand a great deal more about these types of affairs. We can cut our ties when we head back to Town. Just as we did in the past if that is what you wish." Genny couldn't help but take a huge swallow of the champagne before delivering the rest of her short speech. "I'll not force or trap you into a marriage you do not want."

"And if I don't want to leave?"

She shut her mouth with an almost audible snap and tilted her head to the side in question. "What exactly do you want from me?"

"The only thing I know with certainty is that this isn't the same as it was four years ago."

And wasn't that the truth. She was going in with both

eyes wide open this time, and she still wanted something more, even though by all appearances this was only an affair.

"I didn't want to leave you the first time," he said. "But was convinced otherwise."

"By whom?"

"I asked my father's advice on marriage . . . his suggestion proved to be unhelpful and not at all what I wanted for us."

"I would like to think we are smarter now than we were then." She took another sip from her refilled glass. What was she supposed to say? Ask him if this was a proposal? If it was, it certainly was the oddest proposal she had ever received.

"All I'm saying is that it doesn't necessarily end here, Genny."

She felt her hopes drop with the suggestion. "So we should carry on our affair in London?"

"That's not precisely what I mean."

She cocked her eyebrow and looked at him questioningly. She'd not play guessing games all evening. And really, he was killing the intimate mood they had shared. She felt silly sitting in the secluded garden maze half-dressed, so she put down her fluted glass and pulled the loose ties together on her night robe.

Leo came forward and grasped both her hands in one of his, effectively preventing her from dressing herself.

"Don't," he said. "I only want to say that perhaps we should have a real go at courting when we are back in London. While the passion between us is very real, I think there is a lot more to be had. You make me want to be a better man. What exactly better means I can't say, but I'm willing to explore it with you."

It was the most utterly romantic thing anyone had ever said to her. And she wanted to believe she could so easily give herself over to her wants, but life was never so simple, especially with the current position she was in.

She laughed bitterly even though the situation didn't warrant any such reaction. She couldn't help it since it was derived from sadness. Yes, she'd hoped for more from him four years ago, but everything was different now. She wasn't in a position to be courted. Lord Ponsley would certainly object, not only because she would become a spectacle if things turned sour between her and Leo but because he'd already warned her about any association with him.

"My circumstances don't allow for more than what we share now."

He sat next to her on the bench again. "I think that's a poor excuse, Genny."

"I assure you, it is not. Lord Ponsley will never allow it. I'm to be here for his daughter until she is wed."

"And after?"

"Are you suggesting you will wait?"

He paused, obviously mulling over his answer. "No, I refuse to wait. This will happen. Run away with me now, we'll obtain a license to marry without delay."

Genny placed her palm along his cheek. Life had never been more unfair than it was now. "I've been given very specific instructions to avoid contact with you. You cannot go against my benefactor's wishes. To do so would certainly ruin my livelihood. I also cannot leave Charlotte in the middle of the season, for it would taint her reputation as well."

"I will not let the bastard have the last say in this."

"For now, it has to be." Genny pressed her forehead to his.

"Trust me to find a way around this."

"Why not wait until Charlotte is married?" Maybe they could run away together.

"Why should we wait at all?" He kissed her cheek.

She leaned in and kissed him tenderly on the lips, lingering for some moments in the warm closeness of their bodies. She had never felt more right than when she was in his arms. That had been the reason she'd turned down two offers of marriage from other suitors. How could she betray her heart when she certainly couldn't betray the kind men who had offered for her when they deserved someone who could return their affections wholly and completely?

Could she trust Leo after everything they'd already been through? She had no answer to that.

She pulled back from his lips and whispered, "Make love to me, Leo."

"As the lady wishes."

So many thoughts went through Leo's mind when he should be focused on the one thing he could give Genny at the moment.

A night never to be forgotten.

He'd make her crave his touch so thoroughly that it would be impossible for her to go back to London and forget their time here together. Ponsley was another matter entirely. The old man hated him for so many reasons already that a courtship with Genny could be nigh impossible. He'd figure it out regardless because he knew without doubt that he'd not be able to walk away from Genny a second time. In fact, he refused to do so.

Pulling the ribbon ties loose at the front of her nightgown, Leo brushed the material aside, giving him his first glimpse tonight of the soft swell of her breasts.

He exhaled a long breath and brushed his knuckles over the plumpness while his gaze devoured every morsel of flesh revealed. Slowly raising his gaze back to Genny's eyes, he could see that her pupils ate up the whiskey-colored irises. Her cheeks were infused with the slightest hint of pink and her lower lip was damp where she'd licked at it.

Sliding his hand over her shoulders and under her loosened robe, he removed the first layer. Her night rail was nothing spectacular, simple white with ruched shoulder caps. An evening corset cinched her waist and the strings wrapped around the front before circling to the back where they knotted. There was something provocative about seeing her breasts bared above her stays, and he was almost tempted to leave it just as it was. Almost.

"It's only fair that you remove an article of clothing, since I have," she said suggestively. The wanton sound lacing her voice had his cock throbbing painfully in his trousers.

"You are wearing significantly more layers than I."

She raised one brow. "And whose fault is that?"

He chuckled as he reached behind his neck and pulled his shirt over his head. Genny's fingers grasped the neckline of the garment to aid him in tugging it off. When he tossed the shirt to the ground, her fingers threaded through his hair, the tips of her nails gently scoring his scalp.

"I always did prefer your hair without the stiffening product you put in it."

Leo closed his eyes and was glad that he had thought to wash it before gathering up all the items they'd need for an evening outdoors. Her fingers worked their magic as they smoothed over the back of his head and then skimmed lower to mold to his shoulders and back.

Leaning closer to her, he pulled her lips between his. He was rewarded with a moan and the thrust of her tongue in his mouth.

"You've missed me, have you?" he said.

"I've forgotten how good it feels to be in your arms night after night."

"Should I feel insulted that I'm not more memorable?"

She playfully shoved his shoulder. "Stop teasing me, you rogue."

"We should get back to removing more of these pesky layers still separating us." He pulled away from their kiss and waggled his eyebrows at her before catching her around the waist and tugging at the strings that held her stays firmly in place. "This should be the first thing to go."

Spanning his hands over the boneless contraption cinching her waist, he slowly worked his fingers over the taut strings at the back, plucking each until he found the knotted ball at the middle of her back and pulling the looped strings to undo the corset.

Running his fingers under the top seam of the garment, he pressed against the heated cambric chemise that covered her from the ribs down. Her breath caught with the intimate touch. He wanted to bury his face between their softness and gently bite the undersides as he teased her nipples between his fingers.

Never had simply touching someone felt so good or made his cock throb so desperately.

Hooking his thumbs behind the edge of the material, he pulled each side of the corset toward her center and released the clasps that held it in place. When the corset fell around her hips, he yanked it away and threw it atop his discarded shirt.

"It's your turn, now," she said. Her mouth was parted, and her breathing came a little faster.

"I feel the odds are in your favor for this game."

"As they should be."

This was the Genny he remembered—playful and daring, not prim and proper.

He cupped her breast through her chemise, taking the whole weight in his hand and then gently plucking the firm tip between his fore and middle fingers before standing.

Resting one foot atop the bench, he loosened the laces on his shoe. "Hmmm, I don't seem to have my valet on hand to help me undress properly."

"Sit down, Leo."

He complied with a smile. "I aim to please, madam."

"Yourself, you mean." She stood and made her way around to face him. When she knelt to the ground and grasped his shoe with both hands, he could see the two perfect swells of her breasts down the front of her gaping chemise. She pulled hard on his shoe and would have fallen solidly on her bottom had he not grabbed hold of her arms to steady her.

"There, now the other one." She seemed pleased with her result.

"I think not, my lady. That would be two articles of clothing to your one. Wholly unfair considering the rules of this game."

He took both her hands in his and bid her stand before him. She placed her hands on his shoulders and looked down at him.

"What shall it be then?"

Grasping the back of her knee, he lifted her leg so her foot rested on the bench beside his thigh. "I think it only fair that I take a stocking for each of my shoes."

Leo pushed the layered underskirts high on her right thigh, taking time to smooth his hands over her fine calves. Never had he touched a more perfect creature.

One of her hands lay relaxed at her side, the other clasped the soft folds of the bunched-up material over her midriff.

She bit her lip, letting him glimpse the white even row of her teeth as she hissed in a breath with his first caress.

Her legs were nicely formed. The muscles rose partially at the backs of her calves and were firm to his touch. He leaned forward, pressing his chest to her raised shin, allowing his hands to sweep over the back of her knees, and finally over her stocking-clad thighs. He stopped his exploration only when he reached the garter and bare skin between stockings and drawers.

He rested his forehead against the material covering her bent thigh and tucked his fingers beneath the edge of her stocking. There was no way he could refuse what she silently asked for when she tilted her pelvis forward in offering. His hands moved higher, finding the slit in her drawers as he sought the sweetest part of her.

When his fingers found her slick center, he slipped his middle finger slowly inside. The silky wetness that met his touch made him want to take her now, in every way imaginable, but he kept his pace unhurried, planting openmouthed kisses against her thigh. With his free hand, he released the tie holding up her stocking and worked it down to just below her knee.

He wanted to taste her skin and her juices on his tongue. Taking the flesh of her thigh in his mouth, he nibbled a hot path along the flesh he revealed in the torturously slow removal of her stocking.

Her fingers brushed through his hair before grasping it tightly as he inserted a second finger into her tight sheath.

The mewl that escaped her mouth had him pumping his fingers a little faster. Not so fast that they were lost in their ecstasy . . . not yet. He wanted to draw this out, have them spend the whole evening so thoroughly wrapped around each other that there was no telling where one of them started and the other ended.

She couldn't believe she was here, doing this with Leo . . . *again*. But the further into their intimacy they got, the less she was able to even think of pulling back. She wanted him more—if such a thing were possible—than she had when she was younger.

Did one's cravings grow stronger with age? She thought maybe they did, because nothing short of scandalous exposure to the rest of their guests could stop her now.

The feel of his teeth nipping at her flesh made her insides melt and her body relax into his. Her juices were thick on his fingers, and she felt her drawers growing damp where he pumped them inside of her. It wasn't his hands or his tongue that she craved deep inside her but another part of him altogether.

"Leo," she said huskily, since her throat had dried out with the panting and sensuous sounds that fell past her lips. "My legs are going to turn to jelly if you don't let me sit down soon."

She swore she heard a frustrated growl from him as he nearly tore the tie off her other stocking so he could pull that one down as well.

"Sit beside me on the bench so I can get my other shoe off."

Instead of doing as he asked, she went down on her haunches once more and pulled off his second shoe. Before it hit the ground beside her, he caught her up by the arms and sat her on the bench facing him.

"Straddle your legs over either side." His hands rested gently against her thighs, urging her to do just that.

It hit her all of a sudden what she was participating in. The gall she must have to do this to herself twice.

He cupped her face, drawing her gaze back to him, and gave her a swift kiss. "You're thinking too hard, love. Just relax and trust me."

"I do trust you." Just as she'd trusted him all those years ago to make sure her reputation was protected and their affair remained discreet. He'd not do her wrong now after so many years of silence.

He straddled the stone bench in front of her and positioned her so her legs were over either of his hips. She locked her ankles at the small of his back. The jut of his cock pressed into the warm vee of her body. Genny wrapped her arms around his shoulders and pulled him in tight to her breasts. She just wanted to feel him like this a little longer, put to memory an imprint of his stronger body crushed to hers in a comforting embrace.

His hands came up and cupped the back of her head. He whispered, "Genny," then clasped his fingers tight in her hair, tilted her head back and slanted his mouth over hers.

The kiss was slow and deep. She lowered her hands to find the buttons holding his trousers in place. She wanted them off. She wanted him naked and pressed tight against her overheating flesh. She wanted their bodies to grow damp as their passion rose.

He placed his knee against the stone, with her still wrapped about his waist. She didn't hold back her desires; it simply wasn't possible to do so. She rubbed her most private area against the top edge of his manhood, needing to feel it so much harder against her and pounding inside her.

She wanted to feel him fully naked against her, all flesh and blood, and all heated and hard man as he laid her out on the bench. One of her legs was urged above his shoulder. He lowered his mouth and kissed softly at her stomach, her navel, and higher between her breasts.

He yanked at the material still covering her, stretching and tearing the seams at the shoulder until the garment could be pulled fully beneath her bared breasts. The cool night air kissed her in the same moment Leo licked his tongue down the center of her sternum. Both of his hands pressed and squeezed at her breasts as he kissed first one and then the other.

When he pulled away, he took her hand and pressed her fingers between her thighs and against the wetness at her core. "How much do you want me?"

"I ache so badly for you," she whispered.

She wanted to rub at the knot of nerves throbbing and pulsating for more, but she also wanted to stretch out the pleasure they shared.

"Touch yourself, Genny. I want to see how you like to be touched."

"I want your fingers back inside me."

"Show me," he demanded.

And she did. She pushed two fingers inside her sheath and couldn't stop the moan any more than she could deny touching herself at Leo's request.

She was forced to pull away when Leo removed her drawers and his trousers. He settled on the bench again, his cock jutting straight up in bold demand to be touched. He pressed her small foot against the rigid length, urging her to stroke it gently as he leaned over to blow a warm stream of air over her wet sheath. Opening the lips of her sex, he swirled his tongue around the tight bundle of nerves, then dipped lower and stroked between the lips of her sex. Finally, he pumped his tongue inside, mimicking the act they would soon engage in.

"Leo," she groaned, hands holding the bench tight in her grasp above her head. When he raised his eyes to hers, tongue lightly rubbing over that most sensitive part of her, she nearly forgot what she was going to ask. "I'm yours to take. Please . . . I need you inside of me."

His hands grasped her hips tight and pulled her down the length of his shaft till their bodies were pressed as close together as was possible. He held her in his immovable grip as he flicked his tongue over one of her nipples and sucked it deep into his mouth. Her hands curled around his head, holding him closer, wanting so much more as her body adjusted to his wide width.

She felt the inner wall of her sheath clenching of its own accord around his heavy, straining length.

And then he was moving in long, even strokes that had her exhaling roughly with each thrust. His hands went under her bottom, squeezing the cheeks of her buttocks as he held her lower body elevated from the chilly blanket-covered stone.

Pressing her fingers along the corded muscle in his back, she held on as the tempo of their lovemaking increased.

"I can't express how much I've missed this," he said next to her ear as he nibbled on the lobe. His tempo slowed to a steady rhythm.

She could be no less than honest with him. "I have, too."

"Say you'll give me more time. Say you won't let this end with the summer break."

"I can't make any promises, Leo."

His hand lowered between them, and his thumb pressed and rubbed her clitoris. She knew the moment he touched her that she'd explode around him.

"You've undone me," she moaned before his mouth descended upon hers. Little stars exploded behind her eyes and lit up every nerve in her body. She was on fire, and the inferno burned through her body in a blazing fire that took some minutes to ebb to a slow simmer.

Leo thrust harder and faster into her, adding to her pleasure. Pulling out at his climax, he took himself in hand, pumping his seed into his palm. Genny sat up on the bench, legs still spread wide and kissed at his pectorals, tracing her fingers over the sinewy sweat-slicked lines of his torso.

He wrapped his arm around her back and held her close as she explored his body with hands and tongue. Scoring the tips of her nails through the coarse hair that speckled the center of his chest. She also drew circles around his small dark areolas before laying kisses upon them.

His hand cupped the back of her head once again and lifted her so he could kiss her full on the mouth.

As he pulled away, she noticed that desire was still etched in his eyes.

"We are so far from done, Genny." Leo pressed her hand against his renewed hardness. "But we'll give you a rest and clean ourselves up."

"You know how to make a lady's heart flutter in anticipation." She batted her lashes teasingly at him.

He grabbed up a cloth that was tossed atop the picnic basket and wiped his hand off. Folding the material, he pressed it between her thighs and wiped away the evidence of their intimacies.

Chapter 18

Salacious scandal is afoot. This bit of gossip took place in Town . . . of all the unfashionable places to be during the summer season . . .
     The Mayfair Chronicles, August 4, 1846

Genny gathered up her peignoir and pulled it over her shoulders. Her night rail had definitely seen better days but she would not sit out in the open, naked to the world. Leo pulled on his trousers, retrieved their champagne, and returned to the bench.

"Shall we gaze at the stars for a bit?" He wrapped his arm around her waist and slid her closer to his side. "You have yet to make an astronomer out of me."

Genny tipped back her fluted glass and looked skyward. "The clouds make it difficult to see any of the patterns. I doubt I could trace a single zodiac. It may clear up in a bit."

His lips pressed against the side of her neck. "Then I will have to think of better things to trace."

Genny closed her eyes and swayed toward him, lost in the sensation of his gentle touches.

"Leo?"

"Hmm?" He couldn't talk when he was nibbling at her earlobe and biting gently at the arch of her neck.

"When I asked you to wait before approaching Lord Ponsley . . ."

The loss of his lips sent a shiver down her spine. She pulled her garments snuggly around her body, not that it helped to warm her any.

"Didn't we decide our course of action . . . for us, that is?" he asked.

"I wanted to tell you that Charlotte will be married come fall. It hasn't been announced yet, and I shouldn't tell you even that much, but I think you need to know." She worried her lower lip. "It won't be a long wait."

"Any time away from you will feel like an eternity."

Her heart beat frantically in her chest, it was so full of joy. Those words further confirmed that he had every intention of marrying her, but she'd still make him wait till her cousin was wed before he so much as attempted to court her.

Closing her arms around his shoulders, she pulled herself over him so she sat astride his thighs. Her hands immediately threaded through his hair, her mouth pressed gently to his. They did no more than kiss for some time, Leo stroking her back, letting her decide the pace and depth of their intimacy.

She'd always felt a deep connection with Leo. As if they were two kindred spirits meant to come together eventually. Being in his arms just felt right.

Was that what love felt like for everyone? Was it the rush of her blood pumping her heart faster, the tingling sensation that made her belly all aflutter with nerves, the happiness that filled her very soul whenever she was by his side and they could forget their positions in society and just be themselves with each other?

She pulled away and stared into his deep brown irises.

"What is it, princess?"

"Did you intend for me to fall in love with you?" she asked earnestly, not sure why she'd said it. "Is that what you were after all along?"

When he didn't answer right away she dropped her gaze from his. His finger lifted her chin, forcing her to look him in the eye again.

"Do you love me?" His voice was deep and husky, as though the very thought of her confession made his passions rise.

"Shouldn't that much be apparent?" she said shyly.

"No, not till you say so."

"I do love you." There was a profound expression of relief in his eyes before he kissed her hard on the mouth.

"Does that mean you return the sentiment?" She was almost afraid to hear his answer if he didn't feel the same way. What if he didn't love her as she loved him?

"I always have." His tone was soft.

She smiled and ran her fingers over either side of his face.

"I don't think I've ever felt this way before."

"Not even four years ago?"

She pushed a few strands of loose hair from her face. "Everything was so different back then."

"Not nearly as fun and freeing as it is now."

"You are teasing me, Leo, and it's putting me all out of sorts."

His finger brushed over her cheekbone. "I like the pretty shade of *rose* you turn when you're miffed."

She put her foot down on the ground, having every intention of leaving him here in the maze with no one but himself to mock. "I've just opened my heart up to you, and you use the opportunity to poke fun at me."

He caught her hand and hauled her back down onto his

lap. "Don't leave me here, Genny. I didn't mean anything by it."

With the guidance of his hands, he bid her to wrap her ankles around his back. Pressing her hips down, she felt the hard ridge of his sex at the dampened folds of her core.

"Many a man would say you have my balls in a noose."

She cringed with the image that presented. "Need you be so vulgar?"

"Another reason I need you in my life." He gave her one of his easy smiles. "You'll set me straight when I need it most."

"You never said it."

"Said what?"

"Leo." She crossed her arms over her chest and gave him a look of pure annoyance.

"Genny. I am falling madly, deeply, and completely in love with you. And waiting even one day to court you and then have to wait a respectable time to marry you is testing my very sanity."

"You intend to marry me?"

"I have since the moment we saw each other again. We should have married years ago. I certainly hope you'll have me." The way he phrased it almost made him sound vulnerable and unsure of himself. She'd never heard him sound this way before now.

She wanted to scream out her joy. But her excitement would have to wait till her cousin was wed because Lord Ponsley wouldn't allow Barrington and her to have a proper courtship. She was sure they'd have to marry either by special license or ride to Gretna Green when the time came. "December. Let us make our intentions clear in December."

His expression brightened. "Is that a promise, Genny?"

Biting her lip to keep from screaming out her utter

happiness, she nodded her head and grinned like the fool she surly resembled.

"I have an idea," he said.

He suddenly lifted her off his lap, tied her peignoir tight around her waist, and dumped their unfinished champagne in a hedge.

"What are you doing?" She had wanted to finish that champagne.

"Taking you somewhere more comfortable for one."

"Back to your room?"

He paused and thought over his answer before giving her a response. "In a sense." Gathering up the blanket and holding it bunched up under one arm, he placed the glasses, the empty bottle, and her stockings in the basket.

"Let me take something," she said.

He handed her the blanket and grabbed her hand with his free one. "Will you give me your complete trust right now?"

"Of course. Haven't I done so at every opportunity?"

"Then we'll go to my house. It's ten minutes there, ten back. It will invigorate us for later," he said with a sly grin. "And no one will see us together there. And we really can be as loud as we like."

"What would your staff think?"

"They'll all be abed. They keep to their country hours. Your reputation is safe with me, Miss Camden."

"They won't talk to Lady Carleton's staff? That's often the way rumor spreads. I don't want to be the one whispered about come morning."

"You won't. My staff is loyal. Besides, if you still agree to marry me in five months' time, they'll be yours to command."

She frowned. "I'll not command anyone."

"Then they will adore you all the more. But"—he

stopped to press his mouth to hers—"not nearly as much as I."

It took them nearly forty minutes to reach his estate. It was his fault for kissing her. She hadn't been able to resist kissing him back, which had led to touching, then groping, then them on the lawn with her night rail hiked up to her hips and his trousers down around his shins.

They were both laughing and out of breath when they entered through the back portico. Genny looked around her, and though it was dark, and more clouds filled the sky, she could see that the gardens looked as extensive and well maintained out here as they had in the greenhouse.

The door they entered led to a large parlor. She could not make out the colors or see the furniture layout clearly without light. Leo took the blanket from her and tossed it on a sofa, laid the basket down on the floor, and then he took up her hand and led her through the dark house.

"Will you be showing me your etchings in your room, my lord?" It seemed an appropriate moment for a joke, though it was ruined when she couldn't cover her own laugh.

Leo pressed his hand to her bottom. "If I had any, it would be a novelty to fulfill your request."

"You're a rogue to suggest such a thing."

"Yes." He turned toward her and gathered her close. "But I wasn't the one to mention it, madam."

"You make me think and do very *wicked things,* Leo. I daresay it's your fault I even suggested such a thing."

"That I agree with. Now, come, before we are distracted in here as we were on the field."

When they entered his room, he lit a taper and placed it on a desk. "Make yourself comfortable. I need to retrieve something."

He disappeared in the room beyond his chamber. She

assumed it to be a dressing room. She picked up the candle and looked around the large room. The walls were a fairly light color, indistinguishable in the amber glow of the candle. The bed had four tall posts; she ran her fingers over the grooves of the pineapples carved into the dark wood pillars. It was an unusual design. Perhaps he'd shipped it over from the Americas or the West Indies.

A quilt was folded on an upholstered bench at the end of the bed. Sheets of soft pale satin covered his mattress, perfect for the summer climate. An array of pillows at least three deep adorned the head of the bed. Genny toed off her damp slippers and curled her toes into the plush carpet beneath. Turning, she spied a large painting set above the mantel. It looked to be a family portrait. A young Leo sat in his stepmother's lap. Her hair was dark. His father stood to the left with one hand around his stepmother's shoulder; his other hand was held forward and clasped in Leo's smaller hand.

"I was five when that was done. My stepmother said it was a miracle the artist finished it at all since I could barely sit still long enough for him to make significant daily progress."

"It's a lovely portrait. I only have a small locket, each side containing a painted image of my parents."

Leo pulled her hair over one shoulder and rubbed his knuckles over the little bone at the back of her neck. He kissed her there. "I have something for you."

His arms came around to the front of her, and he held out a gold chain with a ring dangling from it. As he clasped it around the nape of her neck, the weight of the ring fell to mid-breast. She picked it up and looked at the filigree ring. Three large gems were lined up in the center and delicate details swirled in gold around them.

"They're garnets. It's the ring my father gave to my stepmother. I'm giving it to you."

She turned in his arms, tears filling her eyes. "I can't possibly accept something so meaningful and cherished by your family."

When she reached behind her to unclasp and remove it, he stayed her hands.

"Yes you can. It will soon be your engagement ring." He paused, as though waiting for her to gainsay him. "You haven't changed your mind, have you?" His thumb wiped away the dampness from beneath her eyes. "What is all this crying about?"

She smiled through her tears. "I can't help it. I worry that Lord Ponsley will be against our union."

"Then we will forget formalities and ride for Gretna Green."

Gathering up the ring and chain, she tucked it beneath her night rail. "Thank you." She stepped up on her toes and pressed a kiss to his mouth just as the clock struck two. "We have to go back."

He placed a light shawl around her shoulders and led her back to the Carleton Estate.

It wasn't a night Genny would ever forget.

On reaching her room, she whispered in his ear, "Thank you for tonight."

"And every night to come." He kissed her quickly on the lips before ushering her into the safety of her room. She poked her head out to watch him walk down the corridor to his own chamber. A shadow caught her gaze but when she turned toward it, there was only a sheer curtain blowing in the breeze of an open window.

Chapter 19

Now for that scandal I promised . . . It has finally unfurled and is blooming into something so salivating that I can hardly contain my excitement. A certain duke, broken off from his mistress for well over a year now, has been spending an inordinate amount of time at the residence of a new lady. This is no courtship, dear readers, but a liaison if the extended late hours are anything to judge by. What man would steal into the back of a house—through the servants' entrance no less—if it weren't for something forbidden?

The Mayfair Chronicles, August 4, 1846

There was no doubt in his blasted mind—because really, what had he been thinking before now?—that he had to tell Genny the full truth. Even though he'd decided not to go through with the wager, or however the hell one defined his agreement and involvement in this charade, he still had to confess his intentions. This wasn't something he could keep from Genny any longer. She had a right to know the truth. And to judge him for said truth.

And he had to be the one to tell her. Because, so help

him, if she ever found out through another source, there would be no chance for forgiveness. This was assuming she'd forgive him. Last night had been meaningful for them both, though, so perhaps it would hold some weight in her final judgment against him?

They lay in his bed together; Leo traced teasing lines over her shoulder and her side. She brushed her fingers in small circles over his chest. The weight of the ring he'd given her lay between them.

The slow tick of the mantel clock was a constant reminder that the night was growing late. This was, he imagined, worse than a countdown for a public hanging. Time stood painfully still as he tried to find the words to tell Genny the whole truth. He had to stop stalling and spit out the hated words.

His arms wrapped tightly around her, and he kissed her as though this were the first and last time he'd have the opportunity to do so.

He pulled away from the kiss slowly. "The hour grows late."

She looked up at him with those forgiving, innocent eyes and it made him hate himself a little more. "I wish I could stay all night."

"I wish the same thing." He pulled away from her and reached for his trousers tossed near the bed on the floor. With a reluctant sigh, she gathered up her chemise and pulled it over her head.

"We only have a week left," he mused aloud.

"Don't remind me that our time grows short."

He pulled his shirt over his head and took Genny's hand and tugged her down to sit on the edge of the mattress with him. "There is something that needs to be said between us. Before you leave tonight."

"You sound so solemn and very serious." She rested her head on his shoulder and took his hands in her own.

Looking down at her, he saw the ring he'd given her around her neck. It glared at him accusingly. Would she forgive him once the truth was out? Would she still go through with the marriage?

It was hard to find the right words so he started at the beginning. "Do you remember when I asked you how you knew Lady Charlotte?"

She sat up and looked at him. Her happy, sated demeanor vanished and puzzlement filled her normally inquisitive expression. "Yes, I recall that day."

"You were right to distrust me when we first came upon each other at the Randalls ball."

She slid her hands away from his and folded them in her lap. He felt the loss of her touch like a slap to his face.

After a moment of silence, she said, "Precisely what is it you've done?"

He didn't wish to expose anyone else's involvement in the Lady Charlotte charade, but there would never be a chance at forgiveness if he didn't reveal everything.

"Tristan and I made a wager of sorts."

Leo watched her expression closely. Her smile completely vanished, and it was as though she were already putting the truth together for herself.

"What have you done?"

He rubbed his hand over his face. "Lest you judge me for any harm where your cousin is concerned, know that I made sure the wager wouldn't succeed."

Genny folded her arms over her chest. "I'm afraid you'll have to be more specific."

"When the Earl of Fallon passed, he left Jez in quite a state."

"And what has this to do with my cousin?" Her tone was clipped.

"He left Jez without a centime to her name. Mr. Warren stands to inherit everything that is rightfully hers."

"With her reputation, I don't understand how you think her deserving of Fallon's fortune."

Leo reached for her but she evaded him by leaving the bed. "She's a better sort than I ever was, Genny. Society has painted a less forgiving picture of her. This is what often happens to the fairer sex when they are treated as equals among men."

"You'll not convince me of her good name." Genny wiped away the few tears that trickled down the side of her face. "Now tell me the rest."

"She remains the dowager until Mr. Warren takes the seat, marries, and sires children of his own."

She moved farther away from him. "And Charlotte stands to inherit everything that was once the dowager's."

"Yes." Because Genny had figured out the truth on her own, it didn't make telling the rest any easier. Regardless, she deserved to hear the whole sordid tale. "We were to court your cousin and sway her decision to marry Mr. Warren."

"I trusted you, Leo." The way her face scrunched up in sadness and anger was like a punch to his gut. "You let me trust you."

He stood from the bed, shoved his hands in his pockets so he wasn't tempted to reach for her, and walked toward her. "I never wanted to hurt you."

"I see . . ."

Her lip quivered, and he wanted nothing more than to pull her into his arms and comfort her, but he knew she wouldn't allow it right now.

"So you willingly planned to seduce my cousin and ruin her chance for a decent marriage. What was the wager?"

"First man on top won my breeding mare from the Americas." He cringed at his own wording for that. There were a million other more appropriate ways to phrase it.

She came forward and struck him across the face so

hard with her open palm that his head whipped to the side. He'd seen it coming, but really, how could he dare stop her? He deserved that and so much more for the damage he had contemplated doing.

"How dare you," she said. "How dare you lie to me all this time. I can't believe I trusted you. How stupid am I?"

He couldn't keep from touching her, he reached out to hold both her arms in his hands, but she yanked away from him. "Have I done you any wrong so far?"

Looking into her sad eyes, knowing he was the cause of her sorrow, he felt as if his heart were pierced in two.

"You have," she said.

"I meant everything I said to you yesterday. Everything, Genny."

"I can only imagine what you thought on seeing me again. You probably thought to have a good go and get the better of me, didn't you?"

When he didn't respond, she said it more loudly, "Didn't you!"

"Believe me, Genny, I never wanted to hurt you."

Tears flooded her eyes again. "But you have."

He watched as she fought to keep those tears at bay, her mouth quivering and on the verge of sobs.

He had done this to her. He had made her a miserable wreck.

Was there any way to make her change her opinion of him? He doubted it as he watched those damnable tears finally spill over the rims of her eyes and slide down her cheeks.

He had been the sole cause of her sorrow. Her hatred.

And he deserved it.

She turned away, giving him her back as she wiped her eyes on the sleeve of her robe. "How did I ever trust you? For even a moment, how could I dare let my guard down?"

It wasn't a question she wanted an answer to; yet, he

needed to give her more. "I asked you to trust me, Genny. What reason should you have not to?"

"Because . . ." Her voice caught on another sob. "Because you made me believe that there was more than just a liaison between us. That you genuinely cared about me."

"Tell me how I can fix this?"

She turned back to him with tear-swollen eyes, her cheeks damp. "You can never make this better."

When he reached for her to pull her into his arms, she stepped away.

"There has to be a way."

"You have to leave, Leo." She shook her head back and forth. "I can't see you ever again. I *never* want to see you again."

"There has to be something . . ."

"There is *nothing* between us now." She pulled the ring and chain off over her head and balled it up in her fist. "I don't know how you thought I could forgive you for this. I can't. Not now. Not *ever*."

"We have three days left." That was three days to convince her that his feelings for her were genuine and that he would make up for the wrong he'd done for the rest of his days if that was the only way she could forgive him.

"If you respect me, have any feelings toward me . . . you'll go back to London and leave me to live my life out alone."

He shook his head. No, he'd never leave her. "Because I care a great deal for you, I cannot abide by your wishes."

She wiped away the wetness on her cheeks with the back of her hand. "You can and you must." She held out her fist with the ring he'd given her.

"It's yours." He didn't want it back. Taking it from her meant a life without Genny. He stepped away from it. "It's my promise to you."

She turned her hand palm down and let the necklace and ring fall to the carpeted floor. "You are nothing to me."

He did not believe her harsh words when they were accompanied by a fresh deluge of tears.

"You have ruined any possibility of a future between us." She sounded broken.

"Genny," he said, feeling more helpless as the minutes wore on and he made no progress in convincing her to stay and work this out with him.

"Don't." She held up her hand and visibly swallowed back another torrent of tears. "I don't want to see you here in the morning."

"You'll feel differently after a night's rest." She was understandably upset right now. But she'd told him she loved him—that had to count for something.

"How dare you think that I would so easily brush away a plot against my cousin! All you have proven is that I'm a fool for ever trusting you again."

She stormed past him in a flurry of rage, but he caught her arm before she could turn the door latch to leave without giving him so much as an option to make this better. He needed to fix the wrong he'd created.

"Genny . . . you can't leave like this."

She pulled out of his grasp, glaring at her arm and his hand as though he'd burned her with a hot iron.

"I never want to lay eyes upon you or your friends again. And if you are here come morning, I will take it to mean that your intentions to play with my cousin's feelings and life are still strong. And *that* I simply cannot abide. We are no longer lovers and certainly no longer friends, *Barrington*." She put her chin up defiantly. "From this point forward you are dead to me."

He was clenching his jaw so tightly that it cracked. "I refuse to give you up so easily."

"I will find a way to publicly expose your deed if you

don't. And I will make sure that your friend *Jezebel* is never invited to another social event so long as I am in London. I might only be a lowly paid companion, but I do have friends in high places that can make life difficult for your friend."

"I understand that you are upset, Genny, but at least give me time to make this up to you. I couldn't be honest before now. And after everything we've been through these past few weeks, I had hoped that you could at least forgive me my transgressions."

"To forgive you would mean that I condone your behavior, but I would never tolerate any actions that could intentionally harm another. You don't know me at all if you thought that this could be easily brushed under the carpet like yesterday's dust."

He put his hands up in surrender and stepped away from her. Nothing would be won tonight. Not when she was this upset. He'd find her in the morning and try again.

"Tell me what to do, Genny?"

"I want you gone from my life." The defeat was so palpable in her voice that he barely managed to take her in his arms to offer her any comfort he could.

He searched for any possibility of forgiveness in her eyes. There was nothing there but disappointment ... sadness, too.

"I will not leave."

"If you ever cared for me ... if you ever loved me, you'll do as I bid."

She turned away from him again and walked through the door without so much as a look back in his direction. Leo followed her into the hall and made sure no one watched her enter her private chambers.

When he was sure she was safely ensconced in her room, he leaned back against the inside of his closed chamber door. He'd known she would be angered by his deception. Why he'd expected anything less than what had just transpired between them was beyond him.

He still had tomorrow to convince her that he hadn't meant to harm her or her cousin. He would find a way to make this up to her.

Leo's head lightly thunked against the door behind him and he rubbed at his face with a heavy sigh. He'd really messed this up. He wasn't sure how to make it better, but he had to because he loved her.

Chapter 20

What do you suppose will happen if you toss a debutante, a man with only his charm and his father's undistinguished title to rely upon, and a distinguished member of high society all in a bowl as if they were a sticky, messy, commingling trifle? What a love triangle you create.
The Mayfair Chronicles, August 5, 1846

What a terrible muddle this was. How had she ever trusted him, or given in to him, or ever adored and fallen in love with him? She flung her arm over her eyes to block out the light from the morning sun.

A very small part of her stupidly wished he'd ignored her explicit wishes yesterday. What was wrong with her? The man had set out to ruin her cousin's chance at marrying a decent man with a decent title. Thank goodness he had told her before anything more serious could develop in their budding relationship.

Who was she fooling?

Something very serious had happened between them. They'd promised themselves to each other. They'd made firm plans to marry.

She let out a frustrated groan and covered her face with both arms. What did she have to be ashamed of? She'd done nothing wrong, aside from sleep with and fall in love with a man she promised herself years ago that she would wipe from her memory. She needed to pull herself together.

Forcing herself to leave the bed, she sat at her vanity and gathered up the last of her courage as she dressed her hair.

Charlotte exited her private chamber at the same time Genny did.

"No breakfast?" her cousin asked, carefully studying her.

Genny tied her bonnet beneath her chin. "I have a megrim that has diminished my appetite significantly."

"Let us walk this morning instead then," Charlotte said.

"That is just what the doctor ordered."

The sun was high in the sky and white balls of fluff danced across the blue. Genny leaned her head back and breathed in the cooler air. "It's the best day we've had since coming here."

Her cousin made a noncommittal noise, then asked, "Where is Lord Barrington this morning? This will be the first day he hasn't walked with us."

"How should I know what amuses him during the day," she snapped. She clapped her hand over her mouth. "I didn't mean to say it quite like that."

"You have had a row with him?" When Genny didn't respond, Charlotte added, "I wonder what you could possibly argue about; you were getting on famously."

"Lord Barrington has probably found another amusement to occupy his time." Genny took her cousin's arm and walked down the stone path that led to the creek. "Where is Ariel this morning?"

"Dinner was not agreeable to her. She looked green when I checked on her in her room."

"Oh, I do hope no one else is ill."

"Lady Hargrove said she wasn't feeling very well last evening but her illness seemed to pass with a good night's sleep."

Genny locked her arm with her cousin's. "We'll check on Ariel when we are back. See if she wants our company."

Her cousin grinned at her. "Oh, I already told her I would barge into her room after lunch if she didn't come down."

"How thoughtful of you."

Genny was glad for the change of topic so that less focus was put on her sour mood this morning. So far the day held a great deal of promise. However, it did not bode well that no one had confirmed whether or not Leo had left the residence. Perhaps he was preparing his bags right now.

She hated that her feelings were conflicted, that she wanted him both to leave and to stay and try and make amends. However, forgiveness simply wasn't possible after this recent betrayal.

They picked some flowers along the way, both holding a bouquet when they reached the path that led toward the stream. As they walked down the stone steps, they spied Leo sitting on the bench she usually rested on. She gave an unladylike stomp of her foot and slowed her pace intentionally. It was far more preferable to turn on her heel and go back to the house.

She pinched her lips together to keep from making a caustic remark. Charlotte did not need to know any more than she had already guessed.

Charlotte let go of Genny's arm. "He looks very somber this morning. Oddly enough, I would say he is as serious and disconcerting as you, cousin. I'll leave you to speak privately with him." Charlotte plucked the bouquet Genny held and took it with her.

"No . . ." She tried to grab her cousin's arm and drag

her back to her side, but Charlotte was already wending her way farther down the path to give her a moment alone with Barrington.

She supposed she had no choice but to speak with him. Demand once again he do the right thing and leave, even though she preferred not to talk to him at all, because the very sight of him tore at her heart.

She froze to the spot and couldn't seem to take another step forward. It didn't matter, because Leo stood from the bench and approached her with an earnest expression and a slow stride. He removed his hat when he stopped in front of her and twisted it around in his hands.

Genny crossed her arms over her chest.

"I see you're still upset with me."

She raised her brows and waited for him to say more.

"I wanted to apologize, Genny. I wanted to make things better between us. There is no reason—"

"No reason," she cut him off. "No reason for me to be angry? No reason for me to detest you as much as I do right now? You had every intention of ruining an innocent girl's life. Someone in my care. Someone I care for."

He grabbed her arm and hauled her off the path that wound around the gardens and behind a tall tangled mess of roses.

"You'll have the whole household here in a minute if you don't get control over your emotions." Unlike her, he seemed rather calm.

"As if I care right now to control my emotions, Leo. You are lucky I'm doing no more than shout at you."

He scratched his head with the back of his hand. "Have pity on me, Genny."

She wanted to look away from him, walk away, but she knew he'd follow her until he'd said his piece.

He tossed his hat to the ground when she didn't respond

and wrapped his arms around her waist to pull her closer. She turned away before his lips could press against her mouth. It didn't stop him from kissing her elsewhere. The side of her face and neck were exposed to the touch of his whiskers and soft lips.

She closed her eyes for only a moment to enjoy the last touch she would allow herself to have from the man she loved. And despite their earlier "row," as Charlotte put it, she did still love him and would for as long as she lived. It wasn't an emotion easily forgotten or erased once you allowed yourself to embrace it.

She slid her hands up between them and shoved lightly at his chest. He let her go and took a step back.

"I cannot think with you here, Leo. I just want to clear my head of everything that has happened." She looked to the ground so that the top edge of her bonnet covered her face from view and he couldn't see her expression. "Please go . . . you have no reason to be here anymore."

She let him take her hand. His hold was reverent, coaxing. "I'm sorry. I can say it a thousand times, Genny, and it'll never be enough."

"You're right. It will never be enough." She put her head back and looked at him, tears filling her eyes. She prayed they would not fall.

He took her head gently between his hands and his thumbs stroked over her temples. She didn't have the will to push him away again. She was done fighting and arguing. What she would give to trade this in for a bad dream. But this wasn't something she could wake up from. Leo had done the unthinkable.

"I made a promise not to walk away from you again, and I have every intention of keeping that vow."

She shook her head; how wrong he was. "You also promised to never endanger my reputation."

"And I haven't."

"You would have. And knowing now that you could have even contemplated such an act changes everything."

He tilted her head back and kissed the side of her mouth before releasing her.

"I will leave only because you have asked me to. But when you are back in London, this issue between us will be resolved."

"Maybe once you're gone, you'll realize that there is no resolution for the pain you have caused me. *You* have singlehandedly wrecked everything that was perfect between us." She fisted the lapels of his jacket and emphasized her words with small shakes. "You and you alone are the cause of this. I was just the fool who fell for you . . ." She gave a defeated sob, but managed to keep her tears from falling. "Again."

She let him go and stepped out of his reach.

Now was not the right time to persuade her of his good intentions. She needed time even though leaving her was the last thing he wanted to do. More than anything, he wanted to pull her into his arms and kiss the wrongs away.

"I'm sorry, Genny. At least believe that." He held out the chain and ring she'd discarded the previous night. "These belong to you, princess. At least take what is rightfully yours."

With one final long look in his direction, she said, "Good-bye, Leo." The regret in those words was unmistakable to him. Then she gave him her back and walked down the path to join her cousin.

He clamped the ring tightly in his fist. She hadn't even looked at it.

He would fix the damage he'd done.

His first order of business when he returned to Town

would be to see Tristan and make sure the man had found another amusement aside from Lady Charlotte.

And then he'd work up some much-needed courage to confront Jez.

As if the first time she'd asked him to leave wasn't hard enough, now she had to ask him to leave again? Life was unfair and unmerciful.

"What has happened between you two?" Charlotte asked when she was back by her cousin's side. Thank goodness most of her tears had dried up shortly after she left Leo.

"He wanted to tell me he was headed back to London."

Their gait was unhurried as they walked down the stone path flanked with green and red hedges. The birds were chirping loudly around them, as though a storm wasn't far off.

"Why are you lying to me?"

"I'm not." The warm breeze had sweat beading on her brow, which Genny wiped away with her handkerchief. She quickened her stride, as though she'd be able to outrun the questions her cousin would soon ask.

"You're treating me like a child!"

"Charlotte, you haven't been a child for some time." She stopped and turned to her cousin when they reached the neatly clipped grass lawn. "I daresay I'm not sure you were ever a child. But I'm telling you the truth. He leaves for London later today."

Not only did Genny find it humiliating that Leo had duped her twice, she was still hurt by his actions and didn't wish to discuss the details with Charlotte of all people. If she talked about it, she'd cry. And she did not want to return to the house with a tear-streaked face where everyone would be sure to ask what was wrong.

"What was it he tried to give you?"

Had her cousin seen the ring? Or was she just fishing for information so she could solve the puzzle herself?

"A trinket."

"If you won't talk about it now, I'll pester you at the dinner table for more information on your *friendship* with Lord Barrington."

Genny turned and glared at Charlotte. It felt good to replace her feelings of sadness with a slow simmering of rage. "You wouldn't dare."

"Are you so sure?" Charlotte cocked her head to the side and gave her a challenging look.

"When I took this position, I thought I would actually make a difference in someone's life. But you've been a trial that I could have done without. I take back what I said earlier, you do nothing but act like a child."

Genny clapped her hand over her mouth. How could she have said anything so horrible as that? What was wrong with her?

"I'm sorry. I didn't mean it." She was saying a lot of things on the spur of the moment lately.

"Yes you did." Hurt colored Charlotte's voice. "But tell me you wouldn't act the same way if you were told to marry a man you had no desire to marry."

"We've been over this time and time again. You can make this difficult, or you can accept and embrace the new life you'll have."

Charlotte clasped her hands behind her back and continued down the lawn ahead of her. "I know you think me young and naïve."

"I think you are a very intelligent young woman." She followed her cousin, catching up to her at the edge of the stream. She rubbed her hand soothingly over her cousin's arm when they stopped again under the shade of a tall elm. "I really didn't mean what I said."

"You needn't take your words back."

Genny sat down on the grass, uncaring if it soiled her white walking dress. "You guessed right earlier."

"Are we referring to Lord Barrington?"

Her cousin sat next to her and leaned back on her elbows. Genny lay back with a sigh, stared up at the green canopy shading them from the sun, and folded her hands over her midsection.

If Genny explained how she and Lord Barrington could never marry, even if they wanted to, would Charlotte welcome her impending marriage?

"Lord Barrington and I had a disagreement."

"On?"

"His reputation."

"Why would you even discuss his reputation?"

"Because he thought to court me." Genny rolled over onto her side, her head resting on her open palm as she assessed her cousin's expression. "I already know your father won't allow it."

Charlotte gave her a questioning look. "You don't know that."

"Your father and Lord Barrington have very opposing views in political matters."

"Why should that matter? The earl will make an excellent husband with his title and his wealth."

"It matters to your father." Genny plucked at the grass between them. She shouldn't tell her cousin this, but really, what good would it do to hide the full truth from her when Charlotte would find out eventually anyway. "Your father told me to avoid Lord Barrington completely. He specifically said I could never be caught in the earl's company again."

Charlotte sat up, a scowl on her face. She was obviously displeased on Genny's behalf. "Then why did he let us come to the Carleton house party? Surely he knows Lord Barrington is in attendance."

"Because of the exclusivity of this party. To ignore or refuse the invitation would have been a slight toward the Carletons."

"We were only invited because you know Lady Carleton." Charlotte folded her legs up to her chest and wrapped her arms around her shins. She pressed the side of her face against her raised knees.

"I think she's taken a great liking to you and Ariel." Genny sat up and toed her slippers off. "Let us cool off before anyone can catch us being indiscreet."

"An excellent idea." Charlotte removed her shoes and rolled her stockings down. "Why would Papa refuse a courtship between Lord Barrington and you?"

"Quite frankly, they despise each other."

"I don't think Papa likes anyone. He's getting grumpier as he ages. He'll be an old curmudgeon soon and liable to beat anyone with his cane if they get too close."

They both laughed at the image of Charlotte's father doing just that.

"I don't think anyone would believe Lord Barrington's intentions were pure if he were to court me. So I kindly refused him."

They waded into the cool water, holding their skirts above the stream. There was a cluster of large boulders three feet out from the shore that they could perch themselves against, so they headed toward them.

"He's liable to settle down with a wife soon, considering his age," Charlotte said.

"He's not yet thirty. And unlike us mere women, men can sire children at any age."

"True. But I still think you should ask Papa. Or maybe Lord Barrington can present his case? That would be utterly romantic."

"Who would look after you if I am focused on a courtship?"

Charlotte shrugged her shoulders. "If I'm to wed as soon as the fall, Grandmamma can attend events with me."

"I'm not sure your father would agree with this plan of yours." Genny rested her head back on the rocks and let the sun heat her face.

"You will never know unless you ask."

But she'd never ask. Barrington had proven no better than his reputation. Not that she would reveal that to her cousin. That was her secret to bear alone.

"Maybe I will ask your father after you are wed," she said, lying easily. That should pacify her cousin and put off the conversation until a much later date. "Come on, we have to head back; we've been cooling in the water a good half hour."

They gathered up their stockings, stuffing them in their pockets, and slipped back into their shoes.

"Don't mention this conversation again. I don't want anyone to know that Barrington and I might have been more than friends."

"That you have so little faith in me goes to show you don't know me well." Charlotte looped her arm through Genny's on the long walk back to the house. "Your secret is safe with me."

She knew her secrets would be safe with her cousin, but she could never reveal the ugly truth about Barrington and Castleigh. Why should she crush her cousin's heart? Charlotte would eventually figure out that both men were no longer interested in being a part of their lives.

When they reached the back entrance, Lady Hargrove informed them that Lord Barrington had urgent business to attend to in London and had left while they'd been on their walk.

Though she'd expected him to leave, the news still made her heart splinter right down the center. It was better this way, she argued to herself. It would be easier to forget him if he wasn't constantly in her presence.

When they went to their own rooms to freshen up after their walk, Genny tossed her hat on her bed and slumped down on the chaise longue near the fireplace and stared at nothing. She wished she could take one day for herself before having to play the perfect chaperone in two hours' time for luncheon. She'd have to settle for a short nap and hope that her emotions didn't bombard her at an inconvenient time.

When she focused on the mantel clock, she saw a small blue box that hadn't been there when she'd left. Genny tilted her head to the side, spying a folded piece of paper next to the box, which looked vaguely familiar.

She stood and grabbed both items from the mantel and sat back down on the chaise. She held the box in her hand, turning it over, recalling the first time she'd seen it back at her uncle's house.

She set it next to her, not sure she should even open it, and peeled through the wax that sealed the letter.

Princess,

Before you toss away this letter or the present that I bought you all those weeks ago from the jeweler's, please hear me out. I cannot walk away from us with my heart intact. I cannot leave you to a life of uncertainty even if it seems better to find your own way than to ever trust me again.

Everything between us these last two weeks has meant more to me than you can ever know. I love you. I have always loved you and I know that we can start over even if I've been the biggest ass there ever was.

Without you, my life is nothing. I need your smile,

*your laughter, your very presence. You alone make
me a better man, and that is the only reason I confessed what needed to be said. I'm sorry I hurt you.
That I broke your trust in me. But know that no matter how long it takes, I will win you back.*

*Always your
Leo*

Genny had to wipe away more tears that spilled over
her cheeks. She loved him, too, but that didn't mean she
could forgive him.

Lying back on the chaise, she fingered the chocolate-
brown ribbon that sealed the box's contents from sight.
The brown matched Leo's eyes exactly and the compari-
son had more tears gushing down her face. Handkerchief
completely sodden, she gave up wiping the salty liquid
and let them flow freely.

Accepting Leo's gift meant accepting him back into
her life. Should she send the box back to him by post? Or
maybe it was better to open it and give the bauble to someone else? That would be a divine punishment, the only
flaw being that he'd never know.

She slowly pulled the end of the satin ribbon, questioning her sanity until the whole thing unraveled at the center. It was too late to turn back now. She flipped the lid
off, letting it tumble to the floor.

Her breath caught on seeing the beautiful piece inside.
It wasn't any of the hair combs she'd tried on for him.
This one was far prettier than any of those.

White ivory, she guessed, as she lifted it from the box.

Little round carved balls lined the top. A flower bloomed
below the top edge from the center and vines swirled in a
delicate pattern through the rest of it. It was smaller than
the palm of her hand and incredibly beautiful. Five tines
about two and some inches long stretched out below. She

ran her finger over the bottom edge then brought it close to inspect the detailed work of the decorative head.

She could never wear something so beautiful and obviously expensive without anyone asking her where she had obtained such a piece. She put it back in the box.

It seemed pointless to send it back to Leo. He had given it to her, knowing that she might refuse to ever see him again, so it was hers to do with as she pleased. Wrapping it back up, she pulled out her portmanteau from beneath the bed, and placed the box inside where no one would ever know about it.

Chapter 21

*None other than the recently rusticating Lord B——
is back in Town. With him comes a wave of speculation about his current attraction to a young lady. A
reliable source has heard that he escaped from his
holiday the moment he was caught in a compromising position with his young lady friend. Of course
she's been ruined for any others now that Lord
B—— has taken advantage of her. Everyone wants
to know if this is a new entertainment he's partaking
in. In time we will know the answer to this, for the
season has yet to end and there are so many more
spinsters for one such as him to weed out.*
      The Mayfair Chronicles, August 6, 1846*

The unthinkable had happened, and it had necessitated
Genny's quick removal from the house party.

It had been two days ago now that she and Barrington
had fought and she'd said good-bye to him one final time.
It had been forty hours since Barrington had left the Carleton Estate. It had been a mere eight hours since Lord
Ponsley had arrived after receiving a note that his

daughter's chaperone was an unseemly character indulging in a very public affair.

A maid had been sent up to her room to tell her that her uncle wanted to speak with her.

She'd been dreading this moment since she knew her card had been played. This was the moment when everything in her life was about to slip through her fingers and rush downhill faster than she could recover.

With her hands folded neatly in her lap to stop her from fidgeting, her foot tapped restlessly against the carpeted floor.

She'd waited nearly an hour now.

Did her uncle intentionally make her wait, expecting her nerves to wear her down with every minute that passed? Did he want her to feel terrible about her actions and mull over everything that had gone wrong? Why couldn't he just come into the parlor and get it over with?

She couldn't abide the waiting. It was awful. She wanted to scream her frustration. Pound her fists into the cushions beside her. Anything to assuage her need to . . . run.

The absence of sleep did not help this situation. Goodness, she hadn't even seen her cousin since yesterday afternoon.

Genny heaved a sigh and rubbed her forehead and temples. She felt a headache coming on; this was all too much stress. Too much to deal with. Though she'd known this was a possibility when she'd started her liaison with Leo, she'd never expected to actually be caught.

When the door opened, she got quickly to her feet, keeping her head downcast. There was a long pause of silence before the door clicked shut and heeled boots approached her.

She felt her lip quiver and had to bite it to still her outward emotions. Like a drop of water in the bucket of time, she slowly raised her eyes, knowing that this was the end of her comfortable life as a companion.

Lord Ponsley's expression was dour. There was no pity present when he scowled at her as though she were the lowest of life forms. She almost expected a growl to pass his lips where it was kicked up on the left in a vicious sneer.

Even though she wanted nothing more than to be strong and brave and pull back her shoulders and face him head-on, she couldn't. It would do her no good to defend such an indiscretion as the one she'd committed. She lowered her gaze like any good servant and slumped her shoulders forward as she waited for a thorough set down from her uncle.

"You have disgraced my family." His voice reverberated around the room.

"I'm sorry, my lord." What else was there to say? How else could she apologize and make up for her wrongs?

"Not to mention that you have shamed my daughter with this indiscretion." Lord Ponsley leaned up against the mantel, a severe look of disdain settled into the wrinkles lining his face. "How did you ever think you could play the whore and not be found out?"

She gasped. "Whore" was such a vile, dirty word. And she'd done everything in her power to protect Charlotte. She'd even turned Leo away after his confession to her. Tears fell copiously from her eyes. She went to where he stood, fell to her knees, and pulled his hand toward her; intent on kissing the heavy gold signet ring he always wore. The tears wouldn't let up.

"I cannot apologize enough for what I have done." Her voice broke, and the tears didn't let up. "Please take some mercy on me; I am of your blood."

Because she held his hand, she was forced to wipe her running nose on the shoulder of her dress.

He pried his hand away from hers and rubbed it on his trousers as though she were a filthy street urchin covered in grime. "I begin to wonder if your mother was a whore, too. You are no blood of a vicar. You are nothing but a harlot. You are no blood of mine."

"Please." She tried to grasp his hand again but he moved it out of her reach. "Let me prove otherwise. You are the last of my family. How can I possibly go on without your help?"

"You are no longer my problem."

Genny looked up at Lord Ponsley from where she knelt on the floor. His expression was severe. Hard. He had no love for her. There was nothing for him to lose in denying their relation.

"What am I to do?" she cried.

"I do not care." He slapped his gloves in the palm of his hand. "You'd be best suited for a whorehouse. You are familiar with spreading your legs for any man that will take you in your unmarriageable state."

She had to cover her mouth to keep the bile down that viciously rose in her throat. "How dare you suggest such a thing!"

"I'm taking Charlotte home tomorrow." He continued to speak as if she had not spoken at all. "You, on the other hand, I want to leave immediately."

How could anyone be as unkind as he was being? Yes, she'd made a bad choice, but did she deserve this callousness and cruelty? No one did. "Lady Carleton—"

"She cannot protect you. You've brought this upon yourself."

"You—you don't care what happens to me?"

His eyes narrowed in disgust. "No. I don't. Make sure you stay away from my daughter."

And with that, he walked away from her. She sank down onto the floor. She shook so badly that she couldn't find the ability to stand. Lady Hargrove and a couple of the other houseguests must have been listening at the door because they apologized to Lord Ponsley when he exited the room. Then the door slammed in his wake and she was left alone once again.

She wasn't sure how long she sat on the floor, crying silent tears, but someone eventually came into the room and sat next to her. Genny could barely see through her swollen eyes, and she didn't know who it was until she spoke.

"Lord Ponsley was always a pompous ass, dear." Lady Carleton put her arm around her shoulders and pulled her to her side in a tender embrace. "I'll get you back to London and help you find accommodations."

"You're being far too kind." Genny hoped that her tears had started to dry up and that her voice wouldn't catch on another sob as she spoke. "I've made a terrible mistake and I've not only brought shame on Lord Ponsley and his daughter but on this household."

"I'm sure I'll fare better than everyone." Lady Carleton gave her a hug and rubbed Genny's back. "I've had far worse scandals during these parties. They've always worked out for the better."

She and Leo would be the first guests involved in a scandal to not marry, then. But she hadn't the energy to explain that to Lady Carleton. Genny closed her eyes and rested her head on the countess's shoulder for a while. She felt completely defeated and lost.

"Let's get you back up to your room."

"I'm sorry. I didn't mean to stay down here so long." She let Lady Carleton help her back to her feet. "I should go pack my things."

"Hush, this is my house and what I say goes. You'll stay and get some food in you. I can't imagine you've eaten much in the last day."

Genny pulled away from Lady Carleton so she could

look the older woman in the eyes. "Why are you being so kind to me? Shouldn't you be on their side?" Genny nodded toward the door, where she was sure some of the other houseguests were still listening.

"Never you mind them." Lady Carleton brushed the hair away that stuck to Genny's face. "I'll send a maid up to help you with your things. But I'm not letting you leave until you eat something."

"Can I leave in the dead of night?" Genny looked down at her disheveled dress. "I don't want anyone to witness my departure. I already feel dreadful."

"Of course. I'd say you can stay here indefinitely, but we both know that not even my name can stand up to the gossips' lashing tongues for acting against society."

"Thank you, Lady Carleton. I know I don't deserve such kindness, but I can't refuse your help."

"Think nothing of it." Lady Carleton wrapped her arms around her back and led her toward the door. "Now, let me walk you up to your room."

Genny was thankful for that because she needed someone to lean on as they passed nearly everyone in the house on their way up to her room. Most of the ladies cut Genny on sight. The gentlemen snickered and turned their backs. The only person she did not see was her cousin. She wished she could convey how sorry she was to Charlotte. Would she ever see her cousin again? The thought saddened her as much as Ponsley's words had.

Lady Carleton had generously offered her a carriage to take her wherever she needed to go. Genny knew she had to leave sooner rather than later.

After a day of dealing with the repercussions of being discovered with Barrington, she'd hidden in her room and plotted the rest of her life. There wasn't much to plot, for she had few options open to her.

The only certainty she had was that she would never play the role of companion again. She couldn't even show her face in society after this.

She needed to talk to the woman who had started all of this.

She'd chosen the quiet of midnight to leave her comfortable, meek existence behind so no one could further witness her humiliation, aside from Lady Carleton.

Though she'd saved over the years, and received a small inheritance from her great-aunt Hilda on her passing, it wasn't enough to live on for the rest of her days. If she no longer had any relatives she could rely upon, she would start with the Dowager Countess Fallon. She was the cause of all this. Not that Genny hadn't been a willing participant in her affair, but she had to wonder if Leo would have pursued her if his friend hadn't insisted on her game of ruin.

The one good thing in all this was that Charlotte's reputation was spared. She'd grown fond of her cousin in the last few months and wanted her to do well in life. Wanted her to have the comforts that Genny would never have.

She rapped her knuckles lightly on Lady Carleton's bedchamber door.

A maid opened the door in a trice. "That will be Miss Camden, Irene. Tell her to come in."

The door swung open, and Genny slipped through. Lady Carleton was at her boudoir, her hair half down from the updo she'd had it in. The maid returned to her mistress's side and removed the remaining pins.

Genny approached, feeling a fresh wave of embarrassment infuse her cheeks and speed up her heart.

Lady Carleton met Genny's gaze in the looking glass. "You wish to take me up on my offer?"

"Yes, my lady."

"Do come closer, dear, and stop bowing and scraping. You knew perfectly well the danger of your *activities*. At least have the gall to face me like a grown woman and not a simpering miss. I never thought you missish."

"I can't express how sorry I am for my untoward behavior, my lady."

"I doubt you'd have changed your actions any had you known you would be caught." At Genny's blank expression, Lady Carleton said, "Sit down, dear. Let us speak frankly."

There was a tasseled velvet stool next to the countess, so Genny pulled it away from the wall and perched herself on the edge. Would the woman Genny respected as she did her own mother reprimand her? Or offer sage advice on the next steps she should take in life?

"You know I am almost twice your age."

She gave a slight nod of her head, though she'd assumed only a dozen or so years separated them in age.

"You remind me of me when I was younger. When you first came to stay with us five years ago, I wanted nothing more than for you to make a good match. I naïvely thought Barrington would offer for your hand on your second summer here since he was smitten with you."

"My lady, he was no more than a friend."

The countess arched one eyebrow in disbelief. "Don't think I don't know everything that happens under my roof." She pointed at her in the mirror with the silver brush she'd been using. "I was no more blind to your affair with Barrington four years ago than I am this time around."

Genny's brows furrowed. Leo had told her that a friend had figured out their affair. "Why did you never say anything?"

"It wasn't my place." The countess gave a deep sigh filled with remorse. "You are the daughter I would have wanted had God ever gifted me with children. You were always a bright girl, and I knew that the decisions you made were ones you would be able to live with, even if you couldn't get that stubborn man to marry you."

"I feel undeserving, but thank you for your high regard." Genny ducked her head, feeling like a bigger disappointment knowing Lady Carleton thought of her like a daughter. "I was naïve enough to believe that I could change him."

Lady Carleton turned in her seat and reached her hand out to pat her affectionately on the cheek. "Oh, you've definitely changed him."

Genny couldn't explain the whole sordid tale so she gave the countess a weak smile.

"You've hit a patch in your life that is sure to try your patience at every turn. Just remember that you will always have a friend in me."

"I don't want to damage your standing in society by associating with you."

"I'm too old, child, to care what my peers think. While I cannot allow you to stay on for as long as you wish right now due to the other guests in residence, know that my home is open to you at any other time."

Tears leaked from Genny's eyes. She couldn't stop them this time, and she didn't care to.

"I can't thank you enough." This was singlehandedly the kindest thing anyone had ever done for her.

"Thank me by promising to visit after you marry that rascal."

She did weep then but not terrible wrenching sobs, just a quiet sound of heartbreak passing her lips. Lady Carleton offered up a folded and pressed handkerchief, which Genny took to mop up her leaking eyes and blow out her nose in the most unladylike fashion imaginable. When she was done she looked up to the older woman. The countess's expression was sincere, not dismissive.

"I'm sad to say that my circumstance with Barrington doesn't lend itself to a happy ending."

"I have every bit of faith that he'll not let you languish in ruin for long. And should he be foolish enough a man to hold out for any length of time, you should go to him, and demand he do the right thing."

If only life were as simple as that. Genny would not go back to him so he could stitch the remnants of her reputation back together.

"He did not take advantage of me. What we had was something mutually agreeable for the time we were together."

"I never took you for a fool, Genevieve Camden."

She could only shake her head in disagreement because she was the greatest fool there ever was.

Pulling herself together, she took in a deep breath and composed her wayward emotions. She had but one goal in mind. "Might I borrow your carriage as far as the next posting inn?"

"You may take my carriage to whatever location you need to in London."

"You've been so kind to me that I wouldn't wish anyone to see your emblem emblazed on the side of the carriage with me inside."

Lady Carleton stood from her gilded velvet chair and took Genny's hands to lead her from the room. "Did I ever tell you how Lord Carleton came to be my husband?"

She shook her head, not sure why Lady Carleton was asking such an odd question.

"He kidnapped—for lack of a better term—me right out of my bed and we traveled in an unmarked carriage all the way to Gretna Green."

Genny gasped. "I had no idea." They wound their way down the servants' stairs that Genny had become familiar with over the past couple of weeks.

Opening the door at the bottom landing, the countess ushered her through the kitchen and out the back door. "While he had never put me in a compromising position, he was intent on marrying me. But what a scandal it made! Of course it wasn't nearly as disastrous as yours and Barrington's."

"Has it been all but forgotten?"

"No one seems to remember. It's a miracle what an elevated position in society will do for you. My husband is a well-connected man."

As was Leo, she thought. But still, how could she ever trust him again after his betrayal?

They walked at a slow pace over the lawn and toward the stables.

"Lord Barrington won't let you languish long." The countess gave her a grin that was full of wickedness and Genny felt her tear-stiffened face reciprocate the gesture.

"Lord Carleton and I took an extended honeymoon on the Continent immediately after our marriage. Two months to be precise, and enough time to let the gossip die down."

Genny sighed wistfully. Lady Carleton was simply offering up advice should Genny ever reconcile with Leo. "It's a rather romantic story."

"Yes, quite. And he tells me often that there isn't a day that goes by where he can't imagine not having married me."

"Why are you telling me this?"

"Because, dearest, I already told you, you are the daughter I would have wanted, and I'll do everything in my power to help you overcome this scandal." The countess pushed open the door to the stables.

There was a lamp on and someone stood to attention on seeing her ladyship. "My lady," he said.

"Good evening, Oliver. Have the blacks readied for a trip to Town."

"Right away, my lady." He bowed and went to do the countess's bidding.

"You know, the sentimentality of that unmarked carriage resides in the farthest stall in this stable. My husband and I travel to Scotland in it once a year." Lady Carleton brushed some of the hair away from Genny's face. "It's in excellent working order. More importantly, no one will know that I was the one who aided you if that is your worry."

Genny threw her arms around the woman, more tears welling in her eyes. "I can't thank you enough for everything you're doing for me."

Lady Carleton rubbed her back in a motherly fashion, saying, "Tut, tut, let's get you on the road before anyone notices your absence."

Genny squeezed her in a hug a while longer, then reluctantly released the older woman.

"Irene has prepared your bags and will no doubt be down shortly. The carriage I had pulled out yesterday and readied for a journey."

Genny was so shocked by her hostess's generosity that she stood there dumbfounded. Lady Carleton turned to her and said, "Though I cannot offer more assistance than this right now, if you need anything, simply get the message to Oliver and it will be done. Do you understand me?"

"I do." Genny had to wipe the water from her eyes again. "I'm sorry about all my tears. I can't seem to control them."

"I'm doing nothing your mother wouldn't do if she were alive today." Lady Carleton engulfed Genny in a consoling hug. "Now go and bring that rascal, Barrington, in line."

It wasn't Barrington she needed to bring in line, but she understood that the countess wanted her to start on the right foot in her life of ruin. And that would mean marriage to the man who had ruined her. She wasn't ready to take that step, she wasn't sure she would ever be ready for that kind of forgiveness.

"I hope you are right."

Lady Carleton released her and smiled warmly. "I am. Your bags are loaded and the carriage ready. We'll see each other soon enough."

"Your kindness means more than I can ever put into words."

The countess smiled and patted Genny's face again before giving instructions to her stable hand.

"Oliver, I'm leaving Miss Camden in your ever capable and trusting hands. Take her wherever she needs to go. Stable the horses at our London residence and wait there a few days in the event that Miss Camden needs your assistance for anything."

One of the young stable hands took her hand and helped her up the steps of the carriage. When she settled herself inside she drew the blind.

Lady Carleton nodded approvingly. "Keep the curtain drawn when you are closer to London."

With one final nod, Genny gave directions to the driver. She had to confront the dowager countess, because no one could act in the manner that woman had acted and not deal with any consequences. And now that she couldn't protect Charlotte, she had to make the other woman realize the wrong she'd committed, and hopefully, sway her onto a less destructive path where others were concerned.

Perhaps it wasn't her place to do such a thing, but if she didn't, how could she ever live with herself if Charlotte ended up being an old spinster? Genny would ensure that her cousin married Mr. Warren.

Chapter 22

The Dowager F—— received not one but two mid-night visitors last night. She's more usually found out and about town gambling through the wee hours of morning, but this new habit is unlike her. Could this have something to do with her short sojourn from society just after her husband's funeral? Is this a new game that she's caught up in? Oh, the secrets and lies I crave to uncover where she is concerned.
   The Mayfair Chronicles, August 8, 1846

The carriage ride lasted a few hours, the pace remained steady but not rushed so the horses weren't overexerted. Genny thought she had dozed for an hour or two in the even rut of the road, and woken with the first rays of morning light.

As instructed, she shut the blinds when they neared Town. It was quite early in the day, and Genny wondered if the dowager countess would even be awake.

What if Genny wasn't given admittance to the dowager's residence?

It was a silly thought brought on by her exhaustion.

She simply would stand outside the dowager's house until she was allowed to enter if she was refused.

It felt as if she had had no time to prepare what she wanted to say before the door to the carriage was opened, and Oliver was offering his hand to help her down the steps. Gathering her courage, she pulled her hood forward on her cloak before she took his hand to be let down the steps.

"I'll be waiting here for you, miss. Till someone comes out and tells me where you'll be staying this evening. I'll be taking you back to my mistress's house if you haven't a place to stay. My lady's orders."

"You've already done so much for me. You must be as exhausted as I am if not more. Lady Carleton's house is only around the corner from here. I'll be able to find you should I need you. And I might be here for some hours. Please, go and rest."

"I hope you'll understand when I say I can't leave you, miss. Wouldn't be right at this time of the day. Asides, no one will know it's the Carleton carriage waiting outside for you."

He gave her a charming wink.

Genny reached out and squeezed Oliver's callused hands. "Thank you."

She lifted her skirts slightly so she didn't trip on her hem traversing the stairs. Once at the top, she rapped the knocker firmly and stepped back.

A young man dressed in a tailed black suit opened the door.

"If that is Mr. Warren again, tell him I'll have someone tie his balls off before he can so much as scream for his mother." The dowager came into view as the footman opened the door fully. She wore a Chinese robe in scarlet, which was decorated with little gold dragons dancing across the sash and hems. Her hair was unbound and fell in a long braid over her shoulder. She'd been about to shout out some other obscenity, Genny was sure, but paused when she saw it was not Mr. Warren at the door.

"And who are you?" The dowager raised one brow at Genny.

"Miss Camden, my lady." She gave a bow, even though this woman deserved no courtesies, and lifted her chin as she gazed back at the woman who had helped ruin her life.

"Do I know you?"

"No, you don't. But I know a great deal about you. If you would." She indicated with a motion of her hand that she wished to enter. "I have a private matter to discuss with you."

The dowager peered around Genny's shoulder and stared at the unmarked carriage. "Who sent you?"

"I came on my own after learning of your scheme to ruin my cousin's engagement to Mr. Warren."

The countess rushed forward, pulled her through the door without preamble, and slammed it behind Genny's confused and slightly shaken form. "Let's not announce our misdeeds to the world, Miss Camden."

Genny raised her chin and scowled at the woman before her. "They were not my misdeeds."

"Where did you come by this information?"

"Barrington told me what you planned."

"Leo? Why would . . ." The countess had an odd look about her as she accessed Genny with renewed interest. "Come, we'll take this to the parlor."

Lady Fallon turned and left so quickly that Genny was forced to catch up to her at a near jog. The room they entered was dark with all the window shutters closed tight. A single lamp on the center table was the only illumination.

"Please excuse the state of the house. I go from loving

and hating it alternately. When I hate it, things are broken, so we've left the windows dark."

Genny wasn't sure how to respond to the countess's honesty.

"Sit, please. We may be here a while." The countess lounged on a chaise. She motioned to the chairs and settee across from her when Genny stood frozen to the spot.

"I only came to ask that you leave my cousin alone." Genny perched herself on the edge of a chair. There was no sense in getting comfortable, she wasn't staying overly long.

Lady Fallon yawned rudely. "She'd be better without Mr. Warren, you know."

"Whom my cousin should marry is not your decision to make."

"I'll be saving her from a long life filled with nothing but misery."

"Do we even know the same man who is courting my cousin?" Genny frowned. "He's been nothing but kind."

Lady Fallon picked up a fan and flicked it open to fan her face. "They always are in the beginning. It's how they lure in young pliable brides."

"So it's your cynical nature that led you to the simple decision to change the course of my cousin's life."

"Not precisely, but I'm bored with this conversation." Lady Fallon leaned forward. "Now tell me what Leo told you."

"Why should I? Is it not enough that he's told me everything? Shouldn't you feel some sort of regret for your part in this?"

"I feel nothing actually."

Genny closed her mouth. What exactly was the countess referring to? Certainly not her cousin's situation. She leaned back against the cushioned seat. She might have to approach this matter differently. "Why did you do it?"

"You don't know me, Miss Camden. Why would you care what my reasons are?"

"I suppose I don't need to hear your reasoning." Genny knew that once her purpose was stated, the countess might be less than friendly. "I want reassurance that you'll leave my cousin alone."

"I have a suspicion that Lady Charlotte won't need me to persuade her to not marry Mr. Warren." The countess picked up a glass half full of champagne and twirled the flute around in circles. "Not only is Mr. Warren a complete bore, he's an imbecile."

Genny pinched her lips together, knowing that a rebuttal would probably only have Lady Fallon continuing her tirade. She stood from the chair. Her trip here was for nothing. This woman would never listen to what Genny had to say, not with open ears and heart as she'd hoped.

Lady Fallon lowered her fan and eyed her. "Have I already frightened you off?"

Should she admit she had? "It does me no good to talk to a brick wall."

The dowager countess laughed. Her hand clapped against her chest as she fell back on the settee, gales of laughter flowing from her.

"Calculating, frosty, degenerate, harlot, charlatan, and player. Those are the typical choice words society showers down on me." Lady Fallon shrugged. "I don't think I've ever been likened to a brick wall."

Genny just stared at the woman. She was mad, and it had never occurred to her before that the dowager countess might not be in possession of all her faculties.

Backing up a few steps, Genny said, "If you'll excuse me, I have somewhere else to be."

"Don't let me frighten you off."

The way the dowager said it made Genny momentarily forget she was in the lair of someone who had orchestrated her cousin's downfall, and through happenstance, Genny's reputation.

There was a split second where she wanted to give this woman the benefit of the doubt and offer friendship to that lonely voice. But only a split second.

"You are the chaperone Hayden mentioned, so I imagine you are needed back at your duties."

Genny put her shoulders back. She would not cower because she'd been ruined. "*Was* . . ." She held her head high. "I *was* the chaperone."

"Oh, my wicked ears hear a story in the making." The dowager's interest was piqued, and she sat up with renewed interest in Genny. "What has changed your circumstance?"

What did she have to lose in telling Lady Fallon the truth? The gossip was sure to make it back to London in a matter of days, if it hadn't already. "Lord Barrington."

Lady Fallon's sharp gaze pierced right through Genny as though searching for the truth with a mere look.

"So that is what has occupied my friend's attention this past month."

"A ruse, I assure you. One that finally played out in his favor."

Lady Fallon's head tilted to the side. "You have nowhere to go, do you?"

"Does it matter?" Genny responded defensively.

"Perhaps I'm offering a bone." Lady Fallon put her feet on the floor and set her champagne on the side table; probably a good thing since it was far too early to imbibe. "Don't you think you should consider nibbling if only to humor me?"

"No." Genny clasped her hands to keep from pulling at the string on her reticule. She'd expected her meeting with Lady Fallon to be awkward, just not quite this awkward. "I think it most unwise. I only came—"

"To persuade me onto the righteous, more acceptable, and sanctified path I should be following?"

"No. I only wanted you to leave Charlotte alone. She is my closest family—"

"And yet you've been locked out of her life and labeled a harlot."

"I am no harlot." Genny was sick to death of being called that vile name. "And I see my time here is wasted."

Genny made her way to the door. Just before she reached it, the dowager suddenly rushed forward and blocked the exit.

"Where will you go?" Lady Fallon asked with a pensive look.

"Your moral obligation to me is nonexistent. Please, let me by."

Lady Fallon didn't move. "Is it hard to believe that I might have changed my ways?"

"I can't see why." Genny crossed her arms stubbornly over her waist. "Shouldn't you be gloating at your achievement?"

"To do so would mean I indulge in life freely." The dowager set her shoulder against the door frame. "Sad to say, nothing comes free in life. Especially mine."

"You don't enjoy a certain amount of freedom then?"

The countess ignored her question. "You should stay. I have so many empty rooms that it would be a shame to not use them before I'm kicked out of my own house."

Genny looked at the countess for a long moment. She'd nearly forgotten that she was penniless and had nothing left from her marriage.

Was the dowager trying to make amends with her? "Are you feeling remorse for putting me into a destitute situation similar to what you find yourself in?"

"Not at all." She moved away from the door so that Genny could leave if she so chose. "But I'd like the company and I imagine Leo will come looking for you. And if you are not in my possession, I'll not know how to locate you."

Lady Fallon was the oddest woman Genny had ever met. First she showed no compunction in planning to destroy her cousin's path in life, and now she was extending an olive branch to Genny because she'd inadvertently ruined her instead of Charlotte.

"Why should you care?"

"Because Leo is my friend. And he has remained a devoted friend despite what the rags have printed about me." The countess looked vulnerable with that admittance.

The door was open should she wish to leave, so why didn't Genny budge? "Leo's no better than you."

"Prejudice is but one form of ignorance, Miss Camden." Lady Fallon crossed her arms in front of her and tapped her fingers on one arm. "Now, breakfast is being served in one hour. Shall I ask the cook to prepare two dishes?"

Why not? Genny asked herself. Staying with Lady Fallon would give her time to find decent accommodations of her own. And though she wanted to make an enemy of this woman, she couldn't. The dowager was—yet she wasn't—a contradiction to everything printed about her.

Lifting her reticule, Genny placed it on a chair. "There is a carriage outside waiting for my direction. I need to tell him that I've found temporary accommodations."

Lady Fallon motioned to the door. As Genny went out to talk to Oliver, she felt as if she'd formed—not a friendship per se—but an odd alliance with the countess.

Chapter 23

Oh, the betting books are so full of the best fodder! When one can be amused by the actions and failures of others, what does it say about society today? Yet, without the characters that rely upon gossip, wherever would your reliable gossip columnist be?
The Mayfair Chronicles, August 9, 1846

Leo hadn't been his normal self since arriving home two days ago. Tristan hadn't been in residence so he couldn't settle that old score. And he didn't want to face Jez just yet.

To say that he had lived the life of a recluse since arriving in Town might be an understatement. Not once had he left his house. Nor had anyone bothered to visit since his knocker was put back on his door.

And in all the time since he'd been home, he hadn't come up with a decent plan to win Genny back. The house party would be over, and everyone returning to London over the next couple of days, so he had better come up with a plan soon.

Should he formally call upon Genny or even Lord Ponsley and state his intention to court and marry her? The great flaw in that plan was that Genny might refuse to see him. However, that did not mean he would give up his suit.

Marks tied his cravat and helped him into his jacket. Fresh air always cleared his mind, so he stepped out the door for a walk in the park. This afternoon he was meeting with Hayden at the club. Perhaps his friend would have a few ideas for winning back Genny's affections.

He missed her. Missed their walks in the morning, trailing after her cousin, their sultry evenings, stealing kisses whenever the mood presented itself, their nights lying out under the stars. Most of all, he missed hearing about her childhood and family as he told her tales of his life growing up while they lay in bed together.

His cane clicked against the paved path with each step. Every so often he was forced to dip his head and return the gestures of the ladies offering him a hallo, a nod, or an invitation to walk with them. He was too much of a bear right now to spend any time with others. He didn't expect he'd be in a decent mood again till he and Genny had reconciled.

There was definitely something to be said about that. The best thing he could do with regard to Genny was beg her forgiveness and then ask for her hand in marriage every day until she was sick of refusing him.

Who would have thought two months ago that Genny would irrevocably snag his affections all over again, and that he'd want nothing more than to call her his wife?

He stopped on reaching the Serpentine and turned to face the river. The trickle of water had always had a soothing effect on him.

To win Genny back, he needed her forgiveness and that meant confronting Jez. Jez needed to understand the error of what they had planned, and he wanted to ensure that no other young ladies ever need worry for their reputations when Jez—or any of their set—singled them out.

Enough time had passed for her to grieve her loss. She'd be in a much better form to hear what he thought of their latest charade from his own lips if Hayden or Tristan hadn't already discussed it with her.

Attuned to his own thoughts, he took no notice of his surroundings until a short, blonde fairy tugged on his jacket.

Leo stared down into the innocent blue eyes of Ronnie and offered her the first genuine smile he'd had the strength to muster in days.

"Well, if it isn't a little imp tugging at my coat."

"You shouldn't call me that." She put her hands on her hips. "I'm a young lady now."

That made him chuckle as he took her hand and walked toward her picnic party. Tristan lounged on the lawn, a blanket beneath him, Rowan, and Beatrice. Sandwiches and tins for water were spread out in front of them.

"I called out to you three times," Tristan said on his approach. "Ronnie thought it a good idea to make sure you weren't walking in your sleep."

"My thoughts are preoccupied." He tipped his hat to Beatrice. "My lady."

"And a good afternoon to you, Lord Barrington." She was filling napkins with food for the children.

"Parliament matters?" Tristan asked.

"Far from." Leo sat on the blanket next to Ronnie.

"You are back from the Carletons early."

There was a glint in Tristan's eye, suggesting he had knowledge of why Leo was back. Was it so obvious he had had trouble with a lady friend?

"Bea," Tristan said to his sister. "I'm going to have a round of the park with Leo."

They both stood from the blanket and walked back down to the path that twisted around the Serpentine.

"Oddly enough," his friend started, "when you warned

me off Lady Charlotte, I had assumed you'd taken a moral obligation to her."

"So you've decided against ruining her for marriage?" Leo nearly breathed a sigh of relief.

"It doesn't matter what I've decided. I'm just trying to figure out when you became such a hypocrite."

Leo stopped and turned to look Tristan in the eye. "True, I was at a house party with Ponsley's daughter, but I had very little association with her."

"Don't get me wrong." Tristan tapped his cane against the edge of the bench. "I'm not angry, but I can't see why you would warn me off her when you couldn't keep your hands off her chaperone."

"What in hell are you talking about?"

Tristan looked at him quizzically and didn't say anything for a few moments.

"It's all about Town."

"That's not possible." Leo hadn't told a soul. Wouldn't dare reveal to anyone what he'd done. Genny wouldn't, either. Maybe someone had said something about the courting they hadn't bothered to hide from those at the house party.

"The betting books have hit record stakes on whether you've taken a preferred liking to spinsters or if wallflowers will be your next target."

What in hell had happened since he left the Carleton Estate? How had any of this happened? was the more likely question. "Are they betting because I took to courting Miss Camden?"

Tristan's smile faded. "You really don't know, do you?"

"Stop equivocating and spit out what it is you mean to say."

"You were caught red-handed, Leo."

"Son of a—"

Leo walked over to the bench and sat heavily on it.

Removing his hat, he thrust his hand roughly through his hair. Tristan sat next to him.

"Tell me what you know."

"I don't know much more than that. Someone saw you with Miss Camden, and rumor has spread like wildfire around Town. The damn Mayfair Chronicler even made note of it two days ago."

"I need to go back to Genny, ask her for her hand and not take no for an answer."

"You'd really marry the chit?"

Leo stood suddenly from the bench and pointed his cane threateningly in Tristan's direction. "Don't you dare insult the woman I have every intention of marrying."

Leo put his hat back on. Where should he go first?

His friend grinned. "Never thought you'd be the first to go."

"What are you blathering on about?"

"I always thought it would be Hayden," Tristan said. "To marry, you dolt. Only, his split with his mistress seemed to do a great deal of damage. Good Lord, I don't think he's lain with a woman since. His balls are bound to shrivel up from inactivity."

Leo didn't have time for this. He had to find Genny. "I have to go."

"It's a day's ride back to the Carleton Estate. Although I have doubts your lady friend will still be in residence."

"She has nowhere else to go, Tristan. What in hell have I done?" He smacked his cane against the bench. "I promised to keep her safe from gossip. I broke my bloody promise."

"Well, it's not like it couldn't be helped; you were in residence with the biggest gossip the *ton* has ever produced. Why did you leave anyway?"

"I told her."

Tristan put his arm on the back of the bench and gave him an inquisitive look. "You told her what?"

"Our intentions regarding her cousin. What Jez wanted and what we thought to accomplish." Leo sat down again. "She asked me to leave after that."

"Do you know nothing about women?" Tristan crossed his ankle over his knee and leaned back on the bench as though getting comfortable to give a long lecture. "Their honor puts ours to shame. Why in hell would you tell her any variation of the truth?"

"Because she deserved to know what we had planned. Because I couldn't keep it from her indefinitely."

Leo's voice had risen and passersby stared at them, probably curious to know what he was shouting about.

Tristan sat up from the bench and tipped his hat in greeting to those who were walking by and giving them strange looks. "You need to calm yourself, man."

"If you felt the way I do, there would be nothing calm about you. I need to find Genny." Where would she go? If this happened two days ago, could she still be at the Carletons? Would she be with Ponsley? For some reason he didn't think so.

"So you ask the girl to marry you. What happens when she says no?"

"She won't. She can't." Really, she'd have no choice but to marry him if she wanted to save her reputation.

Tristan laughed in that smug way of his. "Oh, I will guarantee that she'll say no."

"I'm glad you find amusement in this." Leo sat on the edge of the bench, knowing he had nowhere to go at the moment. He needed to think. "Lady Carleton was her friend and would probably have invited her to stay on at the estate. It's possible she's still in Hertfordshire."

"Since I seem to be the only rational person here at the moment, can I make a suggestion?" Tristan leaned back again, his smile ever present. "Never did think that kind of sentence would ever pass my lips."

"Start talking," Leo spat out impatiently.

"Let me send my fastest rider to Lady Carleton. He'll be there and back before you make the trip one way. We'll beg her assistance to find where your lady friend has gone. We should have an answer before the day is through."

"And what if Genny hasn't resituated herself?" She could be out on the streets. She could be walking back to London. His thoughts were a bloody mess and he'd get nowhere if he didn't calm himself and let his friend help him think this through. "She could need my help now."

"You'll not find her if that's the case. I have a feeling that if Lady Carleton is a friend, she'll have put her up somewhere safe."

"And what am I supposed to do while you send out your fastest rider?"

"To start . . ." Tristan rubbed at his chin pensively, as he stood from the bench they had occupied for too long. "You might as well set the books straight at the club."

Leo threw up his hands in exasperation. His friend was intentionally trying his patience. "I don't care about the bloody books. They won't matter when I'm married."

"Then you'll need to pay a visit to the archbishop and obtain a special license." Tristan slapped him on the shoulder, put his arm around him, and started walking them both back toward his picnic party. "Really, man, you need to screw your head on a little more straight. How are you going to get on for the next day if you can't see where you're going?"

"What in bloody hell am I supposed to do to occupy me until tomorrow?"

"Language, Leo. My children are about and they don't need to hear anything from your foul mouth." Standing on the edge of the blanket, Tristan said to his sister, "Bea, I have some business that needs to be taken care of right away."

"Papa," Ronnie protested. "You promised a day out with us."

Tristan knelt and put his face level with Ronnie's. "And just as soon as I'm finished doing something very important for Leo here, I will make this up to you. It won't take more than an hour. And when I'm done, I'll take you for ices."

Ronnie crossed her arms over her chest and turned away with a curt, "Fine. But I want two ices."

Tristan chuckled and roughed up Rowan's hair as he stood. "Do you think you'll have two also, champ?"

He nodded his head fervently. "Yes, Papa."

"Excellent. I'll see you back here in an hour."

"Thank you," Leo said as they walked back to their houses.

"Don't thank me yet. I still doubt she'll agree to marry a lout like you."

It wouldn't matter so long as he knew she was safe. "I'll convince her that she has no choice."

"How romantic of you," Tristan said drolly.

"This has nothing to do with romance and everything to do with necessity."

Tristan slapped him on the shoulder and laughed uproariously. "I see you've learned nothing of women in all your years."

"I know what makes them happy."

"In bed perhaps."

"Are you questioning my manhood?"

"Would I dare?"

"Tristan," Leo said in warning. He had no compunction about rearranging his friend's face just as soon as Tristan's rider was sent.

"You deserved it." Tristan backhanded Leo across the stomach in horseplay. "If you like the chit as much as you say, you wouldn't have told her the truth."

"When you are in this position, I will remind you of this conversation."

"You do that." They broke apart on reaching the street. Their houses were a block away. "I will see you at the club this afternoon."

Chapter 24

Oh, sweet revenge, how doth you fare today? Do
you remember the much older ne'er-do-weller mix-
ing with the undistinguished much younger type of
society I mentioned some weeks back?

One Lady H—— has been caught in flagrante de-
licto. The gent filling her secret-spilling, reputation-
damaging mouth has moved up a notch on my scale
for the way in which he handled being discovered
with his trousers around his ankles.

The Mayfair Chronicles, August 9, 1846

License obtained and in his breast pocket, Leo walked into
his club the next morning. He still didn't have word from
Tristan, but would follow up with his friend just as soon as
he finished his task here. Everyone's head turned toward
him and a hush fell over them as he removed his gloves.

Slapping the leather against his hand, he walked to the
mahogany pedestal that held the betting book open for all
to see the latest on dit bid.

Sure enough, there were more than a handful of speculating names that he recognized. Their bets were on
whether he'd seek out another spinster, who she would be,

if he would take a virgin wallflower in her fourth and fifth seasons. The list went on in not very favorable directions.

Naturally, his friends had stayed out of the bidding. A shame they hadn't tried their luck in a more positive direction.

Though it was considered bad form to engage in a wager when you were the one mentioned, Leo called over the steward with a wave of his hand. "Hand me a pen, Brett."

"My lord," the man said in a word of warning.

"Hand me a damn pen." His voice was quiet but as sharp as the tip of a rapier.

No further protest was made as the man went to retrieve the requested writing instrument. Leo's eyes focused on each and every name written in the ledger. Someone in the club started to protest but was quickly shushed. They would all clamor to know what he would write and whom he would side with so the debts could be settled the moment he left.

When the pen was set up in the inkstand on the edge of the pedestal, Leo nodded his thanks and turned the page to read the rest of the names. There were a number of bets against him not only from club members but other men and a few women who obviously didn't want to be excluded from the chance to win the hefty sum entered on each line. That they cared to spend this much thought on his private affairs was simply pathetic. On reading the last name, he dabbed the nib on the blotter and wrote his name on the next available line. Estimating his wager based on the tally, he entered his total.

"Wax, Brett," was his next demand.

Taking up a small handful of sand, he tossed it over the wet ink and waited a minute before blowing it off. And though there were some fifty-odd witnesses to his signing of the wager book, he took the heated wax from Brett, poured a small amount on the ledger, removed his signet ring from his pinky finger, and pressed the griffin fashioned around an old-fashioned letter *B* into the wax. He left the club without talking to anyone on his way out. He knew they'd rush over to the betting book the moment he was out of sight.

And really, none of them mattered.

It was time to find Genny.

He knocked on Tristan's townhouse door. Ronnie pulled the heavy door inward. Rowan was next to the footman who stood to the side expressionless. It didn't surprise Leo that Tristan let his children rule the house and servants much like they ruled his life.

"Papa said you'd come today." Ronnie's smile was a welcome sight even in his current gloomy mood.

Leo went down on his haunches and tapped Ronnie on the nose affectionately. "Did he, then?" He looked to Rowan who nodded emphatically. "Where do you suppose I'll find your father this morning?"

"He's still in bed," Rowan said.

Leo pulled out his watch from his vest and flicked it open. "Since when does your father sleep past half ten in the morning?"

Ronnie crossed her arms over her chest with a pout. "I knocked on his door and he told me he'd see me later."

"Do you think I might come in? I have business with your father."

"You should eat lunch with us. He might come down for that." Ronnie suggested, taking his hand to invite him in.

"I can't refuse your kind offer, my lady."

He stood, patted her head, and put out his hand for Rowan to take.

"Alberts, would you mind notifying his lordship that I am here? He is expecting me."

Alberts, a young footman of average looks, bowed to him. "Yes, my lord."

He hurried to do as Leo bid while the children led him farther into the house. The breakfast room was where they took their casual meals. There was an array of dishes set out in buffet style for the children. A kitchen maid, wearing a French uniform, stood by to help the children with their dishes. He nodded to her. What was going on in the Castleigh house this morning? Everything seemed . . . off.

"Where is your aunt?"

Rowan bounced in his chair, chewing a strawberry openmouthed. "Papa sent her out on errands."

Why would Tristan have his sister, albeit half sister, run errands for him? Leo focused on the maid again. "Has his lordship been down from his room today?"

"No, my lord."

"Has food been sent up?" He leaned back in his chair and folded his arms over his chest.

Her eyes went wide, so he was on the right train of thought. "Yes, my lord."

He leaned in close and whispered, "One or two dishes?"

"Two," she mouthed so the children wouldn't hear their conversation.

"An unusual occurrence," he mused aloud.

The maid put her head down. He hadn't meant for her to feel bad for betraying her employer's trust but he had all the right questions. Though he had no answer as to why Tristan would have a woman here when he had a townhouse three streets over for his liaisons.

"What's unusual?" Ronnie asked.

"Oh, these eggs here have double yolks," Leo quickly said.

"Cook has a special hen that lays those. She says it's double the luck and she lays more eggs than the others."

"Very odd." Leo turned his attention back to the children at the table to make sure they were settled in to their lunch and grabbed a sausage and ate it off a fork just as the butler walked in.

The man bowed again. "If you'll follow me, my lord, I'll take you to his study."

"Excellent." He popped the last of the sausage in his mouth and winked at the children. "Thank you for the lunch offer. We must do this again soon."

Once he exited the room and followed the butler down the hallway, he asked, "Does he plan to be down soon, or should I send a white flag upstairs?"

"He is already waiting for you."

"Perfect." Leo pushed the study door open. The walls all around were paneled and stained in a mahogany four feet up; above the wainscoting was a dark green paper. The heavy desk at the center made the room feel smaller than it really was, but the big leather chairs made this room the most confortable to convene in.

Leo sat and put his feet up on the desk. "I hear you have a guest."

Elbows on the table, Tristan's hands were steepled in front of him. "Or so you've surmised."

"You aren't really going to deny it, are you?"

"I have nothing to deny." Tristan's tone was unusually cool. "Do you want word on your Miss Camden?"

"I do. And while I enjoy your company, I have important matters to look after today."

"My news is not going to make your day any easier."

"Why is that?"

Tristan hesitated. "Your lady friend was forced to flee from the house party. No one knows where she's gone."

Leo put his feet down on the floor and stood, placing his hands flat on the desk in front of him as he leaned closer to Tristan. "Is that what Lady Carleton said?"

"Not precisely."

"Then how do you know anything at all?" he demanded.

"I expect Lady Carleton's response within the hour but gossip has made its way back to me, and it was clear that she had to leave quickly. Miss Camden left the party after Lord Ponsley publicly dismissed her and sent her off with her tail between her legs."

Leo shoved his chair back. "Shit."

"Precisely. I have an account that she took a carriage back to the city. But where she's gone, I can't say for sure."

"And whom did you hear this from?"

"No one of concern."

Leo smacked his hands on the desk for emphasis. "I will drag every last bit of knowledge out of the person you got this information from. Tell me who it is."

Tristan stood, planted his palms on the desk, and shoved his face closer. "Word will arrive momentarily."

"Who is the woman?" Leo pressed. That had to be where Tristan had gotten his information.

Tristan's hands tightened. "There is no woman."

"Tristan, if there is one thing I can tell, it's when you lie to me." He strove for calm and failed. The only thing that mattered was finding Genny. "Who is the woman in your room?"

"She is of no consequence."

"Like hell she isn't!"

"If you don't leave this alone, I will personally throw you out of my house." Tristan tapped his joined fingers hard against Leo's forehead. "Think logically. Where would she have gone?"

Leo stood and rubbed his hand over his head, mussing his hair. "I don't know."

"Does she have family here?"

"No. She doesn't." He sat heavily in the chair. "I don't know if she does or not. I never thought to ask. I'm assuming she doesn't. She would have gone to a friend's."

"Do you know any of her friends?" Tristan asked.

"Just one, and she is in Scotland."

"Would her cousin have given her money to go somewhere?"

"That's assuming her cousin saw her before our liaison was made newsworthy." How in hell was he supposed to find her? "Maybe I should start with Ponsley."

"You have the sugar duties act coming up. Do you think it wise? He'll use this to sway the rest of the house against you."

"I could care less. I need to find Genny. If she has nowhere to go, I don't want to think what could happen to her."

Leo leaned his head back and closed his eyes. He was wasting time here. He needed to think about where she'd go. Why couldn't he come up with one possible place? Waiting here wasn't helping Genny any. He felt helpless, like a damned child unable to do anything for himself right now.

"What if Lady Carleton doesn't know where Genny is?"

"Must you be all doom and gloom, my friend?"

"It's the only thing that has been on my mind for the last twenty-four hours. How can I not think the worst when I know she has no family to turn to?"

Tristan tapped his desk. "There was one other rumor that I dismissed as balderdash."

Leo came to attention in his chair.

"Someone mentioned that the carriage she borrowed stopped in front of Jez's for some time."

He was headed out the door at a run before his friend could finish his theory on the carriage.

Chapter 25

A little bird informed me today that a certain marquess has received a veiled midnight visitor under the safety of a moonless night. I will not speculate just yet as to who the mysterious woman is because there is something far more interesting to the whole scenario, and that is . . . that the lady stayed the night in his private residence.
The Mayfair Chronicles, August 14, 1846

"Jezebel?" Leo shouted as he pounded his first against her door.

It swung open mid-pound. Jez stood on the threshold, expression curious.

"You've scared the butler with the way you've gone on, Leo." Jez stood aside so he could enter.

"I'm sorry." Leo had to lean over at the waist and put his hands on his knees as he breathed in heavily. "I ran here from Tristan's."

Jez pressed her palm to the back of his shoulder and rubbed back and forth. "Why would you do that?"

"Is she here?"

Jez leaned over, bringing her face in line with his vision. "She is."

"Thank God." He stood, grasped her by the arms, and planted a loud kiss against her cheek. "Where can I find her?"

Jez looked at him queerly. "She's in the drawing room."

"Genny," he shouted, as he jogged down the hall. He burst through the drawing room doors and nearly fell to his knees on seeing Genny safe and sound.

She stood in the middle of the room, hands folded in front of her. She was wearing a borrowed dress—Jez's most likely; he knew because it was scarlet satin and the prettiest dress he'd ever seen Genny in.

"Leo."

"Oh, God, Genny. I was so worried." Leo couldn't believe he had finally found her and rushed forward, stopping just in front of her when he realized she might not be so welcoming.

Jezebel clicked the door shut, leaving them alone.

"Why are you here, Leo?"

"I've been a madman worrying about you since I found out you had to leave the Carletons'."

"Don't think because I've been properly ruined that you can offer to marry me and save what remains of my reputation."

He wanted to laugh at her tenacity. "Genny, if we married, it would be because we both love each other and want to spend the rest of our lives together."

When she lowered her head, he shortened the distance between them and tipped her chin up with his fingers. "Don't look so gloomy."

"My life is ruined." She shook her head. "It happened so fast that I was at a loss for what to do."

He couldn't help it; he had to touch more of her, comfort

her, do whatever possible to make her feel better. He pulled her into his arms and just held her close. She rested her face over his heart. Her arms were limp at her sides.

"Let me fix this," he said.

"And what of everything that happened between us? How can I trust you?" She grabbed the material at his waist and scrunched it tight in her fists.

"It may take time before you believe this sentiment again, but you can always trust me."

She looked up at him with sad eyes. "Can I?"

He nodded his reassurance and caressed the back of his hand over her cheek and kissed her forehead.

"I don't even understand how we were discovered," she said. "We were so careful."

He gathered her close enough to hug her tight again. "It's my fault. I should have been more vigilant."

"We were both participants in our affair. It was foolish on both our parts."

"The biggest gossip was at that party, and I didn't take extra precaution knowing that. The fault rests solely on my shoulders." He rubbed Genny's back. "Lady Hargrove's name will not fare any better than ours. She's a ruined woman, too."

Genny pulled away to look up at him. "What do you mean she's ruined?"

"Exactly what I said."

"You mean . . ."

"Yes, it was her in the maze."

Genny's hand came up to her mouth to cover her O of surprise. She was obviously shocked by the news. "It was *her*? You didn't . . ."

Of course Genny would want to know if he'd been the one to spill Lady Hargrove's secrets. It all came back to the trust issue. He couldn't blame her for questioning his integrity. "Not I."

He was rewarded with a smile from her.

"Now, tell me how you ended up here."

"At the dowager's?"

He gave a slight nod.

"That's an interesting and rather long story."

"I've nowhere else to be except here with you."

She indicated the sofa. "Shall we sit?"

He grabbed her hand and led her over to the seating area.

"I wanted to confront her," Genny started. "I was so angry that our affair had not only been discovered but subsequently announced to the world that I wanted to blame someone."

"You should have blamed me."

"Oh, I did."

Leo chuckled. Her hands were folded in his. He massaged her fingers one at a time. He had been carrying his mother's wedding band in his pocket since he'd left the Carletons. Would she accept it now?

"I confess, too, that I wanted to see what kind of woman would go to such great lengths to ruin someone she doesn't even know."

"And . . ."

"I was surprised by the dowager. She's not anything like I imagined before meeting her."

"Jez has always been an outspoken woman who knows exactly what she wants and how to get it in life."

"Except the lands and estates tied up in the title," she reminded him.

"True. But that has to do with legalities beyond her control. If it was a request in the will that she get nothing on her husband's death, everything would be different. She'd find a way around it and make the estate hers. But it's all entailed."

He slid closer to her, wanting no space to separate

them. Wanting to take her in his arms again and feel her warm body crushed to his.

"I thought most estates were set up that way."

"Yes, but one usually leaves their spouse with the means to support themselves and live a comfortable life after their death." God, it had only been a few days and he'd missed her terribly.

"Even though I don't agree with her plans for Charlotte, I do understand her reasons behind the decision." Her gaze was pensive when it met his. "Your friend is very sad, and as much as I wanted to hate her, I simply couldn't."

Leo smiled. "Jez does have a way about her."

"She invited me to stay here until she is thrown out by the new earl." Genny's brows scrunched up. "Do you really think he'll toss her out without caring what happens to her?"

"Yes. I do."

"It's rather dreadful that I spoke so highly of that man to my cousin." Genny sighed and leaned her shoulder against the back of the sofa. "I hope Charlotte can convince her father to change his mind."

This time she took the initiative to tangle her hands through his. Was she accepting him back into her life?

"Genny?"

She leaned closer. "I know what you are going to say, Leo."

"Do you?" His hand fell to her thigh.

"Yes, you want me to agree to marry you."

"And will you?"

"I've had nothing but time on my hands for the past few days." She scooted closer to him on the sofa. "I was so angered by the whole scenario that I failed to truly listen to what you were telling me."

She rested her head back on the sofa and looked at the

ceiling. Leo reached up and touched the ivory hair comb he'd given her. It was buried deep in the twisted bun at the back of her head. It brought a smile to his face. She turned and put her cheek in his palm.

"What is your conclusion?" he asked.

"I remembered the things you said to me. About watching over my cousin while spending time with me."

Leo brushed his thumb over her parted lips.

"It occurred to me that you never intended to stop Charlotte from marrying and that you would make sure your friend had no chance to persuade her otherwise, either."

He leaned in closer to her mouth. He was going to taste her soon. "Will you marry me?"

"There can't be any more secrets between us, Leo. Not like that one." The palms of her hands slid over his chest and stopped.

He inched a little closer. "Never again, then."

"Do you still love me?" Her voice was barely above a whisper.

"Always." He reached into his coat pocket and pulled out the chain and ring. "I believe you forgot something when last we parted."

A smile lit her whole face on seeing the ring.

"I don't think we need the chain anymore," he said, freeing the ring from the chain.

"But we aren't married yet."

He grinned. "I have something else in my pocket if you care to take a look."

She reached inside and pulled out the folded parchment. "What is it?"

"A special license. I don't believe we'll wait till December to say our vows."

She grasped his coat and pulled him down to her lips

for a kiss. When she pulled away she said, "Yes, I'll marry you."

He took her hand and slid the ring on her wedding finger exactly where it belonged, then laid claim to her mouth and heart before she could take her next breath.